D0882801

THE SCOTTIE BARKED AT MIDNIGHT

Also by Kaitlyn Dunnett and available from Center Point Large Print:

The Liss MacCrimmon Mysteries
Vampires, Bones, and Treacle Scones
Ho-Ho-Homicide

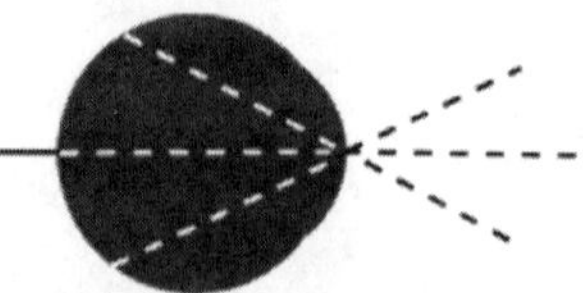

This Large Print Book carries the Seal of Approval of N.A.V.H.

THE SCOTTIE BARKED AT MIDNIGHT

Kaitlyn Dunnett

CENTER POINT LARGE PRINT
THORNDIKE, MAINE

This Center Point Large Print edition
is published in the year 2016 by arrangement with
Kensington Publishing Corp.

The text of this Large Print edition is unabridged.
In other aspects, this book may vary
from the original edition.
Printed in the United States of America
on permanent paper.
Set in 16-point Times New Roman type.

ISBN: 978-1-62899-905-1

Library of Congress Cataloging-in-Publication Data

Names: Dunnett, Kaitlyn, author.
Title: The Scottie barked at midnight / Kaitlyn Dunnett.
Description: Center Point Large Print edition. | Thorndike, Maine :
Center Point Large Print, 2016. | ©2015
Identifiers: LCCN 2015047198 | ISBN 9781628999051
(hardcover : alk. paper)
Subjects: LCSH: MacCrimmon, Liss (Fictitious character)—Fiction. |
Scottish Americans—Fiction. | Murder—Investigation—Fiction. | Large
type books. | GSAFD: Mystery fiction.
Classification: LCC PS3555.M414 S39 2016 | DDC 813/.54—dc23
LC record available at http://lccn.loc.gov/2015047198

THE SCOTTIE BARKED AT MIDNIGHT

Chapter One

Liss Ruskin peered through her windshield into what could only be described as "a dark and stormy night." She knew that phrase was a cliché, but there were times when a few overused and hackneyed words did a better job of summing things up than a whole paragraph of metaphor- and simile-laden description. This was one of them.

March in the western Maine mountains was always unpredictable. Only that morning the sun had been bright, the sky cloudless. Liss had set off for Freeport in good spirits, shopping list in hand. The day had passed quickly. To be truthful, she'd lost track of time, but by late afternoon she'd scored a bonanza of bargains from L.L. Bean and elsewhere, and had headed home a happy camper. When she was halfway back to Moosetookalook, just after the sun went down, the wind came up. Then the heavens opened to spit out sleet, the worst of the worst when it came to winter driving.

For the last half hour, Liss had chugged along the winding two-lane road at a snail's pace, eyes peeled for glare ice on the pavement. Her windshield wipers were barely able to keep up with the precipitation, and she found herself leaning forward over the steering wheel and squinting, as if that would somehow improve visibility.

Even at fifteen miles per hour, her tires kept losing traction on the slick surface. More than once she narrowly avoided sliding sideways into a ditch. Every hill—and there were lots of them—was a challenge, but it wasn't as if she had much choice about staying on the road. If she pulled over onto the shoulder and stopped, she wasn't certain she'd be able to get going again until spring. Worse, she'd be a sitting duck for some other vehicle to skid into.

As she started her descent of a long, steep hill with thick woods on either side, Liss cautiously applied the brakes. Her hatchback fishtailed and briefly crossed the nearly obscured centerline. She regained control, heart thudding, grateful there were no other cars in sight.

"Only a few more miles," she whispered to reassure herself.

The words were barely audible above the racket. Her tires shushed as they rolled onward through accumulated slush. Sleet pinged, loud and steady, on the car's metal roof. Closer still, the hum of the hardworking engine competed with the whoosh of the heater going full blast to blow hot air onto the inside of the windshield. Liss resisted the temptation to drown them out with the audiobook she'd been listening to on the trip south. As soon as the weather closed in, she'd shut off the player, unwilling to risk being distracted when road conditions were so bad.

She let out the breath she'd been holding when she reached the bottom of a hill and started along the long, level stretch at its foot. To unclench the muscles in her back and neck, she lifted one shoulder, then the other, then rolled both. Ever so slightly, she relaxed the death grip she'd had on the steering wheel. Inside her warm winter gloves, her fingers had clenched it so tightly that they'd gone numb. They tingled with a disconcerting pins-and-needles sensation when she flexed them.

It was at that instant that something darted out of the trees and ran right in front of Liss's car. Despite everything she'd been taught about winter driving, Liss braked hard and turned the wheel, the desire to avoid killing a defenseless animal proving stronger than her sense of self-preservation.

The next seconds seemed to last an eternity. One tire hit a patch of black ice. The car slewed toward the side of the road. Liss felt a small bump and hoped it was only the car going over the ridge of dirty, hard-packed snow left behind by a winter's worth of plowing. Then an enormous tree loomed up out of nowhere. Sure she was about to slam head-on into its massive trunk, Liss let go of the steering wheel, squeezed her eyes tightly shut, and covered her face with her arms.

The car went into another spin, slowed, and

shuddered to a stop. Liss's seat belt bit into her waist and torso. Her head jerked. Then a profound stillness settled over everything.

Her heart in her throat, she peeked out from between her fingers. Through a curtain of dark brown hair, she watched the windshield wipers scrape back and forth across unbroken glass. She hadn't hit the tree. She hadn't hit anything. The jolt when the car came to a halt hadn't even been hard enough to inflate the airbag.

Cautiously, she took an inventory of body parts. The seat and shoulder belt loosened, but they'd probably left bruises behind. Nothing throbbed . . . yet. She hadn't banged her head on the steering wheel. Alert for any indication of whiplash, she craned her neck to see where she'd ended up.

The tree she'd nearly slammed into was now off to her right, only inches from the passenger-side door. It didn't look as if she'd even scraped the bark. Not only was she still in one piece, so was her car. The engine continued to run, fueling the heater and the headlights.

"Okay," she whispered. "So far, so good."

Her fingers trembled as she reached out to turn off the ignition. Before she tried to drive away, she'd need to leave this warm little cocoon and check for damage to the tires and undercarriage. If she had a flat or a gas or oil leak, she wasn't going anywhere.

It took her three tries to get her seat belt

unfastened and two to open the driver's-side door. An annoying dinging reminded her the headlights were still on, but she wasn't about to turn them off. The sound also jolted her memory. There had been a reason she'd gone off the road.

She'd caught only a glimpse of the small animal that had dashed in front of her car, but that had been enough to convince her it wasn't a raccoon or a skunk or a fox. She'd braked in an attempt to avoid hitting someone's pet. With a sick sense of dread, she knew she had to find out what had happened to it before she could continue on her way.

That was assuming she was going to be able to go anywhere. Pushing her door the rest of the way open, Liss stepped out into slush. Her left boot hit the icy ground and took off on its own, wrenching her knee. If she hadn't caught hold of the doorframe in the nick of time, she'd have landed in an undignified heap next to her car.

Liss swore under her breath as she righted herself. That blasted knee was the bane of her existence. Years before, it had cost her the career she'd built as a professional Scottish dancer. It still ached on subzero winter nights. And every once in a while, if she abused it or neglected her regimen of muscle-strengthening exercises, it reacted by zapping her with shooting pains and a tendency to give out without warning. Moving gingerly, she tested it. When it took her weight, she breathed easier. Still keeping one hand on the roof of the car for balance, she surveyed her surroundings.

By some miracle, the car was still half on the shoulder. With the help of the bag of kitty litter she always carried in her trunk in winter, Liss was sure she'd be able to get the vehicle back onto the road. The biggest problem was that it was facing the wrong way. The headlight beams picked out the tracks her tires had left as she skidded toward that tree, proof of how narrowly she'd escaped a serious accident.

Her stomach clenched. For a moment she had to squeeze her eyes shut. She'd been lucky. Another few inches, a few miles per hour faster, and there would have been little left of either her or her car. She was shaken up. She'd have a few bruises, but she was alive. She had a lot to be grateful for.

She fumbled in her pocket for her cell phone, turned it on, and was gratified to discover she was not in one of rural Maine's many dead zones. She punched in the code to call home. She might or might not require help to get the car back on the road, but she did, rather desperately, need to hear her husband's voice.

Dan answered on the second ring. Sounding worried, he answered with, "You okay?"

"I'm fine." Except for the fact that her hands were still shaking and her voice had an annoying tremor and it was taking all her willpower not to burst into tears.

Dan wasn't fooled for a second. "What happened? Where are you?"

"The roads are icy. I'm stopped right now, so I wanted to let you know I'll be a little late."

Just hearing his voice made her stronger. She felt along the inside of the driver's-side door for the UNLOCK button. Then, keeping her free hand on the side of the car for balance, she took baby steps toward the back of the vehicle.

"Where are you?" Dan repeated.

"Maybe ten minutes from home. Don't you dare come out after me," she added in a rush, afraid he'd end up having an accident himself.

"What aren't you telling me?"

She opened the hatchback. The kitty litter was right where she'd left it, although she'd have to move several shopping bags to get at it. She'd stocked other winter emergency gear, too, including a heavy wool blanket and an industrial-size Maglite.

"I stopped because I might have hit a dog or a cat," she said into the phone. "It ran right in front of the car. I'm going to take a few minutes to look around for it before I move on."

There was a moment's silence on the other end of the line, but Liss knew Dan would not try to talk her out of searching for the little animal. Neither of them would ever drive off and leave someone's pet injured or dead. If she'd killed the poor little creature, she'd try to find its owner before she went home. She knew how she'd feel if one of her cats got out of the house and was hit by a car. The thought of finding Lumpkin or Glenora lying by the side of the road had her stomach twisting itself into knots and tears springing into her eyes. Losing one of them would be just as painful if the person responsible came and told her what had happened, but it would not be as traumatic as stumbling without warning over the poor, mangled body of one of her babies.

"Do what you have to," Dan said, his voice gruff. "But be careful. And call me again when you're about to get back on the road."

She broke the connection, slipped the phone back into her pocket, and took a deep breath before bending over double to peer underneath the car. She moved the flashlight beam from side to side. No body. No blood. No sign that she'd hit anything except the snowbank.

"So far, so good," she said again.

Before she straightened, she aimed the Maglite at the gas tank, the oil pan, the muffler, and each tire in turn. Everything looked intact.

Upright once more, she examined the ground next to the car. The surface was slick and glistening with a thin layer of ice. With a sense of surprise, Liss realized that the sleet had ended. The wet snowflakes landing on her head and shoulders and outstretched arm were light and fluffy.

Typical Maine weather, she thought. *Wait a minute, and it'll change.*

Moving cautiously, well aware that it was still treacherous underfoot, she widened her search. It had been a snowy winter, and a deep white carpet covered the ground beneath the trees. If she'd hit a cat or dog, it had most likely been thrown in that direction by the impact. Since she'd had an impression of black or brown fur, she kept her eyes peeled for a darker shape against the white. Nothing leapt out at her. Had she been luckier than she'd thought? Maybe she hadn't hit the little animal, after all.

Liss stepped off the shoulder, her boots crunching loudly as she moved deeper into the trees. After a few steps, she stopped and called out, "Here, doggie. Here, kitty."

Shaking her head at the notion that someone else's pet would come for a stranger, she walked parallel to the road, using her flashlight to search for tracks. She left footprints, but it didn't take her long to realize that a small animal wouldn't be heavy enough to make any impression in the thick coating of ice on top of the snow.

Sweeping her light back and forth as she went, Liss started back toward the car. She froze when, for just an instant, the light was reflected back at her—eyes? She held the beam steady on a spot near the tree she'd nearly run into. Was something there? She held her breath and listened, wondering if she'd been making too much noise to hear the faint whimper of an animal in distress.

Nothing moved. No sound reached her, but when she played the light a little to the left, the beam picked out two bright eyes and a bit of dark fur. A small dog crouched between two small birches.

"Stay right there, sweetie," Liss cooed.

Hoping that it wouldn't be spooked by her approach, she moved closer. She breathed a little easier when it emerged from hiding and took a few hesitant steps in her direction. It seemed to be favoring one leg, but at least it was moving on its own.

"It's all right, baby. I'll take care of you," Liss murmured.

She stopped and went down on her knees when she was still a few feet away from what turned out to be a Scottish terrier. Setting her flashlight on the ground, she stripped off one glove and held out her bare hand. The little dog sniffed her fingers, then licked them, apparently willing to accept that she was there to help.

"Okay, sweetie. I'm going to pick you up now. Okay?"

The limp indicated an injured leg, but there might also be internal injuries. Liss didn't intend to take any chances. Her first stop would be the office of the nearest vet.

Continuing to move slowly, she scooped up the little dog and stood. The Scottie squirmed in her arms, trying to reach her cheek with an affectionate wet tongue. Definitely someone's pet, Liss thought, although it wasn't wearing a collar.

Carrying twenty pounds of wiggly dog while juggling a heavy flashlight made the trip back to the car an adventure. Fortunately, Liss was accustomed to lugging Lumpkin around. Her Maine coon cat had tipped the scales at close to that same weight when she'd first inherited him, although since then she'd helped him slim down to a mere fifteen pounds.

With the blanket that was part of her emergency gear wrapped around her new friend, Liss settled the Scottie in the backseat of the car. She remembered reading somewhere that the hard, wiry outer coat of the Scottish terrier was weather resistant, but the poor little thing was shivering with the cold.

Liss had just closed the car door when a sharp cracking sound made her jump. It sounded as if someone had stepped on a twig.

"Is anyone there?" Liss hoped someone was—preferably the Scottie's owners, searching for their missing pet. She called a second time, but no one answered either hail.

Deciding that the sound she'd heard must have

been a branch breaking under the weight of accumulated ice, Liss moved on to the next task, spreading kitty litter beneath her tires so she could maneuver the car back onto the road, get herself turned around, and continue on to Moosetookalook. As she worked, she tried to remember if there were any houses nearby. There were none in sight. That made her wonder where the Scottie had come from. She was still pondering that question when she climbed back in behind the steering wheel. She was just about to start her engine when flashing lights, moving slowly in her direction, appeared in her rearview mirror.

"Hallelujah!" Liss whispered.

It was a town plow, clearing the road and depositing sand and salt in its wake.

In the examining room at Moosetookalook Small-Animal Clinic, Liss's anxious gaze followed the veterinarian's hands as she gently poked and prodded, searching for injuries. She'd already confirmed that the Scottish terrier was female and that she seemed well cared for.

Audrey Greenwood had moved to town three years earlier to set up her business a few blocks away from the town square. Ever since, she had been active in civic affairs, including the Moosetookalook Small Business Association. In a few weeks, she'd be running the information booth during the March Madness Mud-Season Sale, an annual one-day shopping extravaganza sponsored by the MSBA on the last day of the month. She was also Liss's cochair for the event.

"You say she came out of hiding when you called?" Audrey asked without looking up. Her blunt-cut blond hair was just long enough to be tucked behind her ears to keep it out of her way when she bent over a patient. In the bright light above the examining table, her pale, flawless skin, devoid of makeup, looked almost translucent.

"She was a little gimpy, but she didn't seem to be in a lot of pain. And she was good as gold about letting me pick her up. She didn't fuss when I put her in the car, either. Then, with a little help from the plow driver and my handy-dandy bag of kitty litter, I got turned around and brought her straight here."

Liss didn't mention the two quick phone calls she'd made before setting out. Audrey knew about the first because Liss had contacted her to give her a heads-up that she was on her way with an emergency patient. The second call had been to Dan.

"I'm not finding anything worse than a few bruises," Audrey announced.

"You're sure?"

Audrey's manner was brusque and no-nonsense as she straightened. Upright, she was a couple of inches taller than Liss's five-foot-nine. Her rangy, athletic build was the result of many hours of exercise, divided almost equally between the tennis court and cross-country ski trails. She shot an incredulous look in Liss's direction.

"Of course I'm sure. I don't think your car clipped her at all," she added, turning back to the Scottie to tickle her under her chin. "More likely she got hit by a chunk of hard-packed snow when you spun onto the shoulder."

"But what if there are internal injuries? Shouldn't you take X-rays? I'll pay for them. If there's the slightest chance she—"

Audrey raised a hand, palm out, to stop the flow of words. "I'll keep an eye on this little sweetheart overnight, but I don't anticipate any complications. What you need to do is find her owner. She's clearly someone's pet."

"There isn't much I can do tonight, but in the morning I'll put up posters," Liss promised. "Maybe notices in the local newspapers."

"Don't forget the *Daily Scoop*."

"How could I?" Liss grinned. Nine times out of ten, the online newspaper beat the few remaining print versions to breaking stories.

While Audrey got the Scottish terrier settled in a comfortably furnished cage, one of only a half dozen, since there was no room in the small clinic for more, she reeled off additional places for Liss to contact, including the animal shelters in nearby communities. "From your description, the place where you found her isn't in Carrabassett County. Maybe you can get Sherri to put the word out to neighboring police and sheriff's departments."

"I'll ask." Sherri Campbell, the Moosetookalook chief of police, was one of Liss's closest friends.

"Good." Audrey sent her an amused look. "Now go home. You've done all you can for now. And don't you have a good-looking hunk of man waiting for you?"

"And two cats," Liss agreed.

She reached into the cage to give the Scottie a final tickle behind the ear. The little dog had already curled herself into a ball on the padded dog bed. Poor baby. After the excitement of the day, she was all tuckered out.

It had been a long one for Liss, too.

Five minutes after leaving the animal clinic, driving along streets that had been plowed as soon as the snow stopped, she pulled into her own driveway. There, too, Dan had already been out to shovel and sand. Even better, the moment she turned off the engine, he appeared at the front door. Framed in the opening, he'd never looked more appealing. Tall and broad shouldered, his sandy brown hair just a little too long, he was exactly the tonic Liss needed. It took her less than five seconds to get from the car to his welcoming arms. If her bad knee zapped her again en route, she didn't feel a thing.

"Hey!" Dan said with a laugh when she let him

come up for air. “I’m happy to see you and all, but what’s with the extra enthusiasm?”

“I’m just very, very glad to be home.”

And then, because they’d promised not to hide things from each other, Liss filled him in on the details she’d left out when they’d spoken on the phone. Earlier, she’d said only that she was stopped by the roadside to look for someone’s pet. Now she shared the way she’d felt when she’d realized how close she’d come to slamming head-on into a humongous sugar maple.

Bright and early the next morning, Liss was back at Moosetookalook Small-Animal Clinic. “There she is,” she said when Audrey let her in. “She looks happy to see me.”

“Don’t let it go to your head. Anyone bringing food and water would look good to her.”

“Cynic. That little girl and I bonded. Didn’t we, sweetie?” The Scottie looked for all the world as if she was nodding. She did an impatient little dance as she waited for her bowls to be refilled.

“You start baby-talking and I’ll ban you from the clinic,” Audrey threatened. “Here. Make yourself useful.”

As they saw to the needs of the animals in Audrey’s care, Liss outlined her plans for the morning. “A handful of phone calls to start. Then, if no one knows anything about a missing Scottie, I’ll make posters to put up around the area. Then

I thought I'd head back to the stretch of road where I had my accident. Someone who lives nearby may know who owns a Scottish terrier."

"You made one of your famous lists, didn't you?"

Liss laughed. "Of course."

No one had been in touch with any of the animal shelters that she contacted during the next hour. One of the women she talked to reminded her that some people just didn't bother reporting a missing dog or cat. They assumed their pet was lost or dead and went on with their lives.

Liss shook her head. She didn't doubt the truth of the statement, but she found such an attitude hard to understand. If one of her cats went missing, she knew she'd move heaven and earth to find out what had happened. Lumpkin and Glenora were family. As for the Scottie, she hadn't been kidding when she'd told Audrey there was a bond between them. They'd been through a harrowing experience together. One or both of them could have been killed. Liss had been able to drive home and resume her life as if nothing had happened, but her fellow survivor had been set adrift. Until the little dog was safe, her future secure, Liss intended to assume full responsibility for her well-being.

Driving south, approaching the site of the accident, Liss began to feel a bit queasy. The tire tracks she'd left were gone, covered by the slush the plow had thrown onto the shoulder of the road, but she had no trouble spotting the tree she'd come so close to hitting.

She didn't stop. She already knew this wooded area was devoid of habitation. So were the fields on the other side of the road. The last house she had passed leading up to the empty stretch had been some distance back. She planned to stop there on her way home, but for the moment, she kept her eyes peeled, searching for the first house in this direction.

A quarter of a mile passed without any sign of a driveway or side road. Liss slowed to a crawl to make sure she didn't miss anything. There was little traffic at midmorning on a Tuesday. She remembered that it had been clear sailing on the morning the previous day, too. Most adults were already at work. The kids were in school. Just "ladies of leisure" like herself had the freedom to be out and about.

Liss smiled at the notion. There was only one reason she was free to hunt for the Scottie's owner. A few months earlier, she had taken a step back and decided she was driving herself too hard. All work and no play and so forth. Since Monday and Tuesday were traditionally slow days for walk-in customers at Liss's store on the town square, she'd made a change in the hours Moosetookalook Scottish Emporium was open. Wednesday through Sunday, they remained the same, but on the other two days her sign read BY CHANCE OR APPOINTMENT. Ordinarily, she went in to work anyway. She had mail and online orders to deal with. This week was an exception.

A superstitious person with the advantage of hindsight might say she should have stayed at home rather than indulge in her shopping spree. Liss was too practical to buy into such a theory, but she did believe in fate. Things happened for a reason. If she hadn't crossed paths with the Scottish terrier in such a dramatic fashion, she'd undoubtedly have run across the little dog—but hopefully not *over* her—at some later date. There was something special about the Scottie. If no owner turned up, Liss was already considering the possibility of adopting her.

When she finally spotted a house, it was set so far back from the road that she almost missed it. A glance at the odometer told her she'd driven almost a mile past the scene of her accident. That was a long way for a small dog with short legs to wander. She pulled into the driveway, parked in front of a tidy cape with dormers, and went to knock at the door.

An elderly woman was at home. Once she'd turned up her hearing aids far enough to understand Liss's question, she shook her head. "Sorry, dear. I don't remember seeing a Scottie dog or hearing any barking last night. No one in the neighborhood owns a dog except the

Bentleys over on the Leahy Road. They've got a Doberman." She grimaced. "He's a big brute, too. He makes me nervous."

Liss thanked her and went in search of the Bentley house. It wasn't visible from the road Liss had been on, but once she drove south for a bit longer she found a street sign. She understood their neighbor's uneasiness as soon as she got a good look at the dog, but the large, fenced-in area seemed adequate for both the animal's needs and the safety of small animals and nervous passersby. Mrs. Bentley was positive neither had recently ventured onto her property. "Cujo is a terrific guard dog," she boasted. "Just take a look at those teeth."

The remainder of Liss's inquiries were equally fruitless. After the last stop—at the farmhouse north of the accident site—she headed for the Moosetookalook Police Department.

"That is one lucky little dog," Sherri Campbell said when Liss had brought her up to speed.

The two women were in Sherri's office, a cramped space containing two desks, two desk chairs, two hard plastic chairs for visitors, and a large, gunmetal-gray file cabinet. The latter was still in everyday use, despite the advent of "paperless" record keeping. The door behind Liss led to the reception area, furnished with similar plastic chairs and old magazines. Another door, to her left, hid a holding cell, a space so minuscule that Liss had always suspected it had originally been a closet.

"I'm just relieved I didn't actually hit the poor little beastie." Liss took a sip of premium blend from a recyclable take-out cup bearing the logo of Patsy's Coffee House.

Since the café was on her way, she'd stopped there before intruding on Sherri's workplace. Liss and Dan's house was situated in the middle of one side of the town square. She'd walked to the corner, popped into Patsy's, and from there it had only been a few more yards to the back door of the redbrick municipal building. In addition to the police department, it also housed the town office, the fire department, and the public library.

"That dog wasn't the only lucky one." Sherri shifted in her chair, adjusting the pillow tucked in at the small of her back.

"Still hurting?" Liss asked.

Sherri grimaced. She was well into her seventh month of pregnancy and could no longer fit into her trim blue Moosetookalook, Maine, police uniform. Fortunately, as chief, she could get away with wearing civvies on the job. She sat behind her desk, across from Liss, her chair tipped slightly back. Although they were out of sight, Liss felt certain Sherri's feet rested on the small footstool she'd brought from home. Sherri rarely complained, but anyone with eyes could see how uncomfortable she was.

"Drink your milk," Liss said.

Sherri grimaced. She'd said thank you for the chicken-salad sandwich on freshly baked whole-wheat bread and the pint-size carton of milk Liss had brought her from Patsy's, but she gazed at the cup in Liss's hand with the look of desire she usually reserved for chocolate cupcakes and sexy male movie stars. "I'm reduced to getting my caffeine fix from sniffing the air," she grumbled. "I ask you, is that fair?"

Liss knew better than to reply. "When do you go on maternity leave?"

"Bite your tongue. I'd be bored to tears sitting around the house all day. Not that there aren't tons of things to be done, but Pete will pitch a fit if I try to paint the baby's room on my own or, God forbid, do any heavy lifting."

In January, Pete and Sherri, together with their daughter Amber and Sherri's son, Adam, had moved out of their small upstairs apartment overlooking the square and into a four-bedroom house on the outskirts of town. It was a fixer-upper that had been about 80 percent fixed by previous owners. Odd jobs remained, such as putting up the molding in the living room and installing closet doors in the bedrooms. When they could afford it, Sherri wanted to rip out all the wall-to-wall carpeting and restore the oak floors beneath. That was another project she couldn't take on until after she had the baby.

Sherri took a sip of her milk and made a face.

Liss grinned and handed her a napkin. "Mustache."

"Perfect." She scrubbed at her upper lip and then got back to business. "No one's called here about a missing pet, but I'll keep checking around. Will the dog be staying at Audrey's?"

"I'll be keeping her at home with me until I find her owner. Foster care. Audrey doesn't have a lot of room."

"Guilt much? I get that you feel responsible, but we do have a perfectly nice animal shelter in Fallstown for all of Carrabassett County. They never euthanize healthy animals, so you don't have to worry about that."

"I wouldn't feel right abandoning her, and it goes against the grain to keep a dog caged up. She's the sweetest little thing." Liss could feel a sappy smile spreading over her face. "She seems to like me. Scottish terriers don't take to everyone, you know. They can be quite aloof with strangers."

Sherri just shook her head. "I'll keep my ears open and send out some feelers, but if the dog belongs to a tourist or someone deliberately left her by the side of the road, you may end up stuck with a permanent houseguest."

Liss stood, depositing the baggie that had held her ham and cheese sandwich and her empty coffee cup in Sherri's trash can. "I can think of worse fates." She reached for the coat she'd tossed onto the top of the second desk.

"Uh, Liss?"

Already at the door, Liss looked back. Sherri's face wore a look of concern, but Liss also detected a hint of laughter in her friend's eyes.

"Have you thought about how Lumpkin and Glenora will feel about sharing their space? I mean . . . she's a *dog*."

"I'm sure they'll adjust."

Sherri's laughter followed her out of the office.

Second thoughts, and third, assaulted Liss on the short walk to the small-animal clinic, but her first glimpse of the Scottie's expression when she caught sight of Liss vanquished any doubt. She was doing the right thing.

"She does look happy to see you," Audrey admitted, "and this time she's already been fed."

"From the way she's dancing around her cage, I can tell she's not hurting any."

"I told you. Minor bruises. Any luck finding her owner? I can't keep her here much longer. I need the cage."

All the others were occupied. One contained a parrot; the remainder held dogs or cats in various stages of healing. Several people had apparently decided this was the day to "spay or neuter your pet," following the advice so often heard in public-service announcements.

"If you'll sell me a collar and leash," Liss said,

"I'll take her home with me. Temporarily, of course, since I'm sure someone's looking for her."

A short time later, Liss unlocked her back door, scooped up the Scottie, and stepped into the kitchen. Both cats materialized out of nowhere. Lumpkin, the Maine Coon cat, caught sight of the dog first. His head shot up, as did his tail, which instantly puffed up to twice its normal size. Glenora, smaller and coal black, went up on her hind feet, trying to get a better look at the newcomer.

"Now, guys—play nice."

Moving slowly, Liss lowered the Scottish terrier to all fours. She was quivering with excitement, anxious to investigate these new and interesting creatures, one of whom was bigger than she was.

"Lumpkin. Glenora. This is—" She broke off, momentarily stumped. She had to call the dog something. *Sweetie* was just too cutesy. *Wee Jock* was a cliché, aside from being the wrong gender. Pets belonging to past presidents had led to the overuse of *Fala* and *Barney* for Scottish terriers. Then it came to her—the perfect nickname for an animal that had narrowly escaped being run over by a car. "For now, we're going to call this pooch *Lucky,*" she informed her feline housemates. "Be polite to her. She's a guest."

All high spirits and friendliness, Lucky danced up to the two cats. Glenora bristled and spat. Lumpkin's ears went back. That was the only warning before he struck out, slashing at Lucky's nose. The Scottie backpedaled so fast that she tumbled ass over teakettle.

"That's enough!" Liss grabbed for Lucky, meaning to lift her out of harm's way, but the crisis had already passed.

Lumpkin sat down and began to wash his nether regions. Glenora turned her back, flicked her tail, and stalked out of the room. Trailing her leash, Lucky discovered a dish containing leftover dry cat food and chowed down. Liss collapsed onto one of the kitchen chairs.

"That went well," she muttered.

Now all she had to do was figure out how to keep the two cats and the dog apart when she was at work. If she didn't, she had a feeling she'd come home to chaos.

Maybe this hadn't been such a brilliant idea, after all, but she and Lucky had been through a lot together. She wasn't about to abandon the Scottie now.

Liss coped by making a list of all the things she still had to do that day. She'd just finished writing when the phone rang. The caller ID told her Moosetookalook Police Department was on the other end of the line, but she had to let the call go to the answering machine. Lumpkin was stalking Lucky.

He pounced just as Liss attempted to intervene. She separated the two combatants, but not before she acquired a long, deep scratch on the back of her left forearm.

"Good news," Sherri announced after the beep. "I know who owns that Scottish terrier you found. Her name is Deidre Amendole. Give me a call and I'll tell you how to get the pooch back to her."

With mixed feelings, Liss reached for the receiver. Her hand froze in midair when Sherri added one more sentence to her message.

"By the way—she was dognapped."

Chapter Two

"Oh, my God! Is Mama's baby okay? Did the bad man hurt ums?"

Bad *man?* Liss wondered what man she meant, but there was no point in asking. Clutching her lost "baby" tight to her bosom, her face buried in the little dog's wiry black coat, Deidre Amendole rocked back and forth, filling the crisp, early evening air with heart-wrenching sobs. She seemed oblivious to the fact that she was standing in an open doorway in early March.

According to Sherri, the Scottie, whose name turned out to be Dandy, had been spirited away from Deidre's condo on the grounds of Five Mountains Ski Resort the previous afternoon by person or persons unknown. Taken for ransom? It was possible. These condos didn't come cheap. But how on earth had the little dog ended up running loose a good thirty miles to the south?

Liss had to smile at Dandy's obvious delight at being reunited with her owner. It was equally obvious that the dog thought being squashed, even as a display of love and relief, was unnecessary. When a second Scottish terrier materialized from inside the condo to welcome the prodigal pup home, Dandy squirmed in Deidre's arms, anxious to get down and greet her little buddy. The weeping woman wouldn't let go. She hugged Dandy tighter, and the volume of her sobbing increased.

Deidre Amendole was a good two decades older than Liss and at least eight inches shorter. She had deep-set, dark brown eyes and hair that had been dyed jet-black, worn short with over-long bangs. The resemblance to Dandy was remarkable, and it didn't end with her face. Like her dogs, Deidre had a strong, muscular build and short, sturdy legs. She was dressed all in black. The velour tracksuit was a bit too snug in places and emphasized her lack of stature, but it also heightened her similarity to a Scottish terrier.

Left standing on the condo's small front stoop, which was open to the elements, Liss shivered as the last of the day's warmth vanished along with the setting sun. At this time of year, dusk lapsed into night very quickly. It occurred to her that she could slip quietly away, return to her car, and drive home, but the few details Sherri had given her had made her intensely curious.

Another five minutes passed before the water-works shut off. Deidre freed one hand, dabbed ineffectually at her dripping nose with a crumpled tissue, and lifted her head to focus red-rimmed eyes on Liss. "How can I ever thank you for rescuing my baby?"

Too choked up to say more, she scooped up the second Scottie and backed into the condo's small foyer, indicating that Liss should follow her inside. Still sniffling, she led the way into the main part of the condo.

Liss closed the front door behind her and hurried after the trio, stripping off her woolly hat, warm gloves, and heavy winter coat as she went. Three steps down and a left turn brought her into a large living room with a cathedral ceiling and a spectacular view, through floor-to-ceiling windows, of a snow-covered mountainside laced with ski trails.

Avid skiers with less extravagant tastes, or less ready cash, stayed at local hotels and motels, including The Spruces, the hundred-plus-year-old hotel owned by Liss's father-in-law. Since Five Mountains Ski Resort was only a half-hour drive from Moosetookalook, The Spruces ran a shuttle to the slopes several times a day for the convenience of those guests who had come to Maine for the downhill skiing or the snowboarding. Closer to home, The Spruces offered alternative winter sports on-site—ice skating, snowshoeing, and cross-country skiing.

Although Liss had often glimpsed the condos at Five Mountains from the road—there were dozens of them, all identical—this was the first time she had ever been inside of one of the units. The furnishings were as luxurious as she'd imagined, including leather chairs and sofas, an enormous flat-screen TV, a built-in bookcase—its shelves filled with curios and one or two actual books—and a huge stone fireplace containing the ashes of a recent blaze. A small stack of split wood was piled nearby, together with a box of kindling. There were no family photos or other personal touches, making Liss suspect that the place was either a time-share or a rental. The only things in the room that looked as if they belonged to the owner of two Scottish terriers were flung carelessly on an end table—several catalogs for pet products and a copy of the current year's glossy *Fabulous Dogs* calendar.

Two women rose from the sofa as Deidre led Liss in. They were the same height, a few inches shorter than Liss, and both had long dark brown hair. Those were the only similarities between them. Since neither one resembled Deidre, Liss was surprised to hear the older woman introduce the skinnier of the two as her daughter, Desdemona Amendole.

"This is the wonderful woman who rescued Dandy." Deidre started to add a name and realized she'd never asked for one.

"Liss Ruskin," Liss supplied. "Hello."

Desdemona responded by offering to take Liss's coat, although all she did was toss it over the back of a nearby chair. Her attention focused on Dandy, she spoke in quick bursts of sound. "She looks okay to me. I thought you said she'd been hurt."

"Just a few bruises," Liss said before Deidre could answer.

Desdemona took the Scottie from her mother and held the little dog up in front of her, scrutinizing Dandy's movements as she wriggled and tried to lick the end of Desdemona's sharp patrician nose. In the process, Desdemona's sleeves fell back to reveal arms that had shrunk well past thin to enter matchstick territory.

The daughter, Liss thought, looked more like an Irish wolfhound than a Scottish terrier. Or maybe a whippet. Desdemona carried Dandy into the kitchen area, separated from the living room by a waist-high counter. The unmistakable sound of a can being opened caused the second Scottie to try to leap out of Deidre's arms.

She set him down on the carpet. "Go ahead, Dondi. You may have a little snack while your sister eats her din-din."

Liss glanced at the other young woman, who had resumed her seat on the couch. Deidre had not bothered to introduce her, but she obviously felt at home in the condo. Liss put her age at no more than twenty. She had a fresh-faced, schoolgirl look about her, especially where her cheeks retained a hint of baby fat. She wore no makeup that Liss could detect. She didn't need to. She'd been blessed with a peaches-and-cream complexion. Tiny silver hearts dangling from her earlobes were the only ornaments she used to augment her natural beauty.

"Hi. I'm Liss Ruskin." She held out her hand.

Smiling warmly, the young woman grasped Liss's fingers with a firm grip. "Iris Jansen, magician's assistant."

"Excuse me?"

"Didn't you know?" Deidre sounded surprised. "We're here at Five Mountains for the champion of champions competition."

Unenlightened, Liss looked from Deidre to Iris and back again. "Champions of what?"

Deidre blew out an impatient breath. "*Variety Live*. Don't tell me you've never heard of it? It's one of the highest-rated reality competition shows on television."

Liss hesitated before she responded. It probably wouldn't go over well if she confessed that the only televised competition she ever watched was *Dancing with the Stars*, and she wasn't religious about that. In general, she didn't care for televised competitions, and she liked other sorts of reality TV even less. A situation comedy, a British mystery on PBS, or a rerun of *Firefly* was more to her taste. What was even more common at her house was for Dan to watch a Red Sox or Patriots game while she buried her nose in a book.

"I'm afraid I haven't seen it," she admitted.

"Oh, my dear!" Deidre strode straight to the cabinet beneath the flat-screen TV, opened the doors, and pulled out a boxed set of DVDs. "You must take these as your reward for finding Dandy. It's the season we won. Some of our finest performances are here. Of course, Deidre and her Dancing Doggies are working on entirely new and truly spectacular routines for the rest of the current season."

Her mind boggling, Liss took the case Deidre thrust into her hands. "The, er, champions competition?"

"That's right. We're recording the next few shows, including the finale, here at Five Mountains. Iris is the competition," she added, trilling a laugh, "but we love her, anyway."

"She's one of the few Mother doesn't suspect of having a hand in Dandy's disappearance," Desdemona said as she emerged from the kitchen area, the two Scotties trotting after her.

As if the comment embarrassed her, Iris concentrated on coaxing the two dogs to come to her, but patting her lap and making little kissing sounds had no effect. Both Dandy and Dondi ignored her.

Dognapped, Liss remembered. "You said someone took Dandy?"

"It was a blatant attempt to eliminate us from the competition." Deidre stated this so emphatically that Liss had no choice but to believe her.

"I've had some experience with competitions myself," she admitted. "Scottish dancing. Fortunately, no one ever resorted to dirty tricks to keep me from winning."

"Tell us, please, how you found my little darling."

At Deidre's urging, Liss took a seat in one of the armchairs across from the sofa and obliged. As she related what had happened, she couldn't help noticing how twitchy Desdemona was. She started out perched on the edge of one end of the sofa. Unable to sit still, she crossed and uncrossed her legs, then crossed them again and waggled one foot. She put the foot down and began to drum her fingers on one knee. After a minute or two of that, she got up, retrieved the dog dishes from the floor of the kitchen area, and rinsed them in the sink.

"I was already looking for Dandy's owner when the local chief of police contacted me," Liss concluded.

Desdemona wandered over to the window and stared out at the moonlit slopes.

"Until then, I assumed she'd simply wandered off and become lost. Even though she didn't have a collar, it was obvious she wasn't a stray."

Desdemona crossed to the fireplace to begin making random designs in the cold ashes with an ornate poker.

"I just can't thank you enough for bringing her back to me," Deidre said. Once again, there were tears in her eyes.

"Do you have any idea which of your competitors took Dandy?"

Deidre scowled as she knuckled away the moisture. "It could have been any of them. Ruthless. Every one. Vile, villainous, ruthless creatures." She glanced at Iris. "Present company excluded, of course."

Iris's cheeks were tinged with red, but she waved away Deidre's apology. "Not everyone is pleasant to work with," she murmured.

"Why are you so certain Dandy's disappearance had something to do with this competition?" Liss asked.

"What else could it be? Dandy and Dondi have a very high rating among voting viewers. That's why I went straight to hotel security when I discovered my baby was missing, and why I told them they must keep investigating until the police can make an arrest."

"They're not going to do anything now that she's been found." With a clatter, Desdemona thrust the poker back in the rack with the other fireplace tools.

Deidre's lower lip trembled. "But they must."

Liss's heart went out to her. She knew how she'd feel if someone took Lumpkin or Glenora. But Desdemona was right. Even for the private security firm employed by Five Mountains, finding an alleged dognapper would be low on the list of priorities.

"Did they find anything to indicate how Dandy was taken without you being aware of it?"

To Liss's surprise, it was Iris who answered. "They didn't want to believe her at first. They couldn't find any evidence that anyone had broken into the condo, so they said Deidre must have left the door open and Dandy just wandered off. As if!"

"Then they said if she'd really been taken, I'd probably get a ransom note." Sniffling, Deidre had to blow her nose before she could continue. "If only it were that simple. I knew there'd be no demand for money."

Iris reached out to pat her hand. "Don't overexcite yourself, Deidre. Everything's fine now. You have your little Dandy back."

"And I won't let her out of my sight again, believe you me." A fierce gleam in her eyes, Deidre was about to say more when a telephone rang.

Desdemona answered. "Yes," she said to the caller. "I suppose so." With an abrupt movement, she passed the instrument to her mother. "Valentine Veilleux wants to talk to you."

Deidre's eyes glowed with pleasure. Her voice was warm as she spoke into the receiver. "Hello, dear. How nice of you to call. Yes, Dandy's back home. Isn't it wonderful?"

Iris tapped Liss on the arm and handed her the calendar she had noticed earlier. "Valentine is the photographer who took the pictures. Dandy and Dondi are the featured dogs for June."

Liss flipped pages until she came to a shot of the two Scotties. Standing on their stubby little hind legs, with Dandy wearing a skirt, they bore an uncanny resemblance to a couple dancing a waltz. Or maybe it was a cha-cha.

"She's a wonderful photographer, isn't she?" There was a breathy, little-girl quality to Iris's voice when she waxed enthusiastic. "She's been taking pictures for a *Variety Live* calendar for next year. Whoever wins the competition will be on the cover."

Can't top that for an exit line, Liss thought. She gave the calendar back to Iris and stood. "Best of luck to you all. I really have to get going now."

She bent to stroke Dandy in farewell, glad the Scottie was back where she belonged. Deidre was weird, but it was obvious she loved the two Scottish terriers and took good care of them. Liss had no business feeling sad because she had to leave the little dog behind. "Lucky" had never been hers to begin with.

Still on the phone, Deidre sent an absentminded wave in her direction. Desdemona, taking her cue like a pro, restored Liss's outerwear to her and hustled her out the door. Although Desdemona thanked her for bringing Dandy back safe and sound, Liss got the distinct impression that she was glad to see her go.

Shaking her head and smiling to herself, Liss got into her car. She tossed the set of DVDs into the backseat. She doubted she'd ever watch them. Although she wished Deidre and her Dancing Doggies well, she had no interest in the champion of champions competition.

Over a dozen new orders had come in online during the two days Moosetookalook Scottish Emporium had been closed. That counted as excellent news for a hardworking retailer. Liss got busy filling them first thing Wednesday morning. Packaging and shipping occupied her for several hours. During all that time, not a single live customer interrupted her work.

That was *not* good news.

Heating the shop in winter cost money. So did keeping the lights on. Liss reminded herself that this time of year was always slow, and that all the other businesses in Moosetookalook were hurting, too, but she couldn't help but feel discouraged. At The Spruces, business was booming. Surely some of those guests ought to feel an urge to shop for souvenirs of their vacation in Maine.

"Why should they?" she muttered as she ran a feather duster over a display of figurines in Scottish dress. "They're all on the ski slopes. In between runs, they spend their money on overpriced snack-bar sandwiches or buy new helmets, or goggles, or hand warmers."

She put a little too much force into flicking the feathers and nearly sent a bisque bagpiper tumbling to the floor. She caught the delicate knickknack in the nick of time and returned it to its proper place on the shelf. Maybe dusting wasn't such a good idea just now. It wasn't as if anyone was going to come into the shop and run a white glove over the merchandise.

Moosetookalook Scottish Emporium had been founded by Liss's grandfather and carried on by her father and his sister, Margaret MacCrimmon Boyd. When Margaret had decided she'd rather work at the hotel instead, as events coordinator at The Spruces, Liss had bought her out and taken over the business.

She was making a profit, she reminded herself, albeit a small one. So was Dan, with his shop, Carrabassett County Wood Crafts, situated right next door. And at certain times of year the entire village was a tourist mecca. "Summer complaints" came by the busload to shop in the quaint little stores around the town square. They did well in leaf-peeper season, too, but the end-of-winter doldrums still got Liss down. March was such a dismal month.

"And that," she said aloud in a firm voice, "is exactly why the March Madness Mud-Season Sale was invented."

Returning to the sales counter, she pulled out the clipboard that held her to-do lists for the upcoming event. In previous springs, the sale had given her a nice bump in business. With any luck, it would boost the Emporium's profits once again this year. If it didn't, she'd have only herself to blame. She and Audrey Greenwood were the ones in charge. It fell to them to make the March Madness Mud-Season Sale a huge success.

Liss read through her itemized lists, pleased to note that most of the tasks were already checked off. The printer had delivered the flyers in good time, and they had already been distributed all over the county. Posters were up everywhere, too. She'd caught a glimpse of one on the information kiosk as she'd driven past the lodge at Five Mountains Ski Resort. Still, with only a few weeks to go, she didn't dare leave anything to chance. She reached for the phone.

Her first call was to her aunt. On the fifth ring, Margaret picked up. She sounded distracted.

"Is this a bad time?" Liss asked. "I just wanted to go over a few details for March Madness."

There was a long hesitation before her aunt answered. "I'll be home early this afternoon. Why don't we talk then?" Margaret might have sold her share in Moosetookalook Scottish Emporium to her niece, but she continued to live in the apartment above the store.

"Sure," Liss agreed. "That's fine. I—"

She held the phone away from her ear. She was talking to dead air.

Margaret's job at the hotel kept her busy. Not only did she handle arrangements for large groups, she also acted as troubleshooter once a conference or reunion or sales meeting was under way. She was a remarkable woman in every way—cheerful, energetic, and well organized. It was rare that anything left her frazzled. Liss hoped nothing was seriously wrong. She supposed she'd find out in good time.

Meanwhile, she had work to do. Shaking her head, she dialed the next number on her list and was sent straight to voice mail. When the beep to leave a message sounded in Liss's ear, she rattled off the question she had for the owner of the little jewelry store on the other side of the town square. The lucky duck was probably waiting on a customer. Or else she was taking a bathroom break. That was the downside of running a one-person operation. When nature called, Liss had to take the chance no one would come in while she was occupied, or else lock up and put the BACK IN FIFTEEN MINUTES sign in the window.

By the time Margaret walked into the Emporium at three that afternoon, Liss had delegated a half dozen minor tasks and arranged for an ad on the news page of the *Daily Scoop.* She glanced up as the bell over the door jangled, shopkeeper smile in place.

"It's only me," Margaret called out.

"Well, at least now I know the bell still works."

"That bad?"

Liss came out from behind the counter. "Typical March doldrums."

"How well I remember, and back before you created the website and set up online ordering, all we had to fall back on were mail-order sales. Things are better now."

"If you say so."

Liss's brow furrowed as she watched her aunt. Margaret lacked her usual energetic manner. And when had she lost all that weight? Her clothes hung loosely on her frame, as if she'd bought them a size too large. There was something else that was different about her, too, but it took Liss a minute to figure out what it was.

"You're wearing glasses!"

Taken aback by her niece's vehemence, Margaret snatched them off. "What of it?"

"Since when have you needed glasses?"

Although Liss saw her aunt nearly every day, she realized now that she didn't always *see* her. Margaret was nearly sixty-six, and today she looked her age. The lines around her eyes and mouth were deeper than Liss remembered. Laugh lines, Margaret would call them, but to her niece, their presence was worrying.

"For Heaven's sake, Liss. I've worn contact lenses for ages." Jamming the glasses back into place on the bridge of her nose, she headed for the stockroom, where she knew she'd find a pot of coffee that was more-or-less fresh.

"I never knew that." Liss followed her.

"I've had them since before you were born, so I suppose it isn't surprising that you never noticed."

In the distant past, when this building had been a single-family dwelling, the stockroom had been a kitchen. Standing in the doorway, Liss studied her aunt. She'd noticed when Margaret had stopped dying her hair bright red several years earlier. She'd let it go to a natural grayish brown. But when had it turned such a light gray that it was nearly white?

"Why switch to glasses at this late date?" Liss kept her voice level, but it wasn't easy. The fear that something was seriously wrong with her aunt grew stronger by the minute.

Margaret turned, a mug of coffee in one hand. "You should see your expression. It's no big deal. My left eye has been bothering me and the contacts irritate it. Nothing to worry about." Holding a mug full of coffee in both hands—she had a touch of arthritis and tended to be extra careful about avoiding spills—she retraced her steps. "Shall we sit down? I believe you wanted my help with March Madness."

"After you."

Liss watched Margaret with a critical eye as the older woman made her way to the "cozy corner" of the shop. Was she making too much of her aunt's slower pace and the excessive care she took to maneuver around various display cases, clothing racks, tables, and shelving? She wasn't imagining the lack of chatter. Ordinarily, Margaret talked a mile a minute, to match the brisk pace that was her usual walking speed.

"How long have you had that pair of glasses?" Liss asked when the outdated style belatedly suggested a more benign explanation for Margaret's cautious behavior.

"About ten years, and yes, I do need a new pair, but I can manage well enough until my next appointment with the optometrist. Don't fuss over me, Liss. It's a minor inconvenience." She claimed one of the two comfortable armchairs in the cozy corner and set her mug down on the coffee table situated between them. "Now, tell me how I can help with the sale."

Being out of focus explained the stumbling and fumbling, but not the weight loss. Was she just working too hard? Or was something more ominous behind the dropped pounds?

"I appreciate this," Liss said, trying to be subtle, "especially when you're probably right out straight at the hotel."

"Just the usual." Margaret sipped coffee and avoided meeting Liss's eyes.

So much for subtlety. "Ever think about retiring?"

"Retirement is for old people," said her aunt. "March Madness?"

For the moment, Liss gave up trying to get more information out of her and concentrated on the matter at hand. As always, Margaret had good suggestions to offer. She gave Liss's optimism a boost at the same time, despite the fact that their entire conversation took place without interruption by walk-in customers.

"Don't be such a worrywart," Margaret advised as Liss gathered up the lists she'd spread out on the coffee table and reattached them to her clipboard. "You're good at organizing this sort of thing. March Madness will turn out beautifully. You'll see."

"I hope you're right." Liss glanced at her watch. "The ad in the *Daily Scoop* should be up and running by now. Want to see it?"

Liss had brought her iPad to the cozy corner along with her lists, although she hadn't used it. There was something about putting felt-tip pen to paper, and being able to see what she'd scratched out, that gave her a clearer picture of what she was doing. She turned the device on and clicked on the shortcut to the online newspaper. Ignoring the lead news story, she fixed her gaze on the right-hand column, where the ads were located. They were shaped to resemble business cards, and the one Liss had designed was right at the top.

It read: SAVE BIG AT MOOSETOOKALOOK'S MARCH MADNESS MUD-SEASON SALE.

Beneath the text, a small animated moose loped across the bottom of the rectangular space.

"Is the moose too distracting?" Liss frowned, debating whether or not to keep the animation.

Margaret took the tablet from her to study the effect. She had to try several distances before she could see the screen properly, more proof that she needed new glasses. "The moose disappears for a few seconds between passes. That's plenty of time for someone looking at the ad to absorb the fact that the sale will take place on the last day of March from eight in the morning until eight at night."

Relieved, Liss took the iPad back and rested it on her knees. "You're right. And you're probably right about me worrying too much, too." *About all kinds of things,* she added to herself. "Did I tell you there's going to be a feature story in the *Daily Scoop* on the twenty-ninth? I already gave Jerrilyn an interview."

Margaret smiled. "Jerrilyn? Don't you mean 'our intrepid staff reporter'?"

"Right." Liss couldn't help smiling back. Jerrilyn was the editor's college-age daughter. Like most local businesses, the *Daily Scoop* was a family affair.

"No doubt there will be last-minute trouble-shooting to do," Margaret said, "but right at this moment I can't think of anything you've over-looked. Why don't you treat yourself to a few days off while it's so quiet?"

"I've already been closed two days this week."

"Yes. It's called a weekend, even if it is a Monday and a Tuesday. But you still work too hard. You and Dan both. Life is short. You should enjoy it more."

"Look who's talking. When did you last take time off?"

Margaret laughed. "Trust me, I have a well-balanced life. Besides, I love my job."

"And Dan and I took a vacation last November." That it hadn't turned out to be very relaxing hadn't been Liss's fault.

Shaking her head, Margaret drained the last of the coffee from her mug. "There's nothing wrong with taking off more than one week a year."

"I have been thinking I could kick back and relax right here in the shop for part of the day." Liss waved a hand to encompass the cozy corner. "You know—catch up on my reading. Especially if the dearth of live customers continues until the end of the month."

"That's not exactly what I had in mind, but I suppose it's better than nothing. If you have a lull, I say take advantage of it."

"I am tempted," Liss admitted. "I must have bought a dozen novels from Angie's Books and downloaded at least that many again that I haven't had time to read."

As she spoke, she glanced down at the iPad in her lap, thinking of the three apps she had for books, one each for Kindle, NOOK, and iBooks. The *Daily Scoop* was still showing on the screen. A few minutes earlier, Liss had only had eyes for her March Madness ad. Now, belatedly, the lead story on the left-hand side of the page caught her attention.

The headline was in large print: BODY OF WOMAN FOUND AT SKI RESORT.

Margaret reached out to touch her niece's arm. "What is it?"

"I'm not sure." There were plenty of ski resorts in the area. Lots of women stayed at them, but Liss felt a deep sense of foreboding as she scanned the story. Details were sketchy. Earlier that day a guest in one of the condos at Five Mountains Ski Resort had found her mother lying dead on the living-room floor. The dead woman's two little dogs had been standing guard over the body.

Abruptly, Liss handed the iPad to her aunt. There was silence while Margaret squinted at the text, enlarged the print, and read the story for herself. "My goodness! Do you think this is the woman whose dog you found?"

Liss wasn't surprised that her aunt knew about Dandy the Scottish terrier, even though she hadn't gotten around to telling Margaret the story herself. The Moosetookalook grapevine worked at top efficiency at this time of year, reporting news of births, deaths, engagements, and odd occurrences, as well as sharing rumors and spreading gossip.

"I'm afraid it may be. The *Scoop* didn't print any names, but how many women with two little dogs and a daughter are likely to be staying in the condos at Five Mountains at the same time?"

Poor Deidre, Liss thought. She'd been so happy to have Dandy back. And poor Dandy. But at least she still had a home with Deidre's daughter.

Margaret placed the iPad on the coffee table. "It says the police have been called in." She sounded worried.

"That doesn't mean anything. It isn't always easy to distinguish between accidental death and suicide." Liss frowned. "Deidre didn't seem the type to kill herself, but she was the excitable sort. Maybe she had high blood pressure, a heart attack. . . ."

Her voice trailed off at the thought that Deidre had been younger than Margaret was. She sent a surreptitious sideways glance in her aunt's direction, thinking she'd try again to assess the older woman's health, but Margaret was already on the move, picking up her empty mug and heading for the stockroom.

"So sad," she said, "but it just goes to prove what I've been saying—people should enjoy life while they can."

Liss collected her clipboard and the iPad and trailed after her aunt. It was good advice. Deidre Amendole's unexpected death was proof that life could be snuffed out in an instant. Even if you weren't inclined toward suicide, avoided being murdered, and were genetically disposed to escape death from natural causes until you hit one hundred, you could still be hit by the proverbial bus while crossing the street.

Starting tomorrow, she vowed, she'd spend at least an hour a day curled up in a chair in the cozy corner with one of the books from her TBR pile. As for this evening, she had another plan in mind to ensure that she got the most out of life. It was one she suspected her husband would also enjoy.

Chapter Three

Two days later, Liss was in the stockroom at Moosetookalook Scottish Emporium when she heard the loud jangle of the bell over the door of the shop. "Be out in a minute!" she called, hastily applying the last piece of strapping tape to the box she'd been packing for shipment.

A dark-haired woman stood with her back to the stockroom door. Her bulky winter coat hid her shape, but Liss could tell she was thin as a rail, and there was something familiar about her stance. Before she could pinpoint what it was, she heard the click of doggie toenails on the hardwood floor and looked down to see Dandy—or maybe it was Dondi—trotting toward her. The second Scottie appeared a moment later, eyes bright and eager and stubby tail wagging.

"I don't have any dog treats." She spread her hands wide, showing them that they were empty.

One of the dogs—this time she was pretty sure it was Dandy—tilted her head as if she was thinking over what Liss had said. The other pup continued to stare at her, his beautiful dark brown eyes remarkably expressive. She could almost believe he was trying to send her a telepathic message.

"You'll have heard about my mother." Desdemona's words were blunt, her voice harsh.

"Yes. That is, I saw the news stories. I'm sorry for your loss."

A follow-up report had identified Deidre but had not revealed her reason for being at the ski resort, nor had it given the cause of her sudden death.

"Would you like a cup of coffee?" Liss offered.

Desdemona considered the question with far more seriousness than it deserved. "That would be most welcome. Thank you."

Liss waved her toward the cozy corner of the shop. "Have a seat. I'll be right with you."

The Scotties followed her into the stockroom. Dandy and Dondi watched Liss's every move with great interest as she poured two mugs of coffee from the pot she already had going. She placed them on a tray and added packets of sugar substitute, a jar of nondairy creamer, and a plate of Patsy's bite-size corn muffins. Before the two dogs could decide to explore the boxes, bins, and bolts of fabrics stored on floor-to-ceiling shelving, Liss clicked her tongue at them and held the door open. They obliged by nearly knocking her off her feet as they raced past her into the shop. For such little guys, they packed a wallop. Then again, so did Lumpkin and Glenora when either of them took off at full tilt.

Desdemona had seated herself in one of the overstuffed easy chairs, but where most people would have been leafing through one of the coffee-table books Liss left out, or browsing the Scottish-themed titles shelved in a nearby bookcase, Desdemona Amendole just fidgeted. Liss wondered if the other woman was aware of the small nervous movements she made. Although her feet rested flat on the floor, one had a visible twitch, and she drummed the too-thin fingers of her right hand on the arm of her chair, where fabric and thick padding muted the sound.

"Here we go," Liss said in a cheerful voice. She plunked the tray down in front of her guest and settled herself in the other chair.

Desdemona started, as if her thoughts had been miles away from Moosetookalook Scottish Emporium. Hectic color rushed into her cheeks, but she covered her embarrassment, and most of her face, with a toss of the long, luxuriant mane of dark brown hair Liss had admired the day they first met. By the time Desdemona had doctored her coffee and was sitting back to take the first sip, her complexion had returned to normal.

Uncertain what to say next, Liss said nothing. Maybe Desdemona was just the nervous type. That might explain her anorexic appearance, too. In silence, Liss polished off half the coffee in her mug and slipped a muffin apiece to Dandy and Dondi.

"I was gone most of the day," Desdemona said in a rush. "Mother said she had a headache. She planned to take a pill to relax her and lie down for a while after she rehearsed with the dogs. I saw no reason to hurry back. By the time I returned, it was far too late to save her."

"How terrible for you," Liss murmured.

It must have been terrible for the Scotties, too. Looking down into those intelligent eyes, she had to wonder if they'd sensed something was wrong. Had they barked, trying to alert someone? Or had they known it was no use? It wasn't unheard of for the faithful dog belonging to a dead person to guard the body. Some animals pined away after losing their masters. Cats, sad to say, were as likely to take a little taste of the deceased, dead meat being dead meat, as they were to show any signs of mourning.

"They did an autopsy."

Liss made a sympathetic noise. She was neither shocked nor surprised. An autopsy wasn't unusual when the cause of death wasn't readily apparent.

"I was told the preliminary results this morning." The hand holding the mug trembled. Desdemona returned it to the coffee table before any of the remaining contents spilled. "Mother died of an overdose."

"I'm so sorry. What a terrible accident."

Desdemona forced a smile. "Thank you for not immediately leaping to the conclusion that she committed suicide. Not everyone has been so sensitive."

"Your mother didn't strike me as the suicidal type," Liss said, repeating what she'd told her aunt when they'd first heard that a woman had died in one of the condos at Five Mountains.

"Whatever *that* is." Desdemona had folded the napkin in her lap into tiny accordion pleats. With exaggerated care, she smoothed it out again. "I'm afraid my mother traveled with a virtual pharmacy of sleep aids, muscle relaxants, tranquilizers, and pills to perk her up, plus every vitamin known to man."

Too much information, Liss thought. Why, she wondered, was Desdemona telling her all this? Why had she come to Moosetookalook at all? The staff at the ski resort were far better equipped than Liss was to assist Desdemona in making whatever arrangements were necessary, including those having to do with taking her mother's body home for burial.

"Is there anything I can do to help?" She had been brought up to volunteer in times of trouble, but she didn't expect to be taken up on her offer.

"In fact, there is." Desdemona reached for her coffee and took another sip.

Liss waited. *Me and my big mouth,* she thought.

"Mother's contract with *Variety Live* does not have a provision that covers sudden death. The producers say the show must go on or they'll sue her estate to get back the honorarium they paid her to participate."

That the contestants on the show were paid seemed odd to Liss, but she didn't have time to wonder about it. Desdemona was still talking.

"I thought of you at once when I heard that. Did I hear you correctly the day you brought Dandy back? Are you a professional dancer?"

The reason for Desdemona's visit suddenly became crystal clear. "Oh, no." Liss waved both hands in front of her, palms out. "Not a chance."

"Why not? It's only for a few days. And you'll get to appear on national television. You *are* a pro, aren't you? Think what this could do for your career."

"I *was*. Past tense. And even then, I was a professional *Scottish* dancer. In a troupe. Think *Riverdance*, only Scottish."

"Close enough. You just offered to help. Well, this is what I need, someone to take my mother's place with Deidre and her Dancing Doggies."

"Why doesn't the daughter do it?" Dan asked.

They were in the kitchen after supper that evening, and Liss had just broached the subject of spending the better part of the next seven days at Five Mountains Ski Resort. Her husband, predictably, wasn't crazy about the idea.

"Aside from the fact that she doesn't dance, Desdemona says the dogs refuse to cooperate with her. They'll let her feed them and pet them, but they were her mother's darlings. They won't obey her commands." Liss started to clear the table, picking up the plates and silverware.

Dan put away the butter dish and brought their glasses over to the sink. "What makes her think they'll listen to you?" he asked over the rush of hot water filling the dishpan.

Liss had a dishwasher, but she liked washing up by hand when it was just the two of them. She'd gotten some of her best ideas for displays at the Emporium while scrubbing pots and pans.

"That's exactly what I asked her. There was no guarantee that they would, but Desdemona had seen the way Dandy responded to me, so she had me try telling the Scotties to spin. I was sure she was wrong about my ability to control them. Scottish terriers aren't a breed that's particularly easy to train. But what could I do? The woman is in mourning for her mother. I felt sorry for her, so I humored her. I told Dandy to spin, and without a second's hesitation, she did." Liss smiled, remembering. "Honestly, Dan, it was the cutest thing."

"Maybe it was a fluke."

She shook her head. "Dondi was just as obedient as Dandy was."

As Liss washed, Dan dried and put away. They'd been married long enough, over five years, that they performed their allotted roles on autopilot. Liss could feel him watching her as they worked side by side and sensed that something besides a few days' separation had him worried.

"What?"

"Not to sound critical, but committing yourself to something like this on the spur of the moment is impulsive, even for you."

She stuck her tongue out at him.

"I'm sorry the woman died," he went on, "but I don't see where it's your responsibility to take over for her. You only met her once."

"But I rescued one of the dogs," Liss reminded him. "Isn't there some old Chinese proverb about saving a life and then that person becomes your responsibility? Maybe that's what I'm feeling toward Dandy."

"I get that, Liss. I do. But it wasn't Dandy who conned you into volunteering to perform. This Desdemona played on the guilt you're still feeling because you almost hit the Scottie with your car."

Liss started to deny the change, then reconsidered. "You may be right, but does it really matter? This is a chance to try something different—take a break from the routine of the shop and come back refreshed and ready to take on the last-minute chaos of March Madness."

"So you're just going to drop everything to oblige the bereaved daughter of a woman you barely knew? What about your responsibilities here?"

"Desdemona pointed out, quite rightly, that the Emporium didn't seem all that busy. You know I've been thinking the exact same thing myself.

I'd been planning to treat myself to a mini-vacation by goofing off and curling up in the cozy corner with a few good books, but this is so much better. Free lodging at an upscale resort. The chance to dance on TV. A week with those two adorable little dogs."

A reluctant smile tugged at the corners of his mouth. "You really want to do this, don't you?"

"Strange as it seems, I do. The more I think about it, the more I'm looking forward to it."

"Are you going to close up shop for the next week?" He put the last drinking glass away and closed the cupboard door, the dish towel still clenched in one large, capable hand.

"Why not? It really is slow just now. Even the mail orders are down to a handful. I can let them back up for a few days."

"What about March Madness?"

"Everything's right on schedule and Audrey can handle troubleshooting for the week." She emptied the water from the dish pan and left it tipped on its side in the sink to drain. Turning to face him, she pasted what she hoped was a provocative smile on her lips. "You could come visit while I'm at Five Mountains. You wouldn't even have to drive back and forth. Take the shuttle from The Spruces."

Dan studied her for a long moment, his expression solemn. "I didn't realize you missed dancing so much."

Two quick steps brought her into his arms. "Oh, Dan," she murmured against his chest. "I don't. Not really. And these performances are hardly the same as going back to my old life—not that I'd want to, anyway—but it *would* be fun to dance with the Scotties."

She could almost hear Aunt Margaret's voice in her head, advising her to live life to the fullest. She ignored the trick of memory that immediately provided a quotation to suit the occasion: "Eat, drink, and be merry . . . for tomorrow we die."

"How about this, then?" Dan suggested. "*You* commute to Five Mountains. Like you said, The Spruces runs a shuttle."

"True, but I need to rehearse with the dogs and, believe me, you don't want me to keep them here. I told you what Lumpkin thought of Dandy."

"I just—" He broke off to stare at the ceiling. "I'll miss you, that's all."

Held snug and secure in his embrace, Liss felt the tenseness in his muscles. He *would* miss her. She didn't doubt that for a moment because she knew how much she was going to miss him. But that wasn't all that was bothering him. "What aren't you saying?"

"It's probably crazy to worry."

"About what?"

"The woman who died. Deidre Amendole. Are you sure her death was an accident? I mean, one of her dogs had just been stolen. According to what you told me after you returned the Scottie, she believed one of the other contestants was responsible."

Liss stepped far enough away from him to meet his eyes and took a moment to consider the possibility. "Literally killing the competition would hardly be necessary in order to win. There are plenty of less lethal ways to eliminate a rival contestant."

She made a mental note to keep a close eye on Dandy and Dondi while they were in her care. It seemed unlikely they'd win the champion of champions title without their original human partner, but she could certainly protect Deidre's dancing doggies from being the victims of any more dirty tricks.

For Dan's benefit, she downplayed the risks. "Even if Deidre was right about the cutthroat competition, it's a big leap from dognapping to homicide. You can't seriously think that someone slipped an overdose of sleeping pills into Deidre's food or drink just to stop her from performing."

A sheepish grin replaced the look of concern on Dan's face. "When you put it that way," he admitted, "it does sound far-fetched."

The next morning, Saturday, Liss loaded two suitcases and a garment bag into her car and drove to the conference-center hotel at the ski resort. Desdemona had been quite specific in saying that only a week of Liss's time would be required, although by Liss's calculations, several rounds of competition remained before one act could be crowned "champion of champions" on *Variety Live*. That made Liss wonder if she was *supposed* to be eliminated on the next show. That was the first question she intended to ask, although she had plenty of others.

After Deidre's death, Desdemona and the dogs had been relocated to a suite. Liss had deposited her luggage just inside the door and shed her winter coat before she realized that Desdemona had a visitor. A man with a genial smile and a full head of silver hair rose from the sofa.

"Roy Eastmont," he said in a rumbling voice that held the slightest trace of an upper-class British accent. "Master of ceremonies for *Variety Live*."

Liss took the perfectly manicured hand he extended. The skin on his palm was as smooth as a baby's butt, and about as unappealing to grasp. Although he appeared to be in his sixties, his carriage was as erect as that of a much younger man, and he was impeccably dressed in a dark suit, light blue shirt, and colorful but conservative tie. He stood a little taller than Liss, but under the six-foot mark, and met her curious gaze with eyes of a blue so bright that it did not look natural. Liss supposed there was nothing wrong with wearing colored contact lenses, but that he chose to do so made her wonder what else about him was designed to deceive.

"We were all devastated by Deidre's death," Eastmont said. "Just devastated. But I am so pleased we won't be losing her act. Dandy and Dondi are fan favorites and have been a sure bet to make it to the finals from the beginning."

"Yes. The finals." Liss sent Desdemona a speaking glance before she gave Eastmont her full attention. "I wanted to ask about that. This is a live show, right? So each week, one contestant is eliminated, based on scores given by judges and votes cast by viewers?"

"We record live performances." Eastmont smoothed one hand over a tie that needed no straightening.

His evasive answer confused her. "I admit I haven't watched the show, but I assume there's a week between each competition. I don't have that kind of time to devote to—"

"Not to worry, my dear." Eastmont took her arm and steered her to the sofa. When she was seated, he eased himself in next to her while Desdemona took a chair. "I'll let you in on a little secret. The time lapse between episodes is not really a week long. I grant you that we did take a little break to change venues to the ski resort and bring in three new celebrity judges, as is our custom at the halfway point of every season, but we'll be recording all the episodes necessary to reach the finals, together with the finale itself, in which the last three contestants each compete twice, during this coming week."

Liss tried and failed to make that information compute. "What about the fan component to the scoring? Don't viewers call in to vote for their favorites?"

"They do call in, yes." Eastmont left Liss to draw her own conclusions.

"Are you telling me that the show isn't exactly *live* after all?"

"Oh, my dear. Very little on television is ever *real.*"

Liss was not pleased to discover she'd agreed to be part of a deception, but she had to admit that Eastmont had a point. There were some days when she even had her doubts about what she saw on the nightly news.

"Desdemona will provide you with the schedule and all the other information you'll require, but there is some paperwork you need to sign up front. We don't pay you, of course, but there are certain legalities."

His blunt reference to payment, or rather the lack of any, made Liss wonder about the honorarium Desdemona had mentioned and the producers' right to sue for a refund. Were contestants compensated or not? It seemed insensitive to broach the subject with Desdemona right there, but she couldn't help but be curious.

Before she could frame another question, Eastmont reached into the inside pocket of his suit coat and brought forth a thick legal-size envelope. It contained a half dozen pages folded together. He spread them out on the coffee table in front of her, revealing that there were four documents in all. He tapped his index finger on the first.

"This is a waiver. We are conscientious when it comes to safety and we don't expect any accidents to happen, but *Variety Live* can't afford to be held responsible if one does occur."

It didn't bother Liss that she'd have to agree not to sue the production company if she was injured during recording. Such conditions weren't at all uncommon. In fact, the back of every lift ticket sold by the Five Mountains Corporation contained the statement that by purchasing it the buyers agreed not to take the ski resort or its parent company to court if they were injured in an accident while skiing there. Liss hesitated only long enough to be sure she understood all the fine print, then signed.

As she looked over the other documents, which also seemed standard agreements, for all that they were written in legalese, she admitted to herself that Dan had been right. She'd been way too impulsive in agreeing to take Deidre's place. She should have asked many more questions first.

She wasn't going to back out of the deal, but neither would she allow herself to be rushed into leaping before she looked. She ignored Eastmont's restless movements at her side and his frequent glances at his watch and paid careful attention to the convoluted wording. Why, she wondered, was it necessary for lawyers to use a dozen words when one would suffice?

The second paper was a contract. She'd be agreeing to show up, in costumes supplied by the *Variety Live* costume department, at both dress rehearsals and performances through the finale, as required, or pay a penalty. The dates were listed—less than a week, as promised. The third document she agreed not to give any interviews that hadn't been preapproved by the publicity department and agreed to participate in "standard post-production publicity." Finding nothing that set off alarm bells, Liss scribbled her signature on both documents and picked up the fourth one.

"A confidentiality agreement?"

"That's right. Standard practice in the industry."

She didn't know if she believed that claim or not, but what was clear was that *Variety Live* didn't want behind-the-scenes details leaking out either before or after the shows aired. Since she had no intention of providing fodder to supermarket tabloids, Liss signed her name.

Eastmont scooped up the papers, stuffing them back into their envelope. Once again, he glanced at his watch, after which he rose from the sofa and headed for the door, talking as he went. "I fear I must leave you ladies now. I have a meeting with the camera crew. You can introduce yourself to your competition, Ms. Ruskin. All the rooms on this floor are occupied by contestants and production staff. The hotel manager was very good about that. The resort at Five Mountains is providing us with free accommodations and the use of the ballroom in return for the excellent publicity they'll get from having us record the show here. Ms. Amendole, I wish you a safe trip. We'll send flowers."

The door closed behind him on the final word.

Liss looked at Desdemona. "Are you going somewhere?"

Head bent, Desdemona toyed with the ring she wore on the middle finger of her left hand. The fit was loose, and the stone, a garnet so large that it nearly covered her knuckle, slid easily around and around. "I'm leaving shortly to take my mother's body back to Ohio. The funeral is scheduled for Monday."

Liss could have kicked herself. Of course the other woman wasn't going to stick around just to show her the ropes and answer her questions. Still there was one she had to ask. She'd been in the suite for at least fifteen minutes and hadn't seen hide nor hair of the two Scotties.

"Where are Dandy and Dondi?"

"Valentine offered to take them for a walk and keep them while I packed."

"Valentine?"

"Valentine Veilleux. The photographer."

Liss remembered the calendar she'd seen when she'd returned Dandy to Deidre. Iris, the magician's assistant, had mentioned that the same photographer had been hired to take pictures for a *Variety Live* calendar. "Is she staying here in the hotel?"

"She has a room on this floor, but she works out of her RV. She lives in the thing year round and uses it to get from job to job." Desdemona rolled her eyes. "I can't imagine being confined in such a cramped space. I'd go mad inside of a week."

Doing a good imitation of a jack-in-the-box, Desdemona sprang up from her chair and made a beeline for the connecting bedroom. A moment later, she reemerged dragging a bulging suitcase. She was strong for such a skinny female. Somewhere in those sticklike arms there was real muscle. Two more large bags followed, no doubt containing Deidre's belongings as well as Desdemona's.

Liss collected her own luggage and transferred it to the bedroom before asking, "Do you need help getting all that to the lobby?"

"Parking lot," Desdemona corrected her. "Mother had a rental car. I'll return it when I get to the airport." She looked around, checking to see if she'd forgotten anything. "I've left you all the supplies you'll need for the dogs. Food. Toys. Pee pads."

Catching sight of the expression on Liss's face, Desdemona led her into the bathroom to show her where a forty pack of this last item had been stored. The package had been opened, and about a quarter of the pads were already gone.

"This is the best invention since sliced bread. They're sold as aids to house-train puppies, but they're ideal for small dogs, especially if you need to leave them alone for any length of time, or if the weather is so brutal that you don't feel inspired to take them outside to do their business."

Liss had the uncomfortable feeling that, like disposable diapers, doggie pee pads would survive intact for decades, clogging up landfills, but she had to admit that she could see how such a thing might come in handy. "It's too bad dogs can't be trained to use a litter box," she said. "What do you do with the used ones?"

"Heavens! I don't know." Her tone said she didn't care. "Now, these are the plastic baggies Mother used to pick up solid waste when she took the dogs for walkies."

"Wonderful." The snide note in Desdemona's voice bothered Liss more than the prospect of cleaning up after Dandy and Dondi.

"Here's their special food and the vitamins they take daily." Desdemona opened a cabinet in the kitchen area. "Have you ever given a pill to a dog?"

"I assume you manage the same way you do with a cat—open mouth, insert pill, close mouth, rub throat." A rueful smile accompanied the explanation. More often than not there were two more steps—"pick up pill after cat spits it out" and "repeat steps one through four as many times as necessary until the cat actually swallows the pill."

"Whatever works." More and more clearly as she spoke of the Scottish terriers and their supplies, Desdemona's expression showed her distaste for everything to do with them. "Be careful," she warned Liss. "The little devils have very sharp teeth."

"Most animals do. Where is that schedule Mr. Eastmont spoke of?"

Desdemona produced a standard conference registration packet and handed it over. A quick survey of the contents, while Desdemona collected her coat and a scarf from the closet and located her shoulder bag, showed Liss that the material was missing one crucial piece of information.

"I don't see a list of contestants."

"Does it matter? You'll meet them soon enough."

"It would be helpful if you could tell me what you know about the competition before you go." She seated herself at the small desk in the suite's living room, picked up one of the hotel notepads and a pen carrying the Five Mountains Ski Resort logo, and waited.

Desdemona's lips pursed in annoyance. She perched on the edge of a nearby chair, coat clutched in front of her, one foot jiggling. "There are five left." Her fingers toyed with the strap of her purse. "Willetta Farwell is a singer. Hal Quarles is a stand-up comic. Oscar Yates is the magician—The Great Umberto, he calls himself. You've already met his assistant, Iris. Then there's Mo Heedles. Mo is short for Maureen, but she never uses her full name. She juggles. And Elise Isley is an exotic dancer."

"Exotic—you mean she's a stripper?" *Variety Live* might not be live, but it certainly did offer variety.

"Don't let her hear you call her that." Desdemona came close to smiling. "She's also the only other act left that features an animal. She bills herself as Elise and her Mighty Python and performs with a snake named Eudora."

Liss felt her eyes widen. "A *python?* Isn't that dangerous?"

"I'm told Eudora is quite friendly, although it probably wouldn't be a good idea to let her wrap herself around your neck."

"Is there anything else I need to be warned about?"

"I can't think of anything. Of course, I don't know any of these people well. I only visited once during the first half of the competition and I didn't come to Maine until Mother phoned to tell me that Dandy was missing. I arrived on Tuesday, the same day you returned her."

More surprises, Liss thought. She'd been operating under the assumption that Desdemona had been at Five Mountains with her mother all along. "You *are* planning to return here after the funeral, aren't you?"

"Well, I have to, don't I? I'll have to do something about those dratted dogs."

Liss stared at her. Whatever Desdemona had in mind for Dandy and Dondi, it didn't sound as if she intended to provide them with a loving forever home.

Desdemona shot to her feet, overturning her purse as she did so. The papers in the outside pocket spilled out. With an impatient exclamation, she knelt to gather them up and stuff them back in, waving Liss away when she got up to help.

"I need to get going. Give me a hand with the bags and I'll show you where to go to reclaim your dance partners from Valentine."

Liss wanted to tell her she couldn't leave yet, not while Liss still had questions. Instead, she did a quick mental sort and pulled out the most pressing one. "Did your mother keep a written record of her dance routines?"

Desdemona made a brief detour to the desk to rummage through the drawers. "There's a spiral-bound notebook somewhere. The kind students use. Ah, here it is."

She handed it over, then immediately began hauling her luggage into the hallway. Liss had only time enough for a quick peek at the pages, but what she saw was reassuring. Deidre had recorded a series of routines she'd worked out for herself and the two dogs. She hadn't used formal dance notation, but her descriptions and the little diagrams she'd drawn to go with them should be simple enough to interpret. Even so, Liss knew she had some homework to do before she'd be ready for the first performance.

An impatient tapping—fingernails on doorframe—reminded her that Desdemona had a plane to catch. Together they lugged all three bags to the elevator. In the parking lot behind the hotel, after they'd stashed the suitcases in the trunk of Deidre's rental car, Desdemona led the way to an enormous RV. Even before she knocked on the door, extraordinarily loud barking broke out from the other side.

"Good grief! All that noise from such small dogs?" If Liss hadn't known Dandy and Dondi were the ones making the racket, she'd have sworn there was a Great Dane inside . . . or at least a collie. Most dogs the size of the Scotties just yapped, an annoying sound that always reminded her of the toy dog she'd been given for Christmas when she was nine.

A voice, raised to be heard above the din, yelled, "It's open. Come on in."

Desdemona gestured for Liss to enter first. She'd barely stepped inside before the two Scotties threw themselves at her, nearly knocking her off her feet.

"Down!" she ordered, laughing. They responded by circling her in a joyous dance and then, to her delight, stood up on their hind legs and waved their front paws at her. "Does this mean you're glad to see me?"

The look of adoration in Dandy's expressive eyes gave her the answer she hoped for.

"Be with you in a minute." The throaty voice belonged to a strawberry blonde. At first that was all Liss could see of Valentine Veilleux—a mass of hair spilling halfway down her back. The photographer sat hunched over a computer monitor, giving commands with deft clicks of a mouse. Only after she'd saved the file and gone back to her home screen did she swivel her chair around to face Liss and Desdemona.

"Valentine, Liss. Liss, Valentine," Desdemona said.

Valentine Veilleux shoved at glasses that had slipped to the end of her nose and were in imminent danger of falling off. Liss caught a brief glimpse of pretty green eyes before Valentine slid thick lenses in front of them.

"Nice to meet you, Liss. If you ever need to go somewhere dogs aren't allowed, I'm always happy to have their company."

"I'll keep that in mind."

A sharp click sounded as Desdemona attached Dandy's leash to her collar. Dondi eluded her, squirming into the storage space beneath the sofa to avoid being caught.

"Come out of there, you little beast!"

He ignored her. Dandy, deciding this was some interesting new game, barked with delight and tried to crawl in with her brother. Desdemona swore, threatening both dogs with bodily harm if they made her miss her plane. She stamped her foot, looking for all the world like a child on the brink of a temper tantrum.

"Stand back," Liss told her, and got down on hands and knees. "Dondi? Dondi, sweetie. Come here, little one."

As she waited for some response, her butt sticking up in the air and her face all but on the floor of the RV, it occurred to Liss that Desdemona had no need to stick around. She'd already given Liss the key to the suite. She'd brought her to the two Scotties. She was free to leave for the airport at any time. Liss was about to remind her of this fact when a wiry black head popped out from beneath the sofa. Liss snapped the leash in place. Tugging gently, she finished extracting Dondi from his hiding place.

"Wretched creature," Desdemona grumbled. "One more trick like that and he's going to end up in the dog pound, and not one of those humane ones, either."

Liss and Valentine exchanged a look of consternation. Liss hoped Desdemona was just letting off steam, but she had the uneasy suspicion that Deidre's daughter, the new owner of the two Scottish terriers, meant every venom-filled word.

Chapter Four

Once Desdemona had left for the airport, Liss returned to the suite with Dandy and Dondi. They had a lot of work to do to prepare for the dress rehearsal scheduled for the following day. Before she settled in, though, she took a few minutes to explore her new surroundings.

The two rooms in her corner suite looked as if they'd been decorated by the same person who'd done Deidre's condo . . . with a smaller budget. The chairs and sofa weren't leather here, and there was no fireplace, but otherwise the layout was similar. The front room was sectioned off into a minuscule kitchen area, a dining area with table and four straight chairs, and a living area where the furniture was cozily arranged so that the occupant could sit and watch TV, converse with friends, or simply enjoy the spectacular view.

Five Mountains had been aptly named, although someone living in the Rockies might dispute the issue. Such as they were, Mount Dennis, Sandy Mountain, Lawrence Peak, Old Tumbledown, and Pious Ridge rose up to circle the valley in which the ski lodge, hotel, and condominiums had been built. Three out of the five boasted ski slopes ranging in difficulty from bunny to are-you-sure-you're-brave-enough-to-try-this-one?

The vista spread out before the windows in the bedroom was just as impressive. Liss discovered that she had a balcony. It wrapped around the corner, so that if she stepped out through a pair of French doors, she'd be able to see for miles . . . if she wanted to risk frostbite. Fortunately, she didn't need to brave the cold air to orient herself. The windows on one side, like those in the other room, were at the front of the hotel. She was high enough to see most of the long, straight private drive that led from the resort to the highway—a two-lane state road that connected Five Mountains to Moosetookalook, Fallstown, and points south. The rest of the balcony was directly above the driveway that circled the hotel to access the parking lot at the back.

Liss wasn't a skier. Going out to play in the snow had never tempted her. But she could admire the pretty, pristine whiteness, divided by plantations of evergreens and broken by the jagged lines that were, in fact, carefully groomed trails. She stood where she was for a few more minutes, admiring the view.

Dondi let out a yelp when she turned away and nearly tripped over him. Both dogs were right behind her, looking up at her with such hopeful expressions on their faces that she had to laugh. Hands on hips, she sent them what she hoped was a stern look. "You can't be hungry again!"

If she hadn't known better, she'd have sworn Dandy nodded.

Liss led them into the tiny kitchenette and found the dog treats. She checked to be certain there was water in their dog dishes while she was there, aware as she did so that she was procrastinating. It was time to get to work.

After she hunted up the packet of information Desdemona had left for her, Liss ordered a light lunch from room service. While she waited for it to be delivered, she skimmed the contents, looking for any nuggets of information she might have missed earlier. Since nothing jumped out at her, she set the material aside when her food arrived and popped the DVD Deidre had given her into the player. She needed to see what she'd gotten herself into.

This was the season, she remembered, that Deidre and her Dancing Doggies had won their title. That meant none of the other contestants would be the same as those competing in the current show. That didn't matter. What Liss wanted to get a good look at were the dance routines. Although Desdemona had assured her she'd have no trouble getting the dogs to perform, and she had already spent a little time studying the diagrams and instructions in Deidre's spiral-bound notebook, she needed to get a clearer picture of exactly how the routines were executed.

When the acts were introduced for the first time,

Liss waited with keen anticipation for Deidre's appearance. As she'd half expected, given that the woman was dancing with two Scottish terriers, she was wearing a kilt, but it was a kilt unlike any Liss had ever seen. It was *very* short, ending midway down Deidre's thick thighs. The tartan was one Liss was positive no clan would ever claim. The pattern was picked out in bright-colored glitter. On Deidre's short, stocky form, the outfit was not flattering, but it was certainly eye-catching.

All the contestants wore similarly glitzy and revealing clothing. It didn't seem to matter what their talent was. While Roy Eastmont delivered his opening remarks as MC, Liss fished through the material Desdemona had left for her. A page she'd hitherto overlooked, headed POLICY ON COSTUMES, elaborated on the terms she'd already agreed to when she'd signed Eastmont's paperwork.

Variety Live provided contestants with costumes, and the show's costume designer had the final say about what they wore in performances. Liss tried to tell herself that she felt relieved. She'd been saved the trouble and expense of providing her own outfits.

She didn't buy her own argument. The costume policy gave her one more thing to worry about. She had a decent figure and shapely legs and didn't embarrass easily, but she also had a long scar running down one knee. She didn't relish the idea of showing it off to the entire *Variety Live* viewing audience.

Reaching for the clicker, Liss fast-forwarded the DVD to the start of Deidre's first performance. Once she'd gotten past the short kilt and the glitter, she realized that although Deidre was wearing tap shoes, she only seemed to know one combination of steps. She repeated it several times, but for the most part, her "dance" consisted of posing and using a series of hand signals to get Dandy and Dondi to strut their stuff and look cute.

"Oh, boy," Liss muttered. Was she supposed to perform on Deidre's level, or her own?

Making good use of fast-forward, Liss skipped ahead, viewing only Deidre's dance numbers in each show. In one, the dogs formed a conga line. For another, Dandy and Dondi posed as a canine version of Fred Astaire and Ginger Rogers, much as they had in the calendar photo Liss had seen.

Although the dancing involved was minimal, in the end Liss had to admire what Deidre had accomplished. Liss had always heard that Scotties were a tough breed to train and that they condescended to learn tricks only when it suited them. It seemed to her that they must have been very fond of Deidre. They'd tried hard to please her, even if all they ended up doing were variations of sit, stand, and spin.

In her spiral-bound notebook, Deidre had

written down the hand signals she used as commands. The illusion of dancing came as much from her movements as from what the dogs did. As Liss watched the screen and studied the pages from Deidre's notebook, her admiration continued to grow. Deidre had cleverly designed routines that showcased the dogs. She hadn't been half bad at acting, either, a talent that was part and parcel of any successful dancer's repertoire. Liss anticipated few difficulties in duplicating Deidre's steps, but making the whole package come together smoothly would take practice. Lots and lots of practice.

Liss hit the button to eject the DVD.

The Scotties had fallen asleep on the other end of the sofa. They weren't curled up together, the way cats did when they slept, but each of them had stretched out a leg so that their paws touched.

Did they miss Deidre? Liss wondered. Did they understand that she was gone for good? Liss had caught Dandy, once or twice, looking at the door as though she expected someone to walk into the room any minute.

Then again, perhaps Dandy and Dondi were accustomed to extended separations from their owner. Liss had no idea what Deidre's ordinary life had been like. *Variety Live* might or might not be the first reality competition show the trio had entered.

Liss looked again at the diagrams in the

notebook. She sighed. Time enough in the morning to start putting the dogs through their paces. She set aside Deidre's notes and stared into space. No matter how much she practiced with Dandy and Dondi, chances were good that the act would be eliminated in the next round. If that was the case, it hardly mattered how well they performed their routine.

She wished the current season was already out on DVD. She'd like to take a look at her competition.

The penny dropped a moment later. The champion of champions edition of *Variety Live* might not yet be in stores, but it ought to be available On Demand. A few clicks with the remote took her to an index of episodes.

From the information in her packet, Liss knew that the hour-long show was broadcast on one of the minor networks on Monday nights. On Tuesdays, there was a half-hour results show. The On Demand index listed original air dates, which told her something else. In reality, the surviving contestants had just enjoyed a nice long hiatus. To the show's viewers, the first seven episodes and results shows had been airing "live" each of the last seven weeks. An awards show was scheduled to preempt the coming week's episodes, but when *Variety Live* returned the following Monday, fans would believe that the break had lasted only seven days.

That awards show was a stroke of luck for the producers, Liss thought. If they'd started recording the remaining shows a week sooner, they'd be hard-pressed now to explain how Deidre could still appear "live" after she was dead. Telling viewers their "fan favorite" was deceased would be tricky enough. Liss wondered how big a deal the producers intended to make of it, and how they'd explain bringing her in as Deidre's replacement.

She selected the season premiere and settled back to watch.

After the usual hype and two commercial messages, Roy Eastmont appeared on the screen, smile genial and blue eyes bright as sapphires, to introduce the champions from twelve previous seasons. Six acts would be eliminated in the course of the first seven episodes. Liss identified them as a ventriloquist, a lion tamer, a singing family, a dance troupe, a gymnastics trio, and a singing duet.

The other performers interested her more—the ones who were still in the running. Even though she knew that first impressions were rarely accurate, and that the onstage persona of a performer didn't always match the offstage personality, Liss made a list and scribbled notes beside each name as she watched the show.

Since she was yawning well before the credits ran, she decided against watching the remaining episodes that night. She had turned off the TV and was about to go to bed when both Scotties suddenly woke up and started barking. In unison, they flung themselves off the sofa and raced toward the door to the hallway. The sound of someone knocking could barely be heard over the racket they made.

"Nothing like an early-warning system," Liss said. "Good dogs."

Her years on the road, almost always staying in far less luxurious hotels than this one, had taught her to double lock the door as soon as she arrived and to look through the peephole first if anyone wanted to come in. The latter precaution revealed two visitors. One was Iris Jansen, the magician's assistant she had already met. Standing beside her was a plump, chocolate-skinned woman Liss recognized as another of the remaining contestants—the singer, Willetta Farwell.

Judging by the performance Liss had seen, the woman had a heck of a set of pipes. In the premiere, she'd been wearing a glittery floor-length ball gown. In this more casual setting, she'd opted for stretchy black yoga pants and a long, loose green velour tunic. Aware that Liss would be looking out at her from the other side of the door, she aimed a brilliant smile at the peephole and waggled her fingers in greeting. Liss undid the locks and opened the door.

The dogs retreated, losing interest now that they knew who'd been knocking.

Watching them race away, Iris's eyes filled with tears. "I can't believe she's gone. She was such a nice woman." Sniffling, she accepted the box of tissues Liss grabbed from an end table.

While Iris dabbed at her damp cheeks and blew her nose, Willetta went down on one knee to open her arms to the Scotties. Dondi accepted the invitation and gave her a thorough face licking. She didn't seem to mind. She gave him a head rub and scratched behind his ears. Dandy watched, but didn't come close enough to get the same treatment. With a shrug, Willetta stood up and turned her attention to Liss.

"Hi. I'm Willetta. Liss, right?"

"Right."

Although Willetta's tone of voice was friendly, her gaze was cool and assessing. "I hope we're not disturbing you, but when I heard that Desdemona had found someone to fill in for her mom, I was curious."

"Perfectly natural. Won't you sit down? I was planning to introduce myself to everyone tomorrow." She indicated Deidre's spiral-bound notebook and the clamshell case next to the DVD player and the television. "I thought I should do a little homework first."

"We've all been so upset about what happened."

Iris's voice was so choked up that her words were barely intelligible.

Willetta gave the entire room a long, slow appraisal that ended when she picked up the list of names Liss had been annotating. "Studying the competition?"

Liss twitched it out of her fingers. "In part. Mostly, I'm trying to get a feel for the choreography."

Willetta chuckled. "Even I can tell you what that entails—step, brush, ball-change, step-heel, stamp. Repeat with an occasional shuffle."

"Even a simple routine takes practice." Liss heard the defensive tone in her voice and smiled to moderate the effect. It was foolish to resent any criticism of Deidre's act just because the woman was dead, especially when Willetta had hit the nail on the head.

"You'll have an uphill battle, no matter how much you rehearse. Playing catch-up is no fun."

Liss grimaced. "Isn't that the truth! And I'm facing some pretty stiff competition. I've heard you sing."

Reaching into the pocket of her tunic, Willetta withdrew a package of sugar-free honey-lemon cough drops, the kind that also cleared the sinuses. "The singing I'm doing here isn't my usual," she said, fishing one out and popping it into her mouth.

"What's your usual?" In the premiere, she'd

belted out a show tune in the style and with the volume of the late, great Ethel Merman.

"Opera."

Thanks to the cough drop, the word was garbled, but Liss understood it well enough. "Do you have a cold?" She saw no other indication that the singer might be ill.

"No." Willetta rapped on the top of the coffee table. "Knock wood. I use these as preventive medicine." She smiled again, showing beautifully straight, gleaming white teeth. It was the kind of smile that made Liss want to smile back.

"She has to be careful of her voice," Iris said from the chair. She'd been quick to make herself at home. The waterworks had dried up, but she sounded as if she could use one of Willetta's cough drops to soothe her throat.

"Always," Willetta agreed. "Come on, Iris. We don't want to keep our new colleague from her studies."

Iris obediently stood, stepped over the circling Scotties, and headed for the door Willetta already had open. Dandy made a dash for freedom, but Liss was faster, catching hold of the little dog before she could reach the corridor.

Willetta used one foot to gently discourage Dondi from making the same attempt. "Nice meeting you, Liss."

"See you tomorrow," Iris called.

When they'd gone, Liss set Dandy down. A

vague sense of uneasiness nagged at her. On impulse, she grabbed her key card and stepped out into the hall. Iris had already disappeared, but Willetta was still standing in front of her own room, just two doors down from Liss's, cussing softly at the balky lock.

"Hate these things," she muttered. "What was wrong with old-fashioned metal keys?"

"Not a thing that I can see. Want me to try?"

Even as she offered, Willetta succeeded in getting the little green light to come on. She turned the handle before it could go red again, then glanced Liss's way. "Something you wanted?"

"I was wondering—who told you that Dandy and Dondi had a new partner?"

"Was it supposed to be a secret? Roy Eastmont passed on the good news in an e-mail. Everybody connected with the show probably got one."

"No secret. I was just surprised that word got around so fast."

With a wave, Liss retreated into her own suite, double locking the door behind her. She leaned against the solid wooden surface, wondering why the show's MC had been so quick to let everyone know she was taking Deidre's place. She supposed there was no good reason why he shouldn't have done so. In fact, it made perfect sense to send out that e-mail. So why did she find the fact that he had so troubling?

The answer came to her when Dandy went up on her hind legs to lick Liss's hand. Deidre had been convinced that it was one of her competitors who had stolen the Scottie. If she was right, then that person was among those who'd received Roy Eastmont's e-mail. That meant *Liss* was now on the dognapper's radar. Maybe she had good cause to feel uneasy!

"Cats," Liss informed the two Scotties she accompanied outside at a quarter to seven the following morning, "are much less bother." Especially when it was Dan who cleaned their litter box.

Oblivious to her crack-of-dawn grumpiness, they took their time exploring the area at one side of the parking lot that had been planted with decorative trees and shrubbery and furnished with several benches and a bronze statue of a skier. Every bush, every space between two paving stones, every patch of snow had to be sniffed and marked as Scottie territory. With one leash in each hand, Liss couldn't cover the huge yawn that snuck up on her.

"I'd kill for a cup of coffee," she muttered. She'd had time to start a pot, but not to wait for it to be ready. Dandy and Dondi had made it abundantly clear that they needed to go out *now.* "Little con artists."

When the dogs finally got around to doing what

they'd come outside for, Liss shifted both leashes to one hand, retrieved the plastic bag she'd slipped into her coat pocket, and set to work cleaning up after them. Mission accomplished, she herded her charges back through a rear entrance to the hotel and down a short hallway to the elevators. She pushed the button for the fourth floor. It was also the top floor. Hotels in rural Maine were rarely higher, especially in places where a skyscraper might spoil the landscape.

Just before the car began to rise, the doors opened again to reveal a gaunt, unhealthy-looking man in his sixties. Liss recognized him as the stand-up comic competing to be champion of champions. He carried a take-out coffee from the coffee bar next to the concierge desk and a bakery bag that smelled of cinnamon and grease.

Liss stared at the cup with longing, doubly glad she'd hit the BREW button on the suite's coffee-maker before heading outside with the dogs. There was fresh coffee waiting with her name on it. A few more minutes, and she'd be sitting in a warm room and sipping a cup of hot, reviving liquid wake-me-up.

Her gaze shifted to the man. His appearance was unappealing—sunken chest; narrow, bony shoulders; and spindly legs—but since he specialized in insult humor, she supposed he might consider those features to be assets. He sent an irritated glance in the direction of the dogs, who were sniffing his pants legs, then raised faded gray eyes, a good match for what was left of his thinning hair, to give Liss a baleful look. She saw recognition flare, not because he knew who she was, but because he realized that the person walking Deidre Amendole's two dogs had to be her replacement . . . and his competition.

Don't judge a book by its cover, Liss warned herself, and dialed up the best smile she could manage at this hour of the day. "Good morning. I'm Liss Ruskin. You must be Hal Quarles."

"Must I?" His sneer emphasized sallow, sunken cheeks and made the bags beneath his eyes stand out.

Okay. Not a morning person. She made no further attempt at conversation and was surprised when he spoke again.

"I suppose the daughter was too cheap to spring for the upscale digs."

"I beg your pardon?"

"You don't think the producers put Deidre Amendole up in that fancy-schmantzy condo, do you? She rented that place with her own money—she had pots of it—so she wouldn't have to live cheek by jowl with the rest of us."

"These suites aren't exactly shabby."

He shrugged. "I've stayed in better places."

Liss was relieved when the elevator finally came to a stop. She held the dogs back to let Quarles get off first, then followed him down the hallway. His room turned out to be just before hers on the opposite side of the corridor. Watching him hunch over the door handle, glancing suspiciously from side to side as he used the key card, as if someone might be about to bop him on the head, break in, and steal his possessions, she found herself picturing him in Victorian dress. He'd make a perfect Ebenezer Scrooge . . . with a dash of Ichabod Crane thrown in.

So what if Deidre had been wealthy enough to upgrade her accommodations? Quarles's complaint sounded like the lament of a sore loser to her. Sour grapes. The green-eyed monster.

And that made her wonder if *he* had been the one who'd dognapped Dandy. If he had, Dandy apparently bore him no resentment. The little dog had behaved in a perfectly normal manner around the man.

Good, she thought. One less suspect.

In much better humor, Liss let herself into her own room, inhaling the welcome scent of that long awaited, much anticipated cup of coffee.

Five Mountains Ski Resort's hotel boasted an enormous ballroom on the second floor. A harried-looking young woman carrying a clipboard checked Liss's ID card, or rather Deidre's, which had been in the packet Desdemona had left for her, and directed her to an area marked off on the floor with blue tape and numbered with the numeral three. Similar rehearsal spaces had been allotted to each of the competitors, but at the moment they all appeared to be clustered around two tables set up in front of a bank of windows at the far end of the room. The tables held assorted pastries and fresh fruit, pitchers containing various juices, and industrial-size dispensers of coffee, decaf, and hot water for tea or cocoa.

Liss went first to Area Three to put down her tote bag and the two carriers containing Dandy and Dondi. Out in the open like this, she didn't worry that someone would walk off with one of them. The Scotties would be safe enough for the few minutes it would take her to grab a cup of coffee—her third of the day—and a doughnut.

"Be good," she told them. "I'll be right back."

"Hello, Liss," Willetta greeted her when she joined the throng. "Dig in. The food won't last long with this crowd."

Of the people helping themselves to breakfast, Liss recognized only Valentine Veilleux. She sent the photographer a friendly wave.

"We have to eat when we can," a melodious male voice chimed in. "We never know where our next meal is coming from."

It was the lament of all professional performers. Liss turned, fairly certain it must have been the magician, Oscar Yates, who had spoken. She was right, although he didn't introduce himself by that name.

“I am the Great Umberto,” he said, “magician extraordinaire.”

“Liss Ruskin, dog wrangler.”

They didn’t shake hands. His were already full of food and drink. And yet, when his admiring gaze swept over her, Liss *felt* as if she’d been touched. The Great Umberto had charisma up the wazoo.

Seeing his act on the season premiere hadn’t prepared her for the impact of meeting him in person. Although he’d given a smooth, polished performance, it hadn’t included any illusions Liss hadn’t seen before. Up close, though, he gave off vibes strong enough to make her think that he really could work magic. Oscar Yates had been blessed with the kind of rich blue-black hair that reflected sunlight. In combination with olive skin and regular features, the result was a striking appearance.

Liss cleared her throat and reached for a plate. “I’m looking forward to meeting the rest of the contestants this morning.”

“And here we all are.” Willetta sounded amused.

Liss stole a sideways glance at Yates, who stood just a little too close to her at the buffet. He radiated animal magnetism, but he wasn’t really her type. For one thing, the sideburns, mustache, and short, neatly trimmed beard made him look a little too much like a nineteenth-century music-hall villain.

At least two dozen people swarmed around the two tables, making it difficult for Liss to locate the two competitors she had not yet encountered. While watching the first episode of the season, she'd noticed that they were both redheads, but she'd been paying more attention to what they did than to how they looked.

Yates kept pace with Liss as she collected her second breakfast of the morning. "I was sorry to hear about Deidre," he said. "How are her canine partners doing?"

"They don't seem to be pining."

Reminded of her responsibilities, Liss craned her neck for a better line of sight with the dog carriers. Two members of the production crew were walking in the direction of Area Three, but neither showed any inclination to stop, let alone a propensity for dognapping.

"I'm a little surprised to hear that." Yates unleashed the full impact of his dazzling smile. "There always seemed to be such a strong bond between Deidre and her doggies."

Liss started to reply, but the magician's assistant, Iris, chose that moment to materialize beside him. She slid her fingers into the crook of his elbow and gave Liss a nod in greeting, but the welcome was noticeably colder than at their two previous meetings. Liss would have had to be blind to miss the possessiveness in Iris's manner.

"Ready to rehearse?" she asked her boss.

Iris had changed her earrings, Liss noticed. At Deidre's condo she'd been wearing little silver hearts. Last night it had been small gold hoops. This morning the earrings du jour were tiny bouquets of flowers.

Yates kept his voice smooth and a pleasant expression in place, but he didn't look at his young assistant. "I'll be with you in a minute, Iris. Here. Take my plate and go wait for me in our rehearsal area."

Was he oblivious to Iris's feelings, Liss wondered, or was he ignoring them in the hope that she'd grow out of her crush on him? It was impossible to tell.

Reluctantly, Iris released her grip on his arm and relieved him of the food he hadn't yet touched—a muffin, an apple, and a glazed doughnut. Yates stayed put, sipping his coffee as she carried them toward a tall, brightly painted magician's vanishing cabinet.

After one more sip, he made a face and abandoned the cup on the small table set up to collect empties. "Bitter. I prefer things sweet."

His smile and the flash of deviltry in his dark eyes made Liss think he was considering kissing her hand. There was something suave and Continental about him. Instead, he clicked his heels and gave a small bow. "A pleasure to meet you, Liss Ruskin, dog wrangler. I hope we will have another chance to talk together soon."

Charmed in spite of herself, Liss watched him glide away. No other word would do to describe the smooth way he moved. "That man took dance lessons as a kid," she said to no one in particular. "I'll bet good money on it."

"Is that how he developed those magnificent buns?" The voice was female, sultry, and amused.

"Could be." Liss turned her head, expecting to see either Elise Isley or Mo Heedles . . . and came face-to-face with the curious gaze of an enormous snake. She took an involuntary step backward. "Yikes!"

She was proud of herself. She didn't turn and run, and she didn't scream. She'd have been entitled to do both. Even though she'd been forewarned about Eudora the Mighty Python and had even seen her performance on the TV screen, Liss was not prepared for the reality. Eudora looked a lot larger in person, especially when she was draped over the shoulders of a woman who could not be more than five-foot-two. Elise's stare was less curious and more suspicious than that of her pet.

Trying to ignore the fact that a four-foot-long reptile was close enough to touch, Liss addressed the small human beneath the big snake. "Hi. I'm Liss Ruskin. You must be Elise Isley."

The exotic dancer wore such heavy makeup that it was hard to guess her age, but she had sharp facial features and masses of dark red hair artfully arranged to veil the front of her body and play peekaboo with ample breasts. Elise fit the stereotypical image of a stripper—stacked, with shapely legs and toned arms. Both arms and legs were bare, showing skin of a shade somewhere between Willetta's dark chocolate and Oscar Yates's olive.

"I hear you're a pro," Elise said. "Ballroom?"

"Scottish. I'm also retired."

"This is Eudora." Elise reached up to stroke the snake looped around her neck. "You can pet her if you like."

"Thanks anyway. My hands are full." Thank goodness! The last thing Liss wanted to do was extend a hand in Eudora's direction. "Um, isn't it dangerous to carry her that way?" Pythons, Liss recalled, tended to squeeze the life out of their prey before they made a meal of it.

"Not at all," Elise said.

The booming voice of Roy Eastmont, sounding cheerful and well rested, distracted her from whatever she'd been about to add. "Morning, everyone. Ready to rehearse?"

Elise sidled up to the MC as he reached for a bear claw. Whatever she whispered into his ear made his hand clench on the pastry. The smile Liss had begun to think was permanently affixed on his face wavered and, for a split second, completely disappeared.

"Elise is lobbying to get her own show." The comment came from Mo Heedles, the only one of the remaining contestants Liss hadn't yet met. She had circled the table and now stood beside her. Like Elise, she was not very tall and had red hair, but there the similarities ended. No one would ever call Mo voluptuous. She was a ginger-haired elf of a woman, probably somewhere in her late twenties.

"Stripping for fun and profit?" Liss doctored her coffee and took a swallow to the sound of Mo's chuckle. The magician had been right. Why did hotels always seem to make their coffee so strong and bitter? She added another packet of sweetener.

"Be careful Elise doesn't hear you call her a stripper," the other woman warned her as they started to walk toward Area Three together. "We must all use the politically correct term *exotic dancer.* As for the show she wants, it's to be a competition something like this one, only with poles."

"What's next? Mud wrestling?"

Mo's answer was a thunderous sneeze. She managed to turn her head aside and get her arm up in time to protect both Liss and her food, but from the look of her scrunched-up face, more explosions were imminent. "Sorry," she got out before the second one hit.

Turning back to the buffet tables, Liss abandoned her plate and cup and grabbed up a handful of napkins.

"Thanks." Mo sneezed again. "You must have dog hairs on your clothing. I'm allergic." The fourth sneeze was even more violent than the first three.

"I'm so sorry." Liss backed up, retrieved her food, and kept several feet of space between them.

"Not your fault." Mo fumbled in the sleeve of her sweater to pull out a man's white handkerchief. "Happens all the time." She dabbed at her nose. "I don't usually sneeze so much. I just get really stuffed up."

Willetta hovered nearby, finishing off a croissant. Liss expected the singer to offer Mo one of her honey-lemon cough drops, but if the thought occurred to her, she didn't have time to act on it. Mo took off, eyes streaming, heading for her allotted rehearsal space. It was located as far away from Area Three as it was possible to get and still be in the ballroom. Someone on the production staff, Liss thought, deserved a gold star.

In the suite, Liss had run through the routine Deidre had devised for this week's show a half dozen times. She'd committed both the steps and the hand signals to memory. The dogs had cooperated beautifully. Rehearsing in the ballroom was a different story. Not only was it more open, it was noisy and full of distractions. Most disconcerting of all, Liss could swear she felt unfriendly eyes boring into her as she opened the two carriers and gave each Scottie an affectionate cuddle.

In her previous career, Liss had been part of a troupe of dancers. Even when she'd had a solo bit, she'd been surrounded by the rest of the company. She wasn't sure she liked being the center of attention. The "live" performance was sure to be even worse. When she and the dogs danced before the cameras, she'd be wearing a skimpy costume. She hadn't tried it on yet, hadn't even seen it, but she had gotten a phone call just before she left the suite for the ballroom. She was to report for a fitting after the lunch break.

Suck it up, she told herself. *You're a pro.* Makeup would probably hide the ugly scar left by her knee-replacement surgery.

According to the schedule, dress rehearsal was twenty-four hours away. The show would be recorded a few hours later, at two o'clock the next afternoon. Liss frowned and took another look around the ballroom. Where were they going to put the audience? There was a stage at one end of the room, but she saw no tiers of seating. Of course, there were no cameras yet, either. Perhaps it was just too early for both.

She fished an MP3 player loaded with Deidre's music and a set of earbuds out of her tote bag. Tomorrow, a professional sound system would be in place to blare out the tune. For now, she'd have to move to sounds audible only to her.

Fortunately, the dogs responded to visual cues.

"Okay, guys," she whispered, "time to strut our stuff."

The number started well enough. Dandy and Dondi loved to do tricks. But Deidre had taught them more than one dance, and Liss was still a novice at giving hand signals to her two canine partners. She finished a second pirouette only to discover that the dogs had broken formation completely. They were supposed to be standing on their hind legs with Dandy's front paws resting lightly on Dondi's back. Instead, both sat on their rumps, their big, expressive brown eyes following her movements as if they were spectators instead of part of the act.

Liss couldn't bring herself to scold them. She knelt down, murmured a few words of encouragement, and began the routine a second time. On the reboot, the two Scotties made it to the halfway point before they began to improvise.

Liss sensed someone standing behind her a moment before Elise Isley made a tut-tut sound and added a critique: "Pitiful."

The stripper and her snake watched from just outside the blue tape that marked off Area Three. The woman's lips were twisted into a look of disdain. The python expressed her opinion by flicking her tongue in Liss's direction. Was that a show of contempt, Liss wondered, or of hunger?

She tried ignoring her unwelcome audience, but

once Dandy and Dondi became aware of Eudora, they lost interest in dancing. Fascinated, they wanted to investigate up close and personal. Liss had to haul them back by their collars. She was still holding on to them when Hal Quarles joined the party.

Careful to keep his distance from Eudora, he ignored Liss and addressed Elise. "No need to worry about this act anymore."

"I'd like to see you do better with only one day's practice," Liss muttered under her breath.

Quarles laughed and directed his trademark sneer at her. "Do try not to embarrass yourself. From the looks of that performance, you'll be out of the running after the next show."

"She might get the sympathy vote from the judges." Elise looked down her sharp little nose at the dogs. Her voice dripped sarcasm. "Poor orphaned puppies and all."

"They're not good for anything without Deidre." Quarles rubbed his bony hands together and an evil glint came into his eyes. "Elise, my dear, why don't you make Deidre's daughter an offer? Once the dogs are eliminated from the competition, I'm sure she'll be happy to sell them to you. After all those live chickens you've been feeding her, Eudora must be longing for a change of diet."

Chapter Five

Back in her suite a few hours later, Liss was still fuming over Hal Quarles's sadistic comment. She told herself she was being paranoid to feel threatened by it, but the fact remained that *someone* had dognapped Dandy.

A glance at her watch told Liss she still had forty-five minutes before she was due for her fitting. Valentine Veilleux had agreed to look after the dogs for the hour or so it would take, and Valentine, Liss realized, was the only one associated with *Variety Live* she was sure she could trust. If the show's photographer had wanted to harm the two Scotties, she could have done so on Saturday when Desdemona left them in her care.

"Walkies!" That single word, combined with jingling the leashes Liss retrieved from the end table, was enough to have Dandy and Dondi prancing in a circle around her, eager for their next adventure.

She clipped the leashes to their collars and set out. If she arrived at Valentine's RV a little early, she'd have time to ask a few pertinent questions before her appointment with the wardrobe mistress.

Ten minutes later, Liss was seated in the motor home's comfortable lounge area, a mug of hot chocolate in hand. Valentine had set Dandy and Dondi loose to sniff the more interesting corners of the RV, tossed their leashes onto a pullout countertop extension in the midcoach galley, and joined Liss on the sofa.

"This is some rig," Liss said.

"I like it. Plenty of cupboards, closets, and other storage space. Adequate bathroom. Big bed." Valentine shoved her glasses back into place a millisecond before they slipped off the end of her nose. "The only tricky part is finding parking. With the slide-out sections I expand to use nearly three times as much space."

Liss gestured toward the computer workstation that was hardly standard equipment for RVs. It had been built into the space where a U-shaped dinette would normally be located. "What, exactly, is it that you do?"

Valentine chuckled. "I travel around the country taking pictures and creating specialty calendars for groups, especially those used for fund-raisers."

"And you can make a living at that?"

"I can, although I wouldn't say it was a *good* living."

Good enough, Liss thought. From the entrance she'd been able to see the length of the vehicle, clear into a master bedroom dominated by what looked like a queen-size bed. Valentine's home also boasted a combination convection oven and microwave in the galley, blackout roller shades on all the windows, and at least two TVs. At a guess, this rig had cost her upwards of $250,000—more than most Maine people paid for a house.

Dondi trotted up to them and put one paw on Valentine's knee. She laughed and scooped him into her arms. "How's my favorite boy today?"

Dondi licked her face. Dandy hopped up onto the sofa beside them.

Liss turned so she could see Valentine's face, tucking one leg beneath herself. "Deidre believed a competitor spirited Dandy away."

The hand stroking Dondi's back stilled. "Yes, she did."

"Any idea which one she suspected?"

"I wish I did."

"Do you know if any of the other contestants have had any trouble?"

For a long moment, Valentine was silent. Then she set Dondi aside and moved from the couch to the chair in front of her computer. A few clicks brought up a photograph.

Liss rose and went to stand behind her. The picture on the monitor showed a jumble of objects inside a closet. "What is all this stuff?"

"Mo Heedles's equipment. The props she juggles in her act. Or rather, this is what was left of them after somebody got into her suite and wrecked them."

"When did this happen?"

"Thursday. Mo was out all day. She decided to take advantage of our location and go skiing. When she came back and opened the closet where she had everything neatly stored, she found this mess." Valentine depressed another key to start the slide-show function, and similar images appeared, one after another, on the computer screen. "She didn't want to call the police. I don't think she even reported it to hotel security. But she wanted a record of what had been done to her."

"For an insurance claim?"

"I doubt she has insurance. All I can tell you for certain is that she asked me to take these pictures before she cleaned up the pieces."

Image after image of broken and battered objects flowed past. What had once been colorful silicone balls looked as if they'd been stomped on. Wooden clubs had been reduced to splinters. "What did this guy use, a chain saw?"

"I was thinking an ax, but you may be right. Look at the edges." Valentine hit the key to pause the image on the monitor, then enlarged a section of it.

Liss leaned closer, shaking her head. "This isn't just random vandalism. There's real viciousness behind it."

"I agree."

"That's not all that's strange. What sense does it make to wreck props? Take Dandy out of the act, and Deidre and her Dancing Doggies couldn't continue to compete, but equipment isn't irreplaceable. Mo obviously got hold of more balls and hoops and fire torches. She was able to rehearse her act this morning in the ballroom."

On the screen, the slide slow resumed. More shots of the damage scrolled by, all much the same . . . except for one.

Liss blinked. "Stop."

"What do you see?" Valentine hit the pause key just a second too late.

"Go back one. Yes. Now, can you zoom in on the upper right-hand corner?"

"Well, I'll be darned," Valentine murmured, staring at the screen. "That's not a belt, is it?"

"It looks to me like part of a harness, one that would fit a small dog, say the size of a Scottish terrier. In fact, there's one just like it in the doggie paraphernalia Desdemona left with me." It hadn't occurred to Liss until that moment that there should have been two harnesses.

"You think Mo was the one who took Dandy?" Valentine shook her head. "No. I don't buy it. For one thing, she's allergic to dogs."

Liss stood up, easing the kink in her back from leaning over Valentine's shoulder for so long. Dandy and Dondi sat beside the photographer's chair, looking for all the world as if they, too, had been studying the pictures on the screen. "Too bad Dandy can't talk. She must have known the person who took her. How else could the dognapper have gotten her out of the condo without her raising a ruckus?"

"According to Desdemona, her mother was deeply asleep at the time."

"Had she taken sleeping pills?" Liss remembered Desdemona saying that her mother had traveled with a pharmacy.

"Probably. She didn't hear a thing. I know that much."

"I wonder if Deidre suspected Mo. Maybe she's the one who—" Liss broke off, assembling the timeline in her head. "Dandy was taken on Monday afternoon and I returned her on Tuesday. Deidre died the next day, on Wednesday, but the vandalism to Mo's props occurred on Thursday."

"Right," Valentine said. "So unless Deidre came back as a ghost to wreak vengeance on Dandy's abductor, she wasn't the one responsible for wrecking Mo's equipment."

"And we're back to square one."

Valentine sighed and left her computer workstation to reheat her hot chocolate in the microwave. She rummaged in one of the cabinets and produced a package of gingersnaps. Liss checked her watch, saw that she still had time, and once again settled in on the cushy sofa, this time noticing that it had a multiposition feature and pullout ottoman.

"You do live in the lap of luxury."

"I figure I deserve my creature comforts. You want yours hotted up?" Valentine asked as she removed her mug from the microwave.

"I'm good."

"It isn't as if I have anyplace else to go home to," she added, and smiled at Liss's look of surprise. "I told you, I *live* in my RV—all the time, not just to travel around the country and take photographs." Leaning back against the counter, she sipped thoughtfully, then turned the conversation back to Mo Heedles. "It's not just her allergy that makes her an unlikely dognapper. She was a victim, too."

"I suppose it's possible that whoever destroyed her props also planted the harness there to cast suspicion on her. I'd like to eliminate Mo as a suspect in Dandy's dognapping. But if I were the one who'd caused all that trouble, I'd make sure it looked as if I'd had some myself. Wouldn't you?"

"I would," Valentine agreed, "although I wouldn't have planted a dog harness on myself and then asked a third party to take pictures of it."

Dandy, sitting on the floor next to Liss, nuzzled her hand until she responded with long, firm strokes down the Scottie's back. She'd already caught on to the fact that this was the method of petting both dogs preferred over pats on the head. "If Mo didn't say a word about what happened to her to anyone but you, maybe she's not the only one keeping mum."

"I haven't heard of any other dirty tricks, but you could be right. There's no particular reason why any of them should confide in me."

"You've been with the show all season."

"That doesn't mean I've gotten close to the competitors. To tell you the truth, I've tried to stay well away from them. I don't enjoy a constant diet of backbiting and petty jealousies."

Dondi went up on his hind legs, put his front paws against Valentine's thigh, and did his best to look both adorable and hungry. The photographer fed him a tiny bit of the cookie in her hand. After offering Liss a second gingersnap, she moved the bag farther out of canine reach.

"If this is about eliminating the competition," Valentine mused, "I can understand why Dandy was targeted. Everyone knew going in that Deidre's act was the one to beat. But why play such a dirty trick on Mo? After Deidre, it's always been Willetta who was the most likely contestant to take home the prize."

Liss polished off the last of her lukewarm hot chocolate and stood. If she didn't get going, she'd be late for her fitting. "I have no answers," she admitted, "just a bit of advice found in almost every mystery novel I've ever read: suspect everyone."

Valentine grinned at her. "By that token, Liss, you shouldn't be one hundred percent sure you can trust me, either."

• • •

A hotel room had been designated as the show's costume shop and wardrobe storage area. At first, Liss didn't think anyone was there. Huge racks, thickly hung with colorful, glittery costumes, seemed to take up every inch of available floor space, blocking her view.

She cleared her throat and ventured a tentative, "Hello?"

An arm, bare but heavily tattooed, shot up at the back of the room. "With you in a minute."

"No rush." Reluctantly fascinated, Liss examined a few of the costumes nearest her. Elise Isley must feel right at home on this show . . . except for the fact that most of the clothes wouldn't leave her anything to take off during her performance.

A woman in her midthirties wearing a tank top, jeans, and more tattoos than Liss had ever seen on one person before, wormed her way through the narrow space between two racks. "Liss Ruskin, right?"

"Yes. And you are?"

"Just call me Mel. For my sins, I'm costume designer on this train wreck. And wardrobe mistress. Hell, I'm the whole damn costume department!" With a practiced, professional eye, she made a preliminary evaluation of Liss's appearance. She couldn't tell much. Liss still had on the coat, hat, and gloves she'd worn to take the dogs to the RV. Mel gestured back the way she'd come. "Believe it or not, there's an open space through there. Let's get you stripped down and see what I've got to work with. You got any ideas yourself?"

"A muumuu would be nice."

She'd never minded wearing costumes onstage, but since *Strathspey* had been structured around Scottish history, that had meant skirts no shorter than knee-length. Most of the outfits she'd worn to dance in had been even longer, covering her nearly to the ankles and matching that look on top with high necklines and three-quarter-length sleeves. Even a peasant blouse would have been considered too revealing for their target audience, unless there was a shawl draped over it. On tour, they'd most often performed for the middle- and high-school crowd.

"In your dreams," Mel said with a laugh.

An old hand at costume fittings, Liss had worn an easy-to-slip-in-and-out-of sweatshirt and jeans beneath her outerwear. When she was down to bra and panties—and woolly socks, since floors were apt to be cold—Mel took measurements. As Liss expected, the other woman noticed the scar.

"Knee replacement?"

"Partial. Maybe a caftan?"

"It's not that bad. A little makeup, a little fancy camerawork, and you'll be all set. The scratch on your arm will be more of a challenge to hide. Cat?"

"Yes, but about the knee—the Scotties will be dancing at that level."

"Not to worry. Leave everything to me." She disappeared into the forest of fabric and glitter. "Pity you can't just wear Deidre's costumes," her disembodied voice continued, "but your body shapes are way different. I'll make some new things for you to wear the rest of the week. Not much I can do in time for the first show, though."

Liss had a feeling budget considerations played into that decision, too. "So, you'll do what? Try to squeeze me into something you have available?"

"Give the lady a prize." Mel emerged with a single garment draped over one arm. "Slip into this."

"This" turned out to be a skintight gold lamé bodysuit.

"I feel like Catwoman," Liss complained as she tugged and smoothed the fabric into place.

"The underwear will have to go," Mel said.

"Uh, Mel? A little loose here." It was a strange complaint considering how snugly the bottom half of the costume fit, but the top gaped, much too generously cut for Liss's modest bosom.

"Not to worry," Mel said again. "I'll make alterations."

"I'm not sure that will help." Looking down at herself, Liss could see all the way to her belly button. "What's your track record on wardrobe malfunctions?"

Mel chuckled. "We'll use tape to keep things in place, although some people would be perfectly happy to have you pop out of that top. Does wonders for the ratings."

Liss held her breath while Mel inserted pins to mark the places she'd need to take in. The outfit was surprisingly comfortable. She'd be able to dance in it. She'd just have to remember not to bend too far forward.

On the other side of the clothing racks the door opened and closed. Roy Eastmont's distinctive voice, deliberately cheerful, boomed out. "Everybody decent?"

"Come on back," Mel hollered.

"Would that, by chance, be the 'some people' you mentioned?" Liss asked in a low voice.

"Got it in one."

Eastmont pushed his way through to the small oasis where Liss and Mel waited, showing little care for the costumes he shoved aside. "Is that the best you could find?" he asked, looking Liss up and down. "The outfit you made for the lion tamer? The shape's nice but the viewers like to see skin." He sent Liss what was probably meant to be an ingratiating smile. "Fact of life, I'm afraid. We don't have to like it but we do have to play to it."

"I didn't realize the show's MC had so much to do with other aspects of the production," Liss said.

Eastmont's smile widened. "Who said I was just

the MC? I own a piece of *Variety Live.* A big piece."

"Which is why he produces, directs, and generally meddles," Mel chimed in. "Fortunately, most of the time, he listens to the experts he hires to handle individual departments. She's not showing skin, Roy. This is better."

He put both hands up, palms out. "Whatever you say, Mel. I make it a practice to never argue with a woman who has access to a big sharp pair of scissors and a drawer full of pins and sewing needles."

Liss was on her way back to her hotel suite after retrieving Dandy and Dondi from Valentine when she noticed that the photographer's RV was not the only distinctive vehicle parked behind the hotel. THE GREAT UMBERTO was emblazoned in large multicolored letters along the side of a bright blue van. Oscar Yates was just sliding the side door shut as she passed by with the two dogs. Like the entrance to Valentine's motor home, it closed with a metallic thump.

Yates waved and trotted toward her. Liss had no particular reason to be wary of the magician, other than his tendency to intrude into other people's personal space, but she was careful to keep the dogs between them as they walked together toward the back entrance of the hotel.

"Are you anticipating more trouble?" he asked.

"I couldn't help but notice that you're very careful never to leave the dogs unattended."

"Just a precaution." Liss manufactured an air of unconcern. "After all, I'm responsible for them until Desdemona returns."

Yates looked surprised. "She's coming back?"

"After her mother's funeral."

"Ah. Hmmm."

Liss slanted an inquisitive look his way. "How about you? Any problems?"

"No one has messed with any of my illusions, if that's what you mean, but Iris and I are keeping a close eye on our props." He held the door open for her.

"So you know what happened to Mo's equipment?"

"Iris overheard her talking to Valentine about it and told me. It appears that someone is trying to cause trouble for the rest of us. I was keeping some things in the van, but it seemed prudent, under the circumstances, to move them into—well, let's just say *a safer place*."

"Wise of you not to trust me, either," Liss said. "You don't know me from Adam."

"Eve," he corrected her, and let her precede him into the elevator with Dandy and Dondi. When her back was to him, he spoke again, his voice mellow and almost hypnotic, with just a hint of an intriguing accent, something she hadn't noticed the last time they'd talked. "I wouldn't mind getting to know you better, Liss Ruskin, dog wrangler."

By the time she turned around, his back was to her. He pushed the button for their floor.

"Are you *flirting* with me?" He had to know she was married. At the moment, her wedding ring was hidden beneath her glove, but it had been in plain sight the first time they met.

Yates favored her with a charming, charismatic smile. "Do you really mind if I am?"

The last thing Liss wanted to do was encourage him, but she found it difficult not to smile back at him. He was a good-looking guy, and he knew it. "Maybe not, but my husband would."

The elevator rose with excruciating slowness toward the fourth floor.

Before the situation could become more awkward, Liss asked, "Why *Umberto?*"

"*Oscar the Magnificent* just doesn't have the same flair."

"The Amazing Oscar?" Liss suggested.

"Only if I wanted to limit myself to performing at children's parties. Sad to say, despite the fact that so many youngsters delight in magic kits during their formative years, magicians are accorded only slightly more respect than ventriloquists."

The ventriloquist, Liss recalled, had been the first to be eliminated from the champion of champions competition, although he had won in his own season, just as Oscar Yates and all the rest of the contestants had won in theirs.

The elevator doors opened. Dandy and Dondi tugged at their leashes in unison, jerking Liss forward. Yates caught her elbow to keep her from losing her balance and kept hold of it as they exited. He had a firm grip, the kind it would take considerable effort to break.

"My room is next to the stairs," he informed her.

That was the one farthest from the elevator. Its location explained why Yates was accompanying her down the corridor, but not why his fingers still circled her arm. He wasn't much taller than she was, but it was obvious he was much stronger. She doubted she could free herself until he was ready to let go.

They turned the corner and stopped in front of her door. Fumbling for the key card in her coat pocket gave her a reason to pull away from him, and to her relief, he released his grip. She had to juggle the leashes. The dogs, sensing that they'd arrived at their temporary home, danced around her ankles, eager to get inside.

Yates turned up the charisma. "You should be safe enough in your suite, but if there's ever anything I can do to make you feel more secure, please feel free to call on me. Anytime. Anytime at all."

There was a decided *warmth* in his voice, the kind that called up images she'd prefer to reserve for her husband. "I'm sure that won't be necessary. After all, I have these two ferocious watchdogs."

She rammed the key card into the lock, but the little light refused to turn green.

Yates gave an indulgent chuckle. "These little guys?"

"They have a nice loud bark." She tried the key card again, more slowly this time, but it still wouldn't work. Nerves on edge, she blurted out the first thing that came into her head. "The breed originated in Scotland and the Scots believe that dogs can see wraiths where human eyes see nothing."

"Wraiths?" For the first time since Liss had met him, Yates sounded uncertain.

"Ghosts."

The little red light finally went green. Liss turned the handle and shoved, anxious to get the door open before it decided to lock itself again. She shooed the dogs inside and started to follow them, pausing only long enough to look over her shoulder and finish what she'd been about to say: "A dog, howling in the night, heralds the approach of death."

This bit of folklore had a peculiar effect on her audience. Liss hesitated in the doorway, bemused, as a subtle change came over the Great Umberto. His appearance didn't alter. He was still good-looking, with those dark, sexy eyes and handsome features. But now that he'd stopped trying to hit on her, he also seemed to have dropped his stage persona. The charisma remained, but in muted form.

"They didn't, you know."

"Who didn't what?"

"Deidre's dogs. According to the people in nearby condos, they didn't make a sound the day she died." Yates turned away, heading toward his own suite.

She watched him go, wondering how he'd come by that bit of information. Had he been questioning Deidre's neighbors? She could think of no reason why he should have. That was something the police might do, but only if they were suspicious about the cause of Deidre's death.

Yates did not look her way again. Neither did he have any trouble with his key card. It worked just fine on the first try.

A moment after his door clicked shut, Liss heard a second door close. The sound came from the other direction, the way they'd just walked after leaving the elevator. From her corner suite, Liss could see the entrances to three others along that corridor. Willetta occupied one. Liss didn't know who had the other rooms. The suspicion that one of her competitors might be spying on her sent her scurrying inside her own rooms without further delay.

"Next *you'll* be seeing wraiths," she muttered.

After discarding coat and gloves, she caught up with Dandy and Dondi, removed their leashes, and set about putting out fresh water for them to drink. Her capricious mind jumped over rival variety acts and charismatic magicians to focus on the misty realms of legend and lore. She'd heard a few more Scottish superstitions about dogs over the years, but she didn't care for the one that came back to her first. A dog, it claimed, would point in the direction of the next person to die.

"There aren't going to be any more deaths," she said aloud.

Dondi cocked his head and sent her an inquisitive look.

She put her hands on her hips and addressed the two dogs. "I don't believe in signs and portents, but I am very glad neither of you stopped in front of any of the doors to the suites we passed on our way back here."

Leaving them to contemplate her words, Liss extracted a small bottle of water from the suite's minirefrigerator, unscrewed the cap, and took a long swallow.

If both Scotties howled at midnight tonight, what would *that* mean?

That you have an overactive imagination, she told herself. *Cut it out. You have too much work to do to waste time imagining wraiths, phantoms, or foreshadowing. Rehearse. Rehearse. Rehearse. Forget everything else.*

She jumped when someone pounded on her door. The bottle slipped from her hand and landed on her foot. Cold water splashed up onto her leg before it puddled on the floor. Dandy, delighted, started to lap it up while Dondi batted the nearly empty plastic bottle out of Liss's reach just as she bent to pick it up.

She said an extremely bad word.

The knocking came again, louder and more peremptory in tone.

Still struggling to calm her frazzled nerves, Liss approached the peephole, took a deep breath, and squinted at the hallway.

"This *cannot* be good," she muttered when she recognized the man standing on the other side of the door. It was a safe bet that State Police Detective Gordon Tandy had not come to make a social call.

Chapter Six

"What are you doing here, Gordon?"

He stared at her, one slow blink the only indication that he was surprised to see her. "I believe I get to hear *your* answer to that question first." He moved past her into the living room of the suite.

Dandy made a beeline for the open door. To keep her from getting out, Liss had to close it. Dondi was more interested in the newcomer. He ran in circles, nearly tripping Gordon before the detective reached the sofa and sat down.

"Dondi, come here."

To Liss's amazement, the Scottie obeyed. Gordon gestured for her to take the seat opposite him. She thought about offering him coffee or a soft drink and decided against it. He'd removed his hat, but still wore his coat. He wasn't planning to stay long.

As soon as she settled into a chair, the dogs took their places, one on each side of her, standing sentinel with eyes bright and ears erect. All three of them stared at Gordon, waiting for him to speak.

Liss hadn't seen Gordon for some time, but the familiar features hadn't changed. His eyes were such a dark brown that they would have looked black if they hadn't contained flecks of a lighter shade. From the look in them, he was not happy. Removing his hat, he ran one hand over thick reddish-brown hair. He wasn't wearing it as short as he once had, but his bearing still was as straight and stiff as a soldier at attention. He had to be pushing fifty, but he'd always looked years younger than he was.

Marriage agreed with him, Liss decided. Once upon a time, she'd thought he might ask her to be his bride. He'd been a serious contender for her affection before she'd decided that Dan Ruskin was the man with whom she wanted to spend the rest of her life. Not long after Liss married Dan, Gordon Tandy and Penny Lassiter, the sheriff of Carrabassett County, had tied the knot.

She wondered what he saw when he looked at her. Physically, she didn't think she'd changed much in the last few years, but she had matured in other ways. At least, she hoped she had.

Belatedly, Liss realized that Gordon didn't intend to say more until she'd answered his question. "I'm dog sitting, as you can see. Your turn. It's obvious you didn't come here looking for me."

"This suite is registered in the name of Desdemona Amendole. She's the one I expected to open the door. Is she here?"

Liss shook her head. "She went back to Ohio to bury her mother."

Frown lines appeared in Gordon's forehead. He started to say something, then thought better of it. "Have you known her long?"

"A few days. Do I get to ask questions after I answer yours?"

"You can ask." No hint of humor leavened his answer. Seeing Deidre's dance notebook on the coffee table, he picked it up and flipped through it.

"Deidre and her Dancing Doggies were contestants on a television show." Liss reached down to scratch Dandy behind the ear. "I'm guessing you already know that. Anyway, Desdemona asked me to fill in for her mother and dance with the dogs so she doesn't have to renege on the contract with *Variety Live*."

"Why you?" He replaced Deidre's spiral-bound notebook and retrieved a smaller one of his own from an inside pocket.

"How soon they forget!" She pointed to herself. "Professional dancer here."

"Retired, as I recall. And just how would Ms. Amendole know that? How did you two meet?"

Knowing it would do no good to ask Gordon why he wanted to know, she obliged him by recounting the story—how she'd found Dandy and returned the Scottish terrier to Deidre and how, after Deidre's death, Desdemona had appealed to her to take her mother's place in the competition for champion of champions. "You already knew about the dognapping, right?"

Gordon hesitated, then said, "Why don't you fill me in?"

She eyed him with suspicion. That had sounded like a "no" to her, but he had his cop face on, an unrevealing expression set in stone. She couldn't begin to guess what was going on in the mind behind the official mask.

"It happened on Monday. Someone entered Deidre's condo while she was taking a nap and walked off with Dandy." Hearing her name, the little dog climbed into Liss's lap. She placed a comforting hand on the Scottie's back. "Deidre reported Dandy missing to hotel security and called her daughter." She paused, frowning. "I don't know where Desdemona was, but she didn't lose any time getting to Five Mountains. She was with her mother in the condo by the time I returned Dandy in the late afternoon on Tuesday. Deidre was convinced that Dandy had been stolen by one of her rivals on the show, someone who hoped to ruin her chances of winning the competition. She was probably right. At least one of the other contestants has also been the victim of foul play. Her stage props were vandalized."

"Did this other contestant report the incident to the local police?"

Liss shook her head. "I don't think so. I don't think she even complained to hotel security."

"Why not?"

"No idea. Maybe she just didn't want to make a fuss."

"Name?"

"Mo Heedles." She watched Gordon scribble it down, hoping she hadn't just caused more trouble for the other woman.

He closed the notebook and started to stand up. Liss stopped him by leaning forward and putting a hand on his arm. "Hold on, hotshot. It's your turn to answer questions. Why are you looking for Desdemona?"

Dandy, dislodged from Liss's lap by the sudden movement, hopped up next to Gordon.

"I'm not at liberty to say."

"Bull!"

The expletive surprised him into a laugh. "You know the rules, Liss. This is police business."

"Yeah, yeah—police business and none of mine. But it looks to me as if I'm right in the middle of this police business, so give me a break, Gordon. That you're here at all means there must have been something hinky about Deidre Amendole's death. Why else would the state police be sniffing around? Desdemona told me that her mother died of an accidental overdose. Was she wrong?"

Although Liss was trying hard not to jump to conclusions, the word *murder* loomed large in her thoughts. Gordon's presence was a dead giveaway. She winced at the unintentional pun as she watched him tuck his notebook back into his pocket.

"Let's just say the cause of death isn't as cut-and-dried as her daughter would like it to be. We're waiting on toxicology results. They take a couple of weeks to complete. Do you have Ms. Amendole's address in Ohio?"

"Don't you?" Comprehension dawned. "You don't, do you? You came to this suite looking for Desdemona because you expected her to be here. Did you tell her not to leave town? Do you think *she* killed Deidre?"

"No. No. Yes. No. And no. And I can't tell you anything else because there's nothing to tell, so please stop speculating." She heard the underlying thread of amusement in Gordon's voice. "I have some questions for Desdemona Amendole. Loose ends to clear up. Nothing major."

"Uh-huh." Liss remained skeptical. A state police detective wouldn't be investigating *before* the test results came back if there wasn't some indication that a crime had been committed.

"Do you have contact information for Desdemona Amendole?"

"She left me her cell-phone number."

Liss got up and went to the desk, with Gordon following close behind her. She tore off the top page of one of the hotel notepads, where Desdemona had written the number down for her, but she took the time to copy it onto the sheet beneath before she handed it over.

He glanced at it, then folded the slip of paper and tucked it into a pocket. "Thanks. Good luck with your competition."

And then he was gone.

The next morning, Liss was ripped from sleep by the raucous ringing of the phone on the bedside table. She fumbled for it, eyes still closed, and managed to get the receiver to her ear on the third try. " 'Lo?"

"You okay?" Dan's voice asked.

Liss mumbled something incoherent and squinted at the clock. Eight-thirty. She had to be at dress rehearsal in an hour.

"Liss?"

"Asleep. Give me a minute." She could barely remember where she was, let alone how to string two coherent words together. Oh, yeah—Five Mountains. *Variety Live.* Deidre and her Dancing Doggies.

She sat bolt upright, dropping the phone. Where were the dogs? Had someone stolen them while she'd been dead to the world?

She scrambled out of bed, stumbling to the door to the connecting room, heart racing until she spotted them. They were sound asleep on the sofa, paws just touching. Dandy was making small snuffling noises, her paws twitching as she dreamed of chasing imaginary prey.

Now considerably more awake, Liss returned to

the bed and retrieved the phone. "Dan? Sorry about that. You know how it is in hotels. I didn't sleep well and then I overslept and now I'm running late. Everything's fine here. I'll call you later today and fill you in on all the details, okay?"

"Promise?"

"Absolutely."

She'd meant to call him before she went to bed, but Gordon's visit had left her feeling edgy, and events earlier in the day hadn't exactly been soothing, either. She'd needed a sympathetic listener. Sherri had been at work and busy, and Margaret hadn't been answering her phone, and she hadn't wanted to annoy Dan, or worry him, by mentioning Gordon.

After Liss hung up, she scrambled to get dressed. When she studied herself in the mirror, she was pleased with the result. Mel had been as good as her word. She'd altered the costume to fit securely, if snugly, and show minimal cleavage.

Although she had practiced the routine with the dogs a dozen times since the debacle the previous morning, Liss worried that they'd be eliminated if their performance wasn't good enough today. Her desire to be the best, to win, had taken her to victory in many a Scottish dance competition. That same spirit came to the fore once again as she tucked the Scotties into their carriers and headed for the ballroom.

Once the dress rehearsal began, the lights, the

music, even the costume, worked a kind of magic. Professionals to the core, Dandy and Dondi performed their parts on cue. And Liss, like an old warhorse taken out of retirement, found herself rising to the challenge of this new battle. She'd gone over Deidre's simple choreography in her head and on her feet until she knew it by heart. The three of them ran through the routine with nary a misstep.

This was just the dress rehearsal, Liss reminded herself as she executed a fancy curtsy at the end, one dog on each side on hind legs and each waving their front paws in the air. She could still blow the "live" performance.

Roy Eastmont rushed up to them. "Perfect," he called to the camera crew. "Keep that one. No need to do it over."

"But there was no audience," Liss protested.

He looked surprised by her objection. "There never is. We add stock shots later, along with canned applause for the sound track."

"Haven't viewers ever noticed that nobody's watching?"

"Of course not." Eastmont seemed amused by her naive question. "We shoot all our performers in close-ups." He glanced at his watch. "Come back in a couple of hours, dressed exactly the same way, and we'll do the postperformance chat in front of the judges and get their scores."

Liss was still staring after him, feeling a bit

bemused, when Willetta came up beside her. "I see the fix is still in."

Slowly, Liss turned her head to study the other woman. "You're joking, right?"

"What do you think?" Willetta asked.

Was the competition rigged? The possibility wasn't as much of a stretch as it should have been now that Liss knew just how bogus the "live" part of *Variety Live* was. She was only surprised she hadn't suspected sooner. Eastmont's phony smile and his even more phony-looking eye color should have tipped her off right at the start.

"Doesn't that make you angry?" she asked the singer.

"I'm philosophical, especially since the runners-up on this show don't do too badly with their careers."

But Willetta, Liss remembered, had already been one of the winners. "What did you get out of being champion the last time around?"

"A recording contract, but only for one album."

"You want more."

"What I really want is the offer of a job with an opera company. That's why I'm playing it smarter this time around. I've been giving interviews all over the place, emphasizing the fact that I only sing show tunes on *Variety Live* for a lark. I've put a half dozen videos up on YouTube to prove I can belt out an aria with the best of them."

"I thought the agreements we signed forbade interviews."

Willetta shrugged. "Let them sue me. That publicity will hurt them more than it will me."

"Good for you. But wouldn't it be even better for your career if you won the champion of champions title?"

"Sure, but the only way that's going to happen is if you quit the show." She popped a cough drop into her mouth. "Any chance of that?"

"Not likely." She'd signed a contract. Willetta might not mind being taken to court, but Liss would just as soon avoid being sued.

"Then let me put it this way, Liss," Willetta said, eyes twinkling. "When I tell you to 'break a leg,' believe that I really mean it."

That afternoon, as soon as Liss walked into the ballroom, once again wearing the glittery gold bodysuit and feeling as if all it needed was a tail to complete the resemblance to Catwoman, the production assistant handed her a black armband. "Please wear this when we record the opening. Mr. Eastmont is going to hold a brief memorial for Deidre Amendole."

"In front of the cameras?" Liss asked.

"Of course."

Liss was tempted to ask if he wanted Dandy and Dondi to sport black collars. And maybe Elise could arrange a tasteful black chiffon scarf around

Eudora's throat. Mention of Deidre's passing seemed appropriate. If nothing else, it was necessary to explain why Liss had been brought in as a substitute. But anything more was milking unfortunate circumstances for the sake of free publicity.

Somehow, she wasn't at all surprised that Roy Eastmont intended to do just that.

The production assistant, fumbling with her clipboard, produced an envelope with Liss's name on it. "Here are the questions you'll be asked."

Things are looking up, Liss thought. It had not been among her major worries, but she had wondered how well she'd do ad-libbing with the MC.

She opened the envelope and drew out a single sheet of paper. The questions were there all right. So were her answers. According to the script, she was an old friend of the Amendole family who had stepped in to complete the season following Deidre's tragic and unexpected death from a heart attack.

Startled, Liss spoke aloud. "Heart attack?"

"What's that?" asked the production assistant.

"It says here that Deidre had a heart attack. Does whoever wrote this know something the medical examiner doesn't?"

Overhearing her question, Roy Eastmont stepped in to answer it. "Her heart stopped, didn't it?

Relax, my dear. A simple story is best. We don't want to confuse our viewers."

Or, apparently, tell them the truth about anything.

She kept her opinion to herself. No one cared what she thought.

The next hour passed quickly. To Liss's relief, Eastmont kept his remarks about Deidre brief and tasteful, but she'd overheard him give instructions to the camera crew. They were to make sure they got close-ups of the armbands and give viewers a glimpse of Deidre's grief-stricken fellow competitors. If a few of them were caught shedding a tear or two, so much the better. In the hope that she could avoid being included in this travesty, Liss kept her facial expression carefully neutral.

After the requisite "moment of silence," Eastmont segued into the usual beginning of *Variety Live*, the introduction of the contestants. Each of them in turn would swan onto the set in full regalia for their question-and-answer session, remaining there until everyone was assembled. Liss and the dogs were scheduled to enter last, which gave her an opportunity to watch the others interact with the MC.

Elise went first, wearing a skimpy little costume, more glitter than cloth, with Eudora draped over two of the more strategic bits of flesh in order to keep the show G-rated. Liss had to give her credit.

Elise knew how to work a crowd. She stroked the python with one hand and used the other to appropriate the old-fashioned handheld microphone Eastmont passed her. Caressing it—there was no other word that suited the action—she held it close to her brightly painted lips and, sounding sultry but sincere, thanked all the fans who'd called in to keep her on the show.

"Don't forget," she reminded them, playing to both the camera and the cheap seats, "I need your votes this week, too." With that, she threw the audience a big, Marilyn Monroe–style kiss and handed the microphone back to Roy Eastmont. There was a wiggle in her walk as she returned to the sidelines.

If the fan votes didn't count—how could they when the shows were already recorded?—how *was* the winner chosen? Liss wouldn't put it past Eastmont to bypass the judges, too. Why not? He was clearly the one making all the rest of the decisions.

The Great Umberto was up next, his appearance smooth and sophisticated in a tuxedo. It looked as if it might be the same costume he wore whenever and wherever he performed his magic act and stood out in marked contrast to what his assistant was wearing. Iris's outfit was a little bit of nothing that barely covered the necessities, almost as daring as the costume Elise had on.

Liss rolled her eyes. Now that she thought about

it, the episodes she'd watched had all shown this tendency toward skimpily clad female contestants. It wasn't that the show didn't display men as eye candy, because it did, but the men's costumes were a lot more subtle than those worn by the women. To level the playing field, Oscar Yates would have to be decked out in very tight pants with his chest bare and possibly oiled. He looked as if he had a decent build, even if he was a bit on the husky side.

Contemplating the obvious sexism in the competitors' clothing, Liss missed what the magician had to say. All that registered with her was the melodious sound of his voice and that hint of an accent. Regional? Foreign? She couldn't put her finger on it. It occurred to her that it might be his own invention.

Eastmont turned next to Iris, a patently false sympathetic smile on his face, and thrust his microphone into her face. "You were good friends with Deidre, Iris. You must miss her terribly."

Iris burst into tears.

Eastmont patted her on the back. "There, there, my dear. I know it's hard to lose someone you care for. Deidre Amendole was a lovely person. We all loved her."

Someone hadn't, Liss thought. Deidre had been genuinely distraught over Dandy's disappearance, and the person who'd taken the Scottie hadn't cared.

Now that she thought about it, Liss was surprised Roy Eastmont hadn't seized on the dognapping to generate publicity for the show. He must have known about it.

Her eyes narrowed. She wouldn't put it past the MC to have taken the Scottish terrier himself as a ploy to boost ratings. Maybe he just hadn't had time to get the word out before Deidre's death provided him with an even better opportunity for sound bites on the entertainment news shows and headlines in the supermarket tabloids.

Don't be so cynical, she admonished herself, but as she watched and listened to the remaining Q&A sessions, she didn't find any reason to change her mind. Hal Quarles was dressed as he would be if he were headlining as a stand-up comic in Las Vegas. Mo Heedles and Willetta Farwell were attired Vegas-style, too, but at the showgirl end of the spectrum. Their scripts had been written to tug at the heartstrings of the show's fans. Quarles, sour faced, referred to Deidre as "a good egg." Willetta claimed she'd been a dear friend, and Mo, voice husky, perhaps from getting too close to the dogs, remembered her as generous and kind.

When Liss's turn came, she considered rebelling. She wanted to tell the truth instead of pasting a false smile on her face and lying through her teeth, but she'd agreed to play the game. She could not go back on her word.

"As an old friend of the family, this was the least I could do for poor Deidre," she said for the benefit of the camera.

Hoping that she would cry or otherwise lose her composure, Eastmont asked, "And how are you holding up?"

Liss was supposed to tell him how much Deidre had meant to her. Instead, she went off script. "Dandy and Dondi miss her terribly."

The camera swiveled downward to focus on the two Scottish terriers. Viewers at home, in a week's time, would undoubtedly be dabbing moisture from their eyes as they watched this touching moment unfold on their television screens.

The only live audience in the ballroom, aside from the regular cast and crew, consisted of the three judges, minor celebrities whose main qualification appeared to be that they looked good on camera. Liss recognized only one by sight, an actress she'd seen in a very bad disaster movie on the science-fiction channel. She was not sure why she'd started watching it in the first place, but once she had, it had been like witnessing a train wreck. She'd kept telling herself not to gawk, but she hadn't been able to move on, let alone turn off the TV. She'd sat through the entire thing and then been disgusted with herself for wasting so much time.

The names of the other two judges rang distant bells, but Liss couldn't place either of them. The tall distinguished-looking gentleman might be a reality-TV star. Or a used-car salesman. It didn't really matter, nor would it matter that none of them had seen her performance.

With the cameras off, Eastmont glowered at Liss, but he didn't take time to reprimand her. He barked out orders to his crew. While Liss received her scores, the stage would be set for the magic act. She was awarded two nines and a ten.

Sounding exuberant, Eastmont announced that she was now "on top of the leaderboard."

Liss feigned joy and relief and gave the signal for Dandy and Dondi to stand up on their hind legs and spin in circles. Enthusiastic applause would no doubt be dubbed in later.

With due fanfare and evocative lighting, Oscar Yates and his lovely assistant took center stage. Since performance time was limited by the need to give everyone a turn, record the judges giving their scores, and spotlight the musical number of a better-known celebrity guest, plus commercials, the Great Umberto would perform only one illusion. He'd chosen a complicated version of an old standard. He made Iris disappear, and then, with some sleight of hand Liss couldn't follow, but which probably had a perfectly logical explanation, he switched places with her so that she appeared wearing a skintight version of his tuxedo and he came out of his "magic box" dressed in a long, spangled cape that covered him from head to toe. Only in color and glitter did it match the skimpy outfit Iris had worn at the beginning of the stunt.

At Liss's side, obedient to the commands to sit and stay, the two Scotties watched the show with apparent interest. They were well behaved. They did not bark, nor did either one of them try to sing along when Willetta Farwell took her turn, belting out another well-known show tune at full volume and confirming Liss's opinion that she was the most talented "champion" in the group.

Willetta was receiving her scores from the judges—three nines, which left "Deidre and her Dancing Doggies" still in the lead—when a commotion at the entrance to the ballroom diverted Liss's attention. Three men had cut Elise Isley out of the herd. One wore the uniform of the Maine Warden's Service. Over the general din, she heard the second man, one of the resort's security guards, identify the third individual as being from animal welfare.

Elise's shriek of outrage had every head turning in her direction. "You can't take Eudora!"

"I'm sorry, ma'am, but we've received a complaint. It would be one thing if you kept the snake in a cage, but carrying it around loose like this endangers everyone."

"She. Eudora is a she. And you have no business hassling me about her. I don't need a permit for my python. I checked state regulations before I came here."

"This isn't a matter of having a permit," the animal-control officer said, "and *she* will be taken good care of while the charges against her are being investigated."

Liss gave the man points for tact. If looks could kill, the exotic dancer's glare would already have skewered him. Eudora, supremely unconcerned, remained draped over Elise's shoulders, as if she was waiting patiently for her cue to perform.

"How long will that take?" Elise demanded. "We have a show to do. Besides that, Eudora is accustomed to her little luxuries. She's a *house* pet."

The officer's face wore a pained expression. "It will take as long as it takes. No more than a few days, but—"

This time Elise's shriek was positively earsplitting. "Nobody," she shouted, shaking her fist, "is going to deprive me of my chance to become champion of champions on *Variety Live*."

The game warden stepped in, speaking in a reasonable tone of voice. "We can't ignore a complaint as serious as this one, ma'am."

"Lies! All lies! Someone is trying to make trouble for me!"

Liss, watching Eudora, realized that the snake was showing signs of agitation. The animal-control officer noticed, too. Seeing the python's tongue flick rapidly in and out, he backed up a step.

At a little distance, Iris Jansen looked on, wide-eyed. The expression on Mo's face was one of amusement. Valentine Veilleux was taking pictures, although she was careful to do so unobtrusively. Yates, Quarles, and Eastmont looked torn. Jump in to defend Elise, thus earning points for bravery? Or opt for self-preservation by staying well out of the way?

Concerned that there might be a knock-down, drag-out fight if the officers tried to take Eudora by force, Liss shoved Dandy and Dondi back into their carriers and made sure the catches were secure. No one needed two small dogs underfoot. Both immediately pressed their noses against the plastic grilling, eager as little children to see what was going on, but neither of them let out a peep. It was as if they knew that loud barking wouldn't begin to compete with the racket Elise was already making.

"Who accused my baby?" she shouted. "I want a name!"

The animal-control officer looked at the game warden. The game warden looked at the hotel security guard. The guard shrugged and reached into the breast pocket of his uniform shirt for a small spiral-bound notebook much like the one Gordon Tandy carried. He took his time flipping through the pages, looking for the notation he sought.

"Augustus Brown," he read aloud. "Room 312."

"Get him down here!" Elise demanded. "Let him accuse Eudora to her face!"

At the game warden's nod, the security guard took out his radio and mumbled a few words into it. "Be a couple of minutes," he said when he'd stuffed the unit back into the case attached to his utility belt.

"In the meantime," said the animal-control officer, "why don't we secure your pet so she doesn't get overexcited." He indicated the large cage he'd brought with him.

Elise removed the snake from around her shoulders, but instead of turning Eudora over to him, she cradled her like a baby—a four-foot-long pulsating baby capable of squeezing her to death.

The security guard wandered over to where Liss was standing. "Is she brave or just crazy?"

"Eudora is her pet. Her companion. She's protective of her."

"Crazy." He glanced at the two carriers. "I'd keep a close eye on those dogs, if I was you. Pythons will kill anything they can get hold of, including people. I looked them up online after we got the complaint. There was this guy, young guy—only nineteen—found dead in his apartment, a forty-five-pound, eleven-foot-long python wrapped around his body. The cops figured the snake mistook the guy for its next meal when he was trying to feed it a chicken. A whole chicken.

Can you beat that? Anyway, I guess the python thought the guy would be tastier than the bird." The radio crackled, cutting short his snort of laughter.

Liss continued to watch the drama unfolding in front of her. Elise was all but snarling at the two officers and beginning to sound hysterical. The man from animal control lost his composure and shouted back. Even the game warden wasn't as calm as he had been, raising his voice to be heard over the din.

Roy Eastmont's plummy voice boomed out, silencing all three of them. "We want to keep everything on the up-and-up here at *Variety Live*! Of course Ms. Isley will cooperate with the authorities."

"I will not!" Elise shrieked. "Eudora is as gentle as a kitten. She was bred in captivity. She wouldn't hurt a flea."

Valentine Veilleux snapped one photo after another, catching crowd reaction, contestants' faces, and the whole process of forcibly moving the python from Elise's arms to the cage. One of the show's cameras recorded all the action as well, going in for a close-up when Elise flung herself into Eastmont's arms and buried her face in the front of his designer jacket.

Very dramatic, Liss thought, and Eastmont would milk it for all it was worth as Elise's beloved pet was taken away.

A small movement at the entrance to the ballroom caught her eye. Someone stood on the other side of one of the doors that led from the ballroom into the foyer. Liss shifted her position slightly. A man. No, two men, and the second one was armed with a camera that carried the logo of one of the Portland television stations. A closer look at the first man revealed that he held a microphone in one hand. There was something familiar about him, too. After a moment's thought, it came to her. He was Troy Barrigan, a regular reporter on one of the local evening-news shows.

While the security guard conferred with the animal-control officer and the game warden, the three of them forming a protective circle around the cage that held Eudora, Roy Eastmont signaled for the *Variety Live* camera crew to stop recording. He drew Elise aside, closer to Liss and closer, although he didn't realize it, to the television news team.

"It will be all right, love," Eastmont said in soothing tones. "We have plenty of footage from previous performances. Don't you worry about a thing. We'll fake something up so you can stay in the running for at least the next two shows."

Liss cleared her throat. "Uh, you might want to be careful what you promise."

His smile conspicuously absent, Eastmont glared at her. Liss jerked her head toward Troy Barrigan and his cameraman. From the reporter's cat-that-swallowed-the-canary grin, they'd caught all of Eastmont's attempt to reassure Elise.

Barrigan thrust his microphone into the MC's face. "Any comment you'd like to make for our viewers, Mr. Eastmont? Does what you just told Ms. Isley mean that you'll run clips from past shows and try to pass them off as a live performance?"

An appalled silence fell over the entire cast and crew of *Variety Live.* Liss held her breath, waiting to hear Eastmont's reply.

It took the MC only a moment to regain his composure. "You misunderstood, young man." He gave Elise's hand a final, reassuring pat before he clapped an arm around the interloper's shoulder to steer him toward the exit. "If you'll come with me, I'll give you an exclusive inside look at just how our program brings wonder and delight to our millions of viewers every week."

Seconds later, both reporter and cameraman had been ushered out of the ballroom. Eastmont was quick on the uptake. Liss had to give him that much credit.

The production assistant breathed a sigh of relief. "Excitement's over. Back to work, everyone!"

Elise sent her an incredulous look. "I can't do my act without Eudora!"

Mo sidled up to her. "Cheer up, Elise. You can always dance with a feather *boa* instead of a python."

"My *partner* is not so easily replaced!" In a cartoon, Elise would have been pictured with steam coming out of her ears.

"Neither was my equipment!" Mo shot back.

"Hold on!" Liss thrust herself between them before they could come to blows. "Don't get mad at each other. All of our acts have fallen victim to dirty tricks. It seems to me that means—probably—that they weren't played by any of us."

The sound of a throat being cleared had the three of them turning to look at the animal-control officer. The game warden and the security guard had gone, but they'd left the cage containing Eudora behind.

"Someone played a dirty trick on Miss Isley, all right," he said. "Turns out there's no Augustus Brown registered at this hotel, in room 312 or anywhere else. The complaint of a python attack was a complete fake."

Chapter Seven

"I'm going to go out on a limb here and guess that the same person who took Dandy was responsible for the phony charges against Eudora," Liss said. "And it wouldn't surprise me to learn that it was an anonymous tip that brought that TV news team here."

Hal Quarles had joined Mo and Liss after Elise accompanied the animal-control officer to release her pet python from captivity. "Anyone care to wager on who tipped off the media?" he asked. "My money is on Roy Eastmont. I wouldn't put anything past him, not if it gets free publicity for the show."

"If he called the Portland station, then his plan backfired," Liss said. "That reporter overheard enough to convince him that the series isn't really broadcast live."

But when Eastmont returned to the ballroom, without the news team, he didn't seem at all concerned about bad publicity. His smile, wide and genial, seemed as genuine as it ever did.

"Back to work, everyone! Quickly!" He clapped his hands to get their attention. "The crisis is past, but we have a *lot* of work to do! Mo, you're up next."

The rest of the session went without incident. Liss stayed until the end to watch performances by Mo, Elise, and Quarles. The first was lively, the second strangely fascinating, and the third just plain irritating. Liss had never thought insult comedy was very funny, although she supposed she had to admire Quarles's ability to walk the fine line between making people laugh and provoking outrage, boycotts, and even lawsuits.

"We'll record the results show at ten tomorrow morning," Eastmont announced, "then go right into the next week's performances. Be here, in costume, by nine-thirty at the latest."

The young woman who was Eastmont's assistant was waiting to speak with him, and they were soon deep in conversation. Liss supposed she must have a name, but she hadn't heard anyone use it.

The performers scattered, while members of the production staff went about their various duties. The ballroom cleared rapidly. By the time Liss stepped into the foyer, pulling the two wheeled animal carriers behind her, the area appeared to be deserted. She jumped when Mo Heedles called her name. Dandy gave one short bark and then fell silent.

"Mo. What can I do for you?" She kept walking toward the elevator. She'd pushed the UP button before she got an answer.

"Valentine told me what you noticed in the pictures she took. The dog harness. I don't know where that came from but, I swear to you, I had nothing to do with Dandy's disappearance."

Liss slanted a look her way. In the unflattering lighting in the foyer, Mo's face looked pale and drawn. Guilt? Or understandable concern, considering that the alternative explanation was that someone had tried to frame her?

The elevator door opened, and they got in. From her teary-eyed look, Mo was about to start crying. Instead, she sneezed.

Right, Liss thought. *Allergic to dogs.* She fumbled in her pocket for a clean tissue and offered it to the other woman.

"Thanks." Mo blew her nose with a loud honking sound. "You believe me, don't you? You were right in what you said to Elise. We're all three of us victims."

"I'm keeping an open mind," Liss said. The elevator rose slowly toward the fourth floor. "A clever villain would arrange matters so that she, or he, appeared to be just another one of the trickster's targets."

"Why on earth would I want to cause trouble?"

"I don't know, Mo. Why would you? To eliminate the competition, maybe?"

"If that's what I was trying to do, I'd be better at it." The annoyance in her voice was tempered by the rueful look on her face. "And I'd have put Hal Quarles on my hit list."

Liss fought a laugh and lost. "What could you

do to him? He's got all his jokes in his head. There's no equipment to vandalize. No partner to eliminate."

"All I'd have to do is get him drunk right before his performance."

"Spike his drink? Slip him a Mickey?"

"No need. He's a recovering alcoholic." Mo sighed. "Trouble is, I don't think I could bring myself to do that to him, no matter how obnoxious he is. I wouldn't want his relapse on my conscience."

The elevator stopped, and the door opened on an empty fourth-floor hallway. They walked together as far as Mo's suite, which turned out to be the second one on the left.

The memory of a door closing somewhere along this corridor came back to Liss as Mo went inside. She'd wondered at the time if someone had been spying on her, and who occupied which rooms. Still wondering, she let herself into the Amendole suite. After she freed Dandy and Dondi from their carriers and fed and watered them, she went back out into the hall to study the layout.

She was in one of two corner suites. When she stood with her back to her door, the fire exit was straight ahead of her. Only two doors opened off the short hallway leading up to it, both of them to her left as she faced the stairwell. Oscar Yates was in the one nearest it. She had no idea who occupied the other suite. Looking to her right, she couldn't see Mo's door, but it was only just out of her range of vision. Liss hesitated, then decided she could leave the dogs alone long enough to pay a brief visit to her neighbor.

Mo looked surprised to see her. "Is something wrong?"

"I just wondered—do you know which rooms the other competitors are in?"

"Sure. Valentine Veilleux is in the suite next to the elevator, when she feels like using it. Then me. Iris is on the other side of me and Willetta is next to her in the corner room. Then, between Willetta and you, that's Elise's suite."

"Hal Quarles is across the hall from me," Liss remembered, "and Oscar Yates is next to the stairs. Who has the suite next to Yates?"

"That would be Roy Eastmont. *Variety Live* booked all the rooms on this floor and a good many on the third floor, too. I'm not sure who's where down there besides the costume lady. I've heard that most of them are just regular rooms, though. No suites for the peons."

"Thanks, Mo." Liss started to turn away.

"No problem, but is there some particular reason why you wanted to know where everyone is?"

"Just a minor puzzle that needed solving," Liss said. "I have no plans to sabotage anyone's act."

"*Did* you solve it?" Mo asked, stepping out into the hall and watching Liss insert her key card. For once, it worked on the first try.

"Maybe." Liss ducked inside without satisfying Mo's curiosity. The Scotties were right there to greet her. "Make that almost certainly," she told them.

From the door of her suite next to Mo's, Iris Jansen had a clear line of sight to Liss's room. Given the way Iris felt about the magician she worked for, and how she'd been so quick to steer him away from Liss at the food table that first morning, spying on her boss made perfect sense. Iris had probably been coming out of her room when she'd caught sight of Yates talking to Liss. Naturally, she'd keep an eye on them until Yates continued on to his own suite. As soon as he'd disappeared around the corner, Iris would have retreated back inside her own room to avoid being seen. Only the click of the door as it closed had betrayed her presence.

Liss felt sorry for the young woman. Jealousy was a tough emotion to handle, and one that could really mess with a person's sense of perspective.

After Liss had gone over Deidre's notes for the dance number she had planned for the next show and put Dandy and Dondi through their paces, she took a break. Was it still only Monday? She felt as if she'd already lived through a week of rehearsals and recording sessions.

A glance at her watch told her it was nearly five, late enough for Dan to have knocked off work. He built the jigsaw-puzzle tables he sold online and in Carrabassett County Wood Crafts in the workshop behind their house. First, though, before she called that familiar number, she hunted up the one Desdemona had left for her. Liss needed to give Deidre's daughter an update, too.

After twelve rings, she gave up.

Maybe it wasn't such a good idea to bug Desdemona with *Variety Live* business just yet. Deidre's funeral had been held earlier today. Still, it was odd she wasn't answering her phone, or at least letting messages go to voice mail. Liss wondered if Gordon had been able to reach her, and what questions he'd wanted to ask her. She supposed she'd find out eventually. In the meantime, she had another call to make.

Just hearing Dan's voice perked her up. She told him all about the other acts in the competition—even including the Great Umberto's attempt to hit on her, which struck her as pretty funny in retrospect. He claimed he wasn't surprised to hear how phony the whole thing was, and they laughed together over Liss's account of her first meeting with Eudora.

"Talk about up close and personal," Dan said. "Just how big is this snake?"

"At a guess, about four feet long, but I didn't get close enough to take measurements."

"A small one, then."

"In what universe?"

"No, really. Pythons—Burmese pythons, anyway—are usually much bigger. Around nine to seventeen feet. They run maybe forty pounds for a small one and go up to more than a hundred pounds."

"I doubt *Elise* tips the scales at more than a hundred, lucky thing."

"Eudora is probably a ball python, then. They're smaller and much easier to handle. They got their name because they curl into a ball when they're frightened."

Liss thought of Elise, cuddling the snake against her like a baby. Maybe the snake had been scared, but that didn't make Eudora any less dangerous. She repeated the story the security guard had told her.

"Those incidents are rare," Dan assured her. "Even if Eudora got loose and somehow got into your room, it's unlikely she'd bother you." There was a pause. "You should probably keep the Scotties out of her way, though."

"Oh, thank you very much for the nightmares I'll be having tonight! Do I want to know why you know so much about snakes?"

"Science fair. Seventh grade."

"You've got a good memory."

"It was an interesting project. I really wanted to keep a python as a pet. My mother nixed that idea. She said she could deal with garter snakes, but that was her limit."

"Wise woman. Don't get any ideas about introducing a new pet to our house," Liss warned him. "The cats would freak."

"They miss you," Dan said. "I miss you."

She smiled into the phone. "It hasn't been three full days yet." And only two nights.

"Seems longer. My schedule hasn't been quite as full as yours."

"You don't know the half of it."

As she'd expected, he was more concerned than amused when she told him what had happened to Eudora and Elise that afternoon. There was a little silence on the other end of the phone line after she filled him in on the vandalism to Mo's props and her theory that the dirty tricks were connected.

"Anything else I should know about?" Dan asked.

"Well, yes. There is one thing."

Now that nearly twenty-four hours had passed, Liss felt foolish for having been so unnerved by Gordon Tandy's visit. Although there had been a time, not all that long ago, when she'd have avoided mentioning the state police detective's name to her husband, recent events had taught her that it was always better to share information than to hold things back. If some of what she was about to tell Dan irritated him, she was certain that reaction would be short-lived. She took a deep breath and plunged in.

"He was looking for Desdemona Amendole?" Dan asked when she finished.

"That's what he said."

"But he didn't say why?"

"Does he ever?" Thinking that Dan was taking this better than she'd anticipated, Liss relaxed. She was seated on the sofa, with Dandy's head in her lap. She stroked her absently while she waited for her husband's next comment.

"Does Gordon think Deidre Amendole was murdered?"

Her right hand clenched on the phone. The left froze on Dandy's back. She'd wondered the same thing, but it startled her to hear Dan suggest it. "I have no idea what he thinks. You know Gordon—Mr. Stone Face."

"You said someone's been playing dirty tricks—the dognapping and the vandalism and the phony phone call. And that Deidre's act was looking like a sure bet to win the champion of champions trophy. Is it possible one of the other contestants is deranged enough to, well, eliminate the competition in a more permanent way?"

"Now who's got an overactive imagination?"

"I guess it's pretty unlikely, but let's face it, Liss—you've stumbled into more than your fair share of murder investigations."

"Too many. It's beyond belief that I'd find myself in the middle of another one. Besides, if there was any danger to me, I'm sure Gordon would have warned me. He's still a friend, even if he is a police officer first."

"You're being careful, right?"

"Of course I am. We have a troublemaker in our midst and I'm responsible for keeping Dandy and Dondi safe. In fact, after what happened with Elise, I think I may have to start using the pee pads."

"Pee pads?" She could still hear concern in his voice, but there was a thread of amusement there, as well.

Liss explained, adding, "It would be way too easy to run one of them down in the parking lot on the way to that little park we've been using for walkies."

"Easy to run you down, too." Dan was serious once more. "And for God's sake, if you see someone coming toward you with a pipe or a baseball bat aimed at your knees, run."

A snorted laugh escaped before she could stop it, not that the reference was at all funny. It had been years since ice skater Nancy Kerrigan had been attacked by thugs trying to assure that one of her rivals would have a better chance at a gold medal, but the story was revived every time the Winter Olympics rolled around. Kerrigan had been lucky. She'd escaped with a few bruises when the blow could as easily have broken her kneecap.

"And on that cheery note," she said aloud, "I should get back to work. I plan to order supper from room service and spend the rest of the evening rehearsing. Oh, and watching the news, in case they run a piece on Eudora. Someone gave Troy Barrigan a tip. He was there with a cameraman when the authorities tried to take the snake away from Elise."

"I'll be sure to watch," Dan promised. "Liss? I could drive up there. Stay over."

It warmed her to hear him offer, but she didn't want him making a fuss. Besides, she'd never be able to concentrate on the dance routines if he was with her. "I'd love the company, but someone has to stay home to feed the cats and clean the litter box."

She waited. Her argument didn't hold water when Moosetookalook was only half an hour's drive away. Dan could easily commute, both to work and to look after Lumpkin and Glenora.

"I guess I'm staying put." The reluctance in his voice was palpable. "Listen, here's a thought. Would you consider deliberately throwing a performance? That way, you'd be sure to be eliminated in the next round. You could be home by this time tomorrow."

"Not my style," Liss insisted, but the suggestion stuck with her after she ended the call.

Deliberately perform poorly? The idea went against the grain, and yet if the reason for the dognapping had been to eliminate Deidre and her Dancing Doggies from the competition, losing might be the smart thing to do, a way to keep the Scotties safe.

How hard could it be to perform badly? To make mistakes in the routine would be believable after the way that first rehearsal had gone. The judges would have to give the act low scores, and that would be that. They'd be off the show. No one would have any further reason to harm them.

Tempting, she thought. *Very tempting.*

There was only one problem. Chances were good that no matter what she did, she would not be able to maneuver the judges into booting the act off the show. She'd just embarrass herself if she made a poor showing. Roy Eastmont would simply claim that the viewers at home had voted to keep Deidre and her Dancing Doggies in the running despite a less-than-stellar performance.

Better to figure out who was behind the dirty tricks, she decided, and put a stop to them.

She ordered a light supper from room service and turned on the television with the sound low. She selected Troy Barrigan's station. The first of three nightly half-hour news segments was already over, but the scroll across the bottom of the screen told her that a story titled PYTHON FALSELY ACCUSED had yet to run.

Room service had delivered her meal and Liss had eaten it. She was still waiting for Troy Barrigan's report on *Variety Live.* The last half-hour segment led with a car-truck accident that had snarled traffic on I-95. Liss tuned out and retrieved the notes she'd made when she watched her competitors perform in the season premiere. She scrawled one word across the top: *Suspects*.

Someone had been responsible for three dirty tricks: the dognapping, the destruction of Mo's equipment, and the anonymous tip about Eudora the python. After the names of the five contestants, she added three more: Iris Jansen, Valentine Veilleux, and Roy Eastmont.

Could she cross anyone off?

Her pen hovered over Mo's name. She could be lying about the dog harness.

She started to scratch out Elise Isley. Once again she hesitated. A ball python could not be as easily replaced as Mylar devil sticks, silicone balls, or multicolored beanbags. The old expression "cut off your nose to spite your face" came to mind, and Liss could not think of a single reason why Elise would be that foolish. She wanted to win. She wanted, if Mo was to be believed, to host her own competition. But Eudora had *not* been confiscated. If Elise had set the whole thing up, she'd have known that the authorities would soon learn that there was no Augustus Brown. Instead of running a line through the exotic dancer's name, Liss put a question mark next to it.

Oscar Yates came next. Liss grimaced. He was charming—a little too charming. He was—she searched for the right word and came up with *flamboyant.* In an accountant or a physician or even a custom woodworker, his behavior would be considered outrageous, but Yates was a stage magician. He was supposed to come across as bigger than life. She couldn't eliminate him as a suspect, but she had no particular reason to think he was the culprit, either.

Hal Quarles was a nasty piece of work, but that was his stock-in-trade. Beneath the facade he could well be a charming bon vivant. Mo had said he was a recovering alcoholic. That might account for his sour disposition, but it didn't make him a villain. For all she knew, he had a loving wife and eight kids at home.

And why, she wondered, hadn't she checked into that?

Carrying her list with her, Liss left the table and retrieved her iPad. She'd brought it along as a reader, but the hotel had a Wi-Fi connection. Within minutes, she'd called up all sorts of information on the personal life of the insult comic. The wife and kids she hypothesized did not exist, although there were two ex-wives. Quarles had been around for a while, working mostly in comedy clubs, never hitting the big time until he won his season of *Variety Live.* And after that? Nothing again. No guest appearances on late-night television. No contract with some big hotel in Las Vegas.

She supposed Quarles had reason to be bitter,

but that didn't necessarily translate into using dirty tricks to win the champion of champions title. What good would that do him, especially if it was obvious he'd only won because everyone else had been obliged to drop out?

Now that her mind was running along that track, Liss wondered if any of the winners had reaped significant professional benefits from their victories. Willetta had said she hoped for an offer from an opera company, but she'd already won one season of the show without attracting that sort of attention. The recording contract she'd gotten had expired.

Fingers flying, Liss searched "Willetta Farwell" and came up with plenty of hits, but most just repeated the same information, a vita that sounded like it came directly out of a *Variety Live* press release. Liss had been impressed by her voice, and her YouTube videos had lots of likes, but it didn't look as if anyone in the star-making business had been interested in promoting her career. Her performance credits were mostly local—she hailed from Norfolk, Virginia. The closest she'd come to singing in an opera company had been the role of Little Buttercup in a Savoyards' production of *HMS Pinafore.*

Liss was debating which name to type into the search engine next when she glanced at the television screen. The scroll told her PYTHON FALSELY ACCUSED was up next.

A moment later, Roy Eastmont's familiar face appeared, standing next to Troy Barrigan and smiling into the camera. Liss wasn't surprised that Eastmont was a practiced liar, but she'd been under the impression that the TV newsman was smart enough to dig out the truth. Either he was dumber than he looked or he'd succumbed to a bribe because the story was as much a plug to watch *Variety Live* as a piece on the dirty trick someone had played on Elise and her snake.

While a series of clips ran, obviously provided by Eastmont and even including a bit of Liss's dress rehearsal, the show's MC explained that there would be no episode shown that evening, in the program's regular Monday night slot, because of a long-scheduled awards show. He skimmed over Deidre's death with appropriate expressions of sorrow and had Liss wincing when he referred to her as "a prominent local dancer who stepped in to fill the void." She doubted that he'd abandoned the "old friend of the family" angle. He was just taking advantage of the fact that she lived in Maine to give the story greater appeal in that market.

She had to admire the way Eastmont managed not to dwell on the "tragic loss" while at the same time giving the impression that what the reporter had seen that day was just a rehearsal for the show that would be recorded—live, of course!—in a week's time. As for Eudora's confiscation, that was explained away as a silly practical joke—"You know these show business people!"—already "well on its way to being resolved."

The footage of Elise, Eudora, the warden, and the animal-control officer, which Liss had expected would be the focus of the news story, lasted about three seconds. The piece ended with Eastmont once again smiling into the camera.

Liss was frowning when she clicked off the TV. She looked down at Roy Eastmont's name on her list of suspects. *Variety Live* was his baby. He was good at spinning unfortunate events into good publicity. But what if he was also very good at creating unfortunate events?

She grabbed her iPad, and this time went straight to IMDb, the movie and TV database that contained just about everything anyone ever wanted to know about actors, directors, and the others who worked in those fields. *Variety Live* had an entry. Two more clicks brought up Roy Eastmont's filmography. As Liss already knew, he was more than just the show's master of ceremonies. He was also listed as director and as an executive producer, and the entry hinted that he also owned a large chunk of the show. If ratings had been falling in recent seasons, as the "comments" section indicated, Liss could see how Eastmont might be getting desperate enough to call attention to the current competition in any way he could.

On the other hand, he had a lot to lose if certain aspects of the way the show was produced became public. In addition, he seemed to want Deidre and her Dancing Doggies to win. Liss underlined his name. Twice. She didn't know what to think about Roy Eastmont, but he would bear watching right along with the other suspects on her list.

The hotel phone rang before she could move on to Iris and Valentine. Liss sent it a wary look. She'd been expecting this. Way too many people she knew would have seen that news story, and at least three of them—Sherri, Aunt Margaret, and Dan—knew where to reach her. Others could find out easily enough, and she had no doubt that someone in Moosetookalook had already sent an e-mail to Arizona, where Liss's parents lived, alerting them to the fact that their daughter was going to appear on national TV next week in a skintight gold lamé bodysuit.

She reached for the phone, tempted to answer with "The costume wasn't my idea."

Before she could say anything, Dan spoke. "It's Margaret, Liss. She's in the hospital in a coma."

Chapter Eight

Liss burst into the house in Moosetookalook. "What happened?"

Dan had been watching for her and was already shrugging into his coat. "I'll tell you what I know in the car. She's not in Fallstown Community Hospital. She's at CMMC. Do you want me to drive the rest of the way?"

"Yes. No. I don't know. I can't think straight."

In the half hour it had taken Liss to get home, her imagination had run wild. Guilt had plagued her, too. She'd thought something was wrong with her aunt the last time she'd seen her. She should have pressed Margaret for answers.

"I just talked to the hospital a few minutes ago." Bundled up against the cold, Dan checked to be sure he had his keys and his wallet. "They wouldn't tell me much. Damned privacy laws!"

Lumpkin butted Liss's leg, and she automatically reached down to rub the big Maine Coon cat on the top of his head. Glenora, curled up on a chair, opened one eye but didn't bother to get up and greet her.

Dan was still talking. "Dad's there."

It took Liss a moment to absorb this information. Joe Ruskin was at Central Maine Medical

Center? "Why? I mean, what happened? Was there an accident at the hotel?" Her voice rose with each question.

"Whoa. Calm down." Dan enveloped her in a hug. After a moment he stepped back. "Here's the plan. I filled a thermos with coffee for the trip." He picked up the tote bag he'd left by the door. "I'll drive. Do you need to use the bathroom before we go?"

It was a welcome gift to have someone else making the decisions. Liss couldn't seem to get her head wrapped around what was happening. She felt as if she'd stepped into another dimension.

"Give me five minutes."

She was back in six, having taken time to slosh cold water onto her face. She delayed another minute to make sure the cats had food and water. Then she and Dan were on their way south.

"What *do* you know?" she asked as they drove out of town. It would be over an hour before they reached the hospital. "You said she was in a coma. Was she in a car accident?"

"No. From what Dad was able to find out, she checked into the hospital this morning for surgery."

"Surgery?" The word came out as a squeak. "What kind of surgery?" She held her breath, waiting for his answer, her mind leaping wildly from cancer to appendicitis to open heart and back again to cancer. There were so many forms of cancer, and most of them were deadly.

"Eye."

"What?" Disbelief had her turning in her seat to stare at him.

"Eye," he repeated, keeping his own on the road ahead. "Dad found out that much after he got to CMMC. Margaret went in for some kind of elective eye surgery. Rather than worry her friends and family, she kept it to herself. If all had gone as planned, she'd have been back home tomorrow with no one the wiser."

"What went wrong?"

"It sounds like she had a bad reaction to the anesthesia."

"Oh, God." People could die from that. "And she's in a coma?"

"That's what Dad said, but I doubt anyone would tell him much, either. They'll have to talk to you, though. You're a blood relative. And you're the one she named in her living will."

They lapsed into silence. Liss couldn't remember when she'd been this frightened or felt so helpless. She'd seen that living will. Margaret had forbidden the use of any "extraordinary means" to keep her alive if doctors deemed there had been irreparable brain damage. Up until that point, if Margaret wasn't capable of doing so herself, Liss was the one who would have to make medical decisions. Just the thought of assuming so much responsibility sent Liss into a panic.

Dan gripped her hand, giving it a hard squeeze. “We’ll be there soon.”

He didn’t try to tell her everything would be okay. She wouldn’t have believed him if he had.

Joe Ruskin was waiting for them at the hospital entrance. He was an older, more grizzled version of his son. Liss rushed toward him, a dozen questions ready to tumble out, but her first glimpse of his face did more to ease her mind than any verbal answer. He was smiling.

“Is she—?”

“She’s going to be fine, Liss. I’m so sorry I worried you. She regained consciousness about fifteen minutes ago. She was still woozy, but she was coherent enough to be seriously ticked off at me for contacting Dan. I told her it was her own fault for listing my extension at The Spruces as the first number to call in an emergency.”

A few minutes later, Liss was able to see for herself that Margaret was on the mend. She’d already been moved from the intensive care unit to a regular room.

“Do you have any idea the scare you gave us?” Hands on her hips, her cheeks tear streaked, Liss glared at the woman lying in the hospital bed. Her heart wasn’t in it. She was too relieved. “I thought you were going to go and die on me!”

“Sorry. That was not my plan.”

“Your *plan* was lousy.” Liss perched on the end

of the bed. "Don't you ever do something this stupid again, okay?"

Margaret lifted her hand far enough to make the "okay" sign.

She looked pale, and one eye had clearly been operated on. "I should go. You need rest." But she didn't get up.

"I've been resting. You're here. Stay a little longer. Cheer me up."

Liss didn't argue. She was badly in need of cheering up herself. She also needed reassurance that Margaret was really out of danger. That Liss's family was so small made the possibility of losing one of them all the more wrenching.

"Are the doctors sure you're okay now? What went wrong? Joe said you had a bad reaction to the anesthesia and were in a coma."

"I was *not* in a coma. It just took me a little longer than most people to wake up after the surgery."

Temper, Liss thought. Always a positive sign. Slowly, the knot of tension inside her began to loosen. She dared believe that the crisis was past and that Margaret was on the road to recovery.

"How was I supposed to know I was sensitive to some chemical I've never even heard of? It's not like I've had a lot of operations over the years."

Liss couldn't remember that she'd had any. "So. Elective eye surgery. Are you supposed to keep your head still? Lie flat for a couple of days or something?"

"I did *not* have a detached retina."

Liss waited. Margaret seemed to grow stronger with each passing moment.

"What I had," Margaret said in an exasperated voice, "is the stupidest-sounding ailment I've ever heard of. It's called a macular pucker." She waited a beat. "My optometrist called it a wrinkle on the retina, which sounds even sillier. It's apparently not uncommon in someone my age, and not terribly serious, either, although it does eventually cause wonky vision."

"Anything that affects eyesight is serious. I'm glad you got it fixed, but why on earth didn't you want to tell me beforehand? I already knew you'd been having trouble with your vision."

Margaret bristled. "Because, in case you've forgotten, you have other responsibilities this week."

Knowing the way hospitals worked these days, Liss suspected her aunt would be released as soon as was humanly possible. Too soon, probably. She'd need someone to take care of her once she got home, if only to keep her from doing too much too soon. The obvious solution was for Liss to move in with her for a few days. She'd stayed in Margaret's apartment before, when she'd first come back to Moosetookalook after her years on the road.

"When they let you out," she said aloud, "I'll bunk in your spare bedroom for a few days, just to make sure you don't try to do more than you should."

"I don't need a babysitter. And you made a commitment to *Variety Live*. You can't break a promise. Besides, I expect they had you sign a contract."

"You're more important than some stupid variety show."

"And nothing will do more for me than seeing you perform. What have you done with those adorable little dogs? Don't tell me you left them alone in a hotel room!"

"They're being looked after by a woman named Valentine Veilleux."

"Ah! The photographer."

"Yes, but how did you—?"

"I've seen some of her calendars. In fact, I've been considering hiring her to do one for The Spruces. Twelve scenic views of our historic hotel. We could sell the calendars in the gift shop. I think they would do quite well."

"I'm sure they would, and that she'd do a wonderful job, but I'm not going back to Five Mountains when you need—"

"Amaryllis Rosalie MacCrimmon Ruskin!"

Uh-oh. Whenever her aunt, or her mother, pulled out Liss's full name, she knew she was in trouble. Although she no longer instantly reverted to shy adolescence, it was an incantation that still had the power to make her cringe.

"You agreed to be on the show in Deidre Amendole's place."

That Aunt Margaret sounded more like her old self with every word gladdened Liss's heart, even at the expense of being lectured on her responsibilities. "Yes, but—"

"And you promised her daughter you'd see the competition through. Now I want you to promise me the same thing. I will not be able to relax and recover from this little setback if I feel guilty about taking you away from a chance to dance on live TV."

Liss bit her tongue. Trying to correct her aunt at this stage would take too long, and it didn't matter, anyway. Put to her that way, what choice did she have? She gave her word.

The nurse kicked her out a few minutes later. Joe had already gone home, but Dan was waiting in the parking lot.

She said nothing for most of the drive, sitting slumped in the passenger seat, lost in thought. It was only when they approached Moosetookalook that she roused herself, surprised to see by the dashboard clock that it still lacked a few minutes until midnight.

"I need to go back to Five Mountains."

"We'll stop at the house first. I need to pick up my truck."

She turned her head to stare at him. "You're going to follow me back to the resort and stay over?"

"I thought I would. Do you object?" His hands gripped the wheel with unusual force. Tension radiated from the set of his shoulders, as if he expected an argument.

Liss liked to think of herself as self-reliant and resourceful, but sometimes even the most independent woman needed her man's arms around her through the night. "Not a chance!"

The next morning, Liss hated to see Dan leave. They lingered over their good-byes in the hallway by the elevators, and she cooperated fully when he claimed one last heart-stopping kiss. They separated when a faint ding indicated one of the elevator doors was about to open.

"Love you," he said, stepping inside and pushing the button for the lobby.

"Right back at you." She waggled her fingers at him in a little wave as the door slid shut again. A small sigh escaped her when she heard the elevator start to descend.

"Dreamy. Is he yours?"

Iris's voice caught Liss off guard. She turned so quickly that her elbow slammed into the wall, cracking the funny bone. "Ow. Damn!"

"Sorry. I didn't mean to startle you. Come in here. Let's get some ice on that."

"That's okay." Liss tried to move past Iris's door and around the corner to her own suite, but the other woman caught her undamaged arm and hauled her inside. She was stronger than she looked.

The interior of Iris's suite was a duplicate of Liss's, except that Iris had littered every surface with her personal effects. Earrings were scattered hither and yon, singly and in pairs. Hearts. Hoops. Gemstones. Plain gold. To Liss, who had never had her ears pierced, the variety was a revelation. Bemused, she watched Iris dump the ice in the tray in the room's tiny refrigerator into a towel and bring it like an offering to where Liss was perched on the arm of a chair.

"It's fine. Really."

"And ice will make it better." Without a by-your-leave, she grabbed Liss's wrist, adjusted the angle of her arm, and applied the cold compress to her elbow. "Put your other hand over it and hold it there."

Liss did as she was told.

Iris plopped herself down on the sofa. Her rosy cheeks glowed with good health, and her smile was that of a child anticipating a treat. "Tell me everything. Who was that delicious hunk I just saw you kissing?"

Voice dry, Liss said, "That was no hunk. That was my husband."

"Oh, my goodness!" Iris pretended to fan herself.

"Well, I guess I don't have to worry about *you* then."

Liss adjusted the makeshift ice pack. "*Worry* about me?"

"Worry that you're after Oscar. I wondered, you know, when I saw you together the other day. You're quite attractive." Unsaid were the words *"for someone your age."*

"Ah." Liss had known Iris was the jealous, possessive type and had already concluded that she wasn't above spying on the Great Umberto. "Does he know how you feel about him?"

The smile vanished. Iris's eyes filled with unshed tears. "He doesn't know I'm alive, not as a woman. I'm just another prop to use in his magic act."

"I'm sure it's not as bad as all that. Perhaps he just thinks you're still a little . . . young for him."

"Maybe," she said in a small voice. "It doesn't matter. I won't give up. Someday he'll notice that I'm all grown up. How's the elbow?"

"Better. Thanks." Liss rose and carried the towel, now soaked through, to the suite's small sink and dumped it and the ice. The sleeve of her sweater was damp, too, but it would dry. "I mustn't keep you. You were probably on your way down to breakfast."

"Oh, no," Iris insisted. "I'm in no rush. If you want, I can mind Dandy and Dondi while you go get something to eat."

"Thanks, but I'm all set."

Iris's face fell. "You don't trust me to take care of them, do you? I'm one of your competitors, so you think I could have been the one who took Dandy. But Deidre trusted me. That must count for something."

Had she?

Liss thought back to that first day in Deidre's condo. It had been Desdemona who'd said that her mother didn't believe Iris was the dognapper. She would know, Liss supposed. In her own interaction with the magician's assistant, she could think of nothing to contradict that opinion. Iris was young and immature. She cried at the drop of a hat. She was suffering from a bad case of unrequited love. But none of those things gave Liss a reason to think Iris was the one behind the dirty tricks.

"I was about to collect Dandy and Dondi," she said. "Valentine kept them overnight and she was going to order breakfast for us from room service. Why don't you join us? I'm sure there's plenty to go around."

When Liss knocked on the door to Valentine Veilleux's suite, the response was immediate—joyous barking. A moment later, the photographer opened up. "Come on in. I've already made a start on the coffee." If she was surprised to see that Liss was not alone, she gave no sign of it.

"You're a lifesaver, and not just because you were willing to look after the Scotties at a moment's notice." Liss bent to scratch behind ears and stroke backs but didn't lose any time following Valentine to the table containing an enormous room-service breakfast—bacon, ham, eggs, pancakes, toast, and croissants. The carafe of coffee was a giant economy size and was flanked by a pitcher of orange juice and one of milk.

"No problem on either count." Valentine said. "It's a terrible weakness, but I need fuel as well as caffeine to give me a jump start. And I like dogs. I had one of my own who used to travel with me until he died of old age. He was nearly twenty years old when he went. He had a good life."

"I'm sure he did, but I still feel a little guilty for taking advantage of you." Liss poured herself a cup of coffee and sat down opposite the other woman. Iris was making a fuss over the two Scotties, but they were more interested in seeing what crumbs they could beg from the two women at the table. "I should have come for them as soon as I got back last night, but it was pretty late by then and we had already planned to have breakfast together."

"How is your aunt?" Valentine asked.

"Doing well. It was sort of a false alarm." She explained, trying to make light of her fear, but she had a feeling that Valentine saw right through the attempt. "I talked to her for a few minutes this morning. She thinks she may be allowed to go home later today."

Iris was all ears, but said nothing.

"The dogs were good company," Valentine said. "I hope you don't mind, but I couldn't resist taking a few photos while they were here, even though I didn't have Desdemona's permission."

Before she spoke again, Liss took another sip of coffee and let the warmth of it seep through her. "Have you heard from her?"

"Desdemona? No. Have you?"

Liss shook her head. "I tried to call the other day but there was no answer. I was hoping to find out when she'll be coming back to Five Mountains."

"Is she coming back?" Iris pulled out a third chair and sat, reaching for a piece of toast.

"Surely she will!" Valentine exclaimed. "She left the Scotties behind."

Iris took a bite, looking thoughtful. "I guess. But you know she doesn't like them much."

"No matter how she feels about Dandy and Dondi, she'll have to put in an appearance to retrieve them." Liss bit into a buttery croissant. Her appetite wasn't as good as it had been a few minutes earlier.

"From what I hear," Iris said, "if she wanted to, Desdemona is rich enough that she can afford to hire people to take care of them." She sent Liss a sideways look. "I bet she conned you into doing it for free, though. Am I right?"

Liss frowned. "The subject of money didn't come up."

She'd put her agreement to take Deidre's place into the category of "lending a helping hand." You didn't expect to be reimbursed if you donated clothes to someone whose house had just burned down. Or when you gave blood because the Red Cross had a shortage and there was a hurricane coming.

"Maybe that's how the Amendoles managed to amass their fortune," Valentine mused. "Get people to work for you for free and you can sock away what you'd normally have to pay for a service."

Liss's frown deepened. What was it Hal Quarles had said that day in the elevator? Something about Deidre having pots of money? "I take it the family isn't hurting for cash."

"Not so you'd notice." Iris shared a tiny section of her toast with Dandy.

Valentine nodded her agreement. "I spent some time with both Deidre and Desdemona when I did the shoot for the dog calendar. Deidre didn't like the first set of proofs and offered to pay me out of her own pocket for a second session. Who was I to argue?" At Liss's speculative look, she laughed. "No, I didn't mess up the first time just to create more work. In fact, I thought a couple of shots in that set were better than the one Deidre finally chose." She paused to chew. "I hear you're in retail. You know the rule."

"That the customer is always right? I don't know about you, but I've dealt with some pretty stupid customers."

"I won't argue with you there, but my clients always end up satisfied, which means they pay their bills and I eat regularly and can afford to fill up that gas-guzzler I drive." Valentine poured herself another cup of coffee, having made short work of the first.

Liss sipped and swallowed, her early-morning fogginess now a thing of the past. Since her brain was fully functioning, thoughts began to whirl through it, fast and furious. "I read Deidre's bio for *Variety Live*, but it was more about the dogs than it was about her. I didn't try to find anything on Desdemona. Maybe I should have."

"I doubt there's much to find. From the bits and pieces she told me, she's never worked for a living. When she was younger, she wanted to be a model, but she never grew tall enough."

"If she's wealthy, I don't suppose she needs to work."

Valentine nodded. Her glasses had slipped down to the end of her nose, and she pushed at them in an absentminded manner until they were back in place. "I got the impression that Desdemona's father left healthy trust funds behind when he died, one for his widow and one for his only child. I expect Desdemona will inherit everything, now that Deidre's gone."

Liss returned cup to saucer a little more quickly than she'd intended.

"What's wrong?" Valentine asked. "You have the most peculiar expression on your face."

"I read too much crime fiction," Liss muttered. But she was remembering her visit from Gordon Tandy. Just why *had* he been looking for Desdemona?

Valentine was quick on the uptake. Her eyes narrowed as she caught Liss's drift. "I thought Deidre died from an accidental overdose."

Liss worried her lower lip with her teeth. She trusted Valentine to look after the dogs, but could she be trusted to keep a confidence? She'd been quick to share what Desdemona had said to her. Iris was even more of an unknown.

"I'm sure I'm just letting my imagination run away with me. There's no reason for Desdemona to have been in touch with any of us so soon after her mother's funeral. This must be a difficult time for her."

Iris seemed absorbed in feeding bacon to Dandy, but Valentine made a little humming sound.

"What?"

She shrugged. "I read mystery novels, too. The nearest and dearest always have the best motives." She leaned across the table, her gaze intense. "If

Deidre Amendole was murdered, who'd have a better motive than her daughter?"

"There's absolutely no reason to believe that her death was murder."

Valentine didn't look convinced. "What are you holding back? You know something more."

"Am I that transparent?"

"I'm good at reading people." She shrugged. "I have to be if I'm going to take photos that show more than bland expressions and phony smiles."

"It's probably nothing. It's just that the police haven't closed the case. They're waiting for toxicology results."

Iris's eyes had gone wide, but she didn't say a word.

"Desdemona was the one who had means and opportunity," Valentine murmured. "Easy access to her mother's pills. She could have slipped extras into Deidre's food or drink."

"But matricide? Did you ever see any signs she hated her mother that much? I bump heads with mine all the time, but I'd never harm her."

"I never noticed much affection between them." Valentine sat back, once again sipping coffee as she pondered the question. "Some mothers and daughters never show much. Some fight all the time, but even the ones who yell and scream a lot don't usually try to kill each other. And yet . . ."

"And yet what?"

"Just something Desdemona once said. I

assumed she was joking, but maybe not." She returned the cup to its saucer, picked up her napkin, and crumpled it in one fist. "She doesn't like Dandy and Dondi."

"I told you that," Iris said, sotto voce.

"No, I mean, she *really* doesn't like them. Desdemona said, and I quote, that the 'little beasts ought to be euthanized.' "

Appalled, Liss stared at her. "How could anyone—?"

"I know! The thing is, would a woman who'd consider killing two healthy, innocent dogs balk at killing her own mother?"

Liss had lost her appetite. She'd even lost interest in the coffee. Elbows on the table, she cupped her chin in both hands, fingers covering her mouth, and tried to think rationally. No flights of fancy allowed. They were probably making a mountain out of a molehill. Gordon had said he had questions for Desdemona. That did not mean he suspected her of murder.

But there was another possibility, a second scenario to consider now that Liss was seeing Desdemona Amendole as a coldhearted woman who regularly used people, and pets, for her own ends. "Is it possible Desdemona was the one behind the dirty tricks?"

"She had an alibi for the afternoon Dandy disappeared," Valentine pointed out. "She wasn't even in the state, let alone near her mother's condo."

"She could have hired someone to dognap Dandy."

"Why would she?" Valentine asked.

Iris raised her hand like a schoolgirl. She even bounced a little in her chair. "I know. I know. She wanted to throw everyone off the scent when she went after the other contestants. She could have arranged for that anonymous call that caused Elise so much trouble. And she was at the resort the day Mo's props were damaged."

Valentine removed her glasses and cleaned them with an unused napkin, her brow furrowed in thought. "I admit I've read more than one mystery novel in which someone kills several innocent people to confuse the motive for getting rid of one of them, but all the dirty tricks have accomplished is to annoy everyone. No one's been eliminated from the competition. Even if Eudora had remained in custody, Roy Eastmont would have been able to finagle his way around the problem."

"Someone will be voted off the show today," Liss reminded her.

Shoving her glasses back into place on the bridge of her nose, Valentine gave a derisive snort. "Someone Eastmont picked *before* the first episode of the season was recorded."

"You know that for a fact?"

"Oh, please! If it was any more obvious, there would be a billboard announcing it."

Liss sighed. It wasn't as if Valentine's confirmation came as any surprise to her. "Maybe someone thought he'd make a last-minute adjustment and dump Elise instead. Without the snake, she wouldn't have much of an act."

"Whoever that someone was, I doubt it was Desdemona. It's not like the winner gets a check for a million dollars. The champion of champions is awarded a trophy, like the mirror ball on *Dancing with the Stars*, only cheesier."

Iris started to say something, then stopped, shaking her head when the other two looked her way.

"Since Desdemona is the last person in the world to want to take the act on tour, or into the movies, or whatever," Liss said, taking up Valentine's thread, "she has no reason to care if Deidre and her Dancing Doggies win or not, except for the honorarium, of course."

Valentine looked blank. "The what?"

"I think that's what Desdemona called it." Liss strained to remember exactly what the other woman had said. "She stood to be sued if someone didn't take over Deidre's part in the act. She'd have to return the honorarium paid to all the contestants."

Even before Liss finished her explanation, Valentine was shaking her head. "No. There's nothing like that. Believe me, I'd have heard about it if there was." She shrugged. "People talk to me. I don't know why."

Liss looked at Iris. "No honorarium," the younger woman agreed.

"So Desdemona lied? Why would she, especially about something like that?"

Valentine gave a snort of laughter. "To get you to feel sorry for her and agree to dance?"

"Yes, but . . . oh, this is hopeless. Every time I think I have one thing figured out, someone throws me a curve." She supposed Eastmont could have paid only Deidre, but she couldn't think of a good reason for that, either.

Valentine looked as troubled as Liss felt. Iris's brow was puckered, as if she was trying hard to make sense of what they were saying and having little success.

"Why not just bow out if there's no penalty?" Liss asked. Besides, the show couldn't sue Deidre for not showing up if she was dead.

Glancing at her watch, Valentine rose from the table. "I don't have an answer to that question, or to any others."

"Wow. For a whole thirty seconds there, I thought I could cross Desdemona off my list of suspects."

The other woman chuckled. "You made a list. How efficient. Who else is on it?"

Liss sent her a sheepish smile. "To tell you the truth, Desdemona's name wasn't there, but I did include all the performers and Roy Eastmont and you. No offense."

"None taken."

"I already knew I was a suspect." Iris sounded oddly pleased.

"Well, innocent or guilty, we'd all better get a move on," Valentine said. "It's already after nine."

Liss shot out of her chair. In half an hour's time she was supposed to be in the ballroom, in costume, when the results show was "recorded before a live audience."

Chapter Nine

In costume, smiling, one Scottish terrier on either side of her, Liss watched with reluctant admiration as Roy Eastmont did his MC shtick. A performance by a guest star would be inserted later. Today Eastmont had only to introduce everyone again and then boot one of them off the show.

Deidre and her Dancing Doggies were the first to be pronounced "safe" to go on to the next round. The other acts had to suffer through tease after tease until there were only two left. When the show was televised, there would be a commercial break at that point. Eastmont prolonged the suspense unmercifully even without the interruption.

"Elise and Eudora—did your fans vote to bring you back for another week? The Great Umberto and the lovely Iris—in just a moment, your fate will be decided."

Liss was reminded of the ticking clock on an old game show, only this time the sound was ominous, not upbeat. Iris looked terrified. Her glittery earrings—pendants heavy with rhinestones—caught the light as she turned her head and buried her face in the front of Oscar Yates's tuxedo, as if she couldn't bear to look when Eastmont, in the best awards-show fashion, pulled a card with a name on it out of an envelope.

"Here it is," he announced. "What you've all been waiting for." He took his time opening the large gold-embossed envelope. "The act with the lowest combined score and going home right now is . . . Elise Isley and her Mighty Python!"

Elise let out a screech of disbelief. She refused to take the MC's hand to be led downstage center to make a farewell speech. Instead, she pitched a hissy fit. With an agitated four-foot-long python as her backup group, the exotic dancer's final performance was more than spectacular. It ended with an attempt to scratch out Eastmont's eyes.

Hotel security moved in, but they were so wary of the snake that it took them a good ten minutes to lay hands on either Elise or Eudora. The camera crew never stopped recording. Would they edit the footage, Liss wondered, or just air the whole screaming match? Either way, she felt certain Eastmont would get the bump in ratings he so obviously craved.

Once Elise was removed from the ballroom, it was time to record the show that would be broadcast a week after the first one. The remaining contestants dispersed to change costumes, while the crew made minor adjustments to the set.

Braced to endure whatever Mel had in store for her, Liss was pleasantly surprised to end up in a skirt that came to just below her knees. Of course, it was slit up the side almost to her waist, but the spangled bikini bottom that went with the outfit kept her marginally decent. The top clung to her like a second skin, but the neckline was modest.

"Thanks, Mel," Liss said as she studied her reflection in a full-length mirror. The entire outfit was bright red, and the material was encrusted with glitter.

The costume designer shrugged. "No problem. I know how you hate the thought of titillating viewers every time you bend forward."

Still shaking her head over the other woman's word choice, Liss headed back down to the ballroom, where she'd left Valentine watching the dogs. They'd have about ten minutes for a final rehearsal, and then they'd be "live" once more.

She met Willetta in the elevator. The singer ignored her, engrossed in running through scales as they descended. She unwrapped one of her honey-lemon cough drops and popped it into her mouth when she was through. She had a second cough drop ready in her hand, since her gown, a stunning creation of green velvet, low cut and figure hugging, didn't run to anything so useful as a pocket.

The magic act was up first. Liss didn't pay much attention, although she did notice when the Great Umberto swung his assistant up into his arms and then lifted her over his head to stand on his shoulders as a build-up to the trick du jour. Yates was strong. She'd grant him that much. Iris wasn't tiny like Elise. She was slender but not skinny and at least five-foot-six. The magician was only a few inches taller.

Hal Quarles came next. His insult comedy would have worked better with an audience, but he knew when to pause for the canned laughter. It wasn't until Liss moved into position to begin her dance number with Dandy and Dondi that she realized there were a couple of new faces among the watching cast and crew. Dan had slipped, unnoticed, into the ballroom, and Sherri Campbell had come with him.

With her husband and her best friend watching, Liss couldn't give the performance less than her best effort. Even so, she knew it was only adequate and that, once again, the judges were scoring Deidre and her Dancing Doggies based on a prearranged plan rather than on merit. Smiling, bowing, pretending to be thrilled with her three nines, Liss led the Scotties away and tucked them back inside their carriers.

Placing the carriers where she could keep them in sight, she turned to watch the next act. It was Willetta Farwell's turn, but when Roy Eastmont introduced her, there was a delay before she came onstage. She had a peculiar, pained expression on her face. Liss understood why when she tried to sing. Nothing but a croak came out of her mouth.

Willetta tried again, tears streaming down her cheeks, but the results were just as disastrous.

"What's wrong with her voice?" Liss hissed when Mo appeared at her side. She was scheduled to juggle after Willetta's song received its scores.

The other woman's face had gone pale beneath her makeup. "Sabotage," she whispered. "Willetta popped one of her cough drops into her mouth just as you were finishing up your routine. I saw that odd look come over her face, but I didn't realize—"

"Someone doctored her cough drop?"

Just the thought of it made Liss feel sick to her stomach. This went way beyond the other dirty tricks, and way beyond removing a rival from the competition. Damaging a singer's voice could ruin her entire career. If one of their number was that ruthless, that desperate to win, then the rest of them were in much more danger than she'd believed.

Something had made it impossible for Willetta to sing. She could barely speak. Liss prayed the condition wasn't permanent. It was horrible enough that her inability to perform was about to cost her a place in the competition. The judges stumbled all over themselves expressing their sympathy, but they had no choice but to award her the lowest scores of the season. Even if viewer votes really *did* count, there was no way Willetta would make it to the finals now. This time, the attempt to eliminate a contestant had succeeded.

• • •

After the session was complete, Dan and Sherri accompanied Liss back to her hotel suite.

"How is Margaret doing?" she asked the moment they were inside.

"She's fine. Otherwise, I wouldn't have been calmly watching the show. I'm heading for the hospital to pick her up and drive her home as soon as I leave here, but I'm not going anywhere until you tell me what happened to that singer."

"I don't know much. Willetta goes through cough drops like they were candy. It looks as if someone tampered with one of them." She freed the dogs from their carriers and set out fresh water for them, thinking hard. "Alum would have that effect, wouldn't it?"

She thought she remembered reading that alum could cause the mouth to pucker, but she could be mixing it up with something else. She was no chemist, nor was she an expert on poisonous herbs.

"I don't even know what alum is." Sherri eased her bulky body onto the sofa with a sigh of relief. "What's been going on here?"

"Dirty tricks." Taking the chair opposite, Liss filled her in on what had happened to Mo, Elise, and now, Willetta. "You already know about Dandy being stolen and abandoned in the woods." She reached down to stroke the Scottie, who had curled up at her feet. Dondi was still in the kitchenette, slurping his water.

Dan stood by the window. "So whatever was on that cough drop made her tongue swell up so much that she couldn't sing?"

"Yes. She's already recovering, thank goodness, but it's too late to save her spot on the show."

"On the surface, these all sound like run-of-the-mill juvenile pranks," Sherri said, "except that this last one was played at a moment crucial to the victim's performance. I imagine there are lots of easy-to-obtain substances that someone could use to get that result, but the trickster would have to have access to the cough drop and the opportunity to doctor it."

"One of us. No surprise there."

"And that means whoever is doing these things has too damn many opportunities to try something else. If he comes after you or the dogs—"

"I promise not to get maimed or killed." Liss interrupted, making the cross-my-heart gesture and trying to smile.

Temper flared in Dan's eyes, and he took a step closer to her. "Damn it, Liss, don't make light of this."

"He's right, Liss. You need to be careful." Sherri hesitated. "Are you sure Deidre Amendole's death was an accident?"

"According to her daughter, she took all kinds of pills. She could easily have mixed a fatal cocktail without realizing it."

"Or someone else could have done it for her."

Liss shifted in her chair, uncomfortable with both of them staring at her. "Valentine suggested that Desdemona might have killed her mother. I don't agree. I'm not even willing to concede that there's been a murder. Seriously—what are the odds? I'm just an ordinary person. Ordinary people do *not* keep getting tangled up in murder investigations. It's going to turn out to be an accidental overdose, just like Desdemona said."

"And where, exactly, is Desdemona Amendole?" Sherri asked.

"Ohio, which is why we also ruled out the possibility that Desdemona could be the one behind the dirty tricks. She's not here."

"You're sure about that?"

"That she's not at Five Mountains? Well . . . how about I call her right now?"

Liss dug her cell phone out of the tote she'd been using to lug dog paraphernalia back and forth and punched in the number Desdemona had left for her. It rang eight times before an unfamiliar voice answered with "Amendole residence."

"Hello? May I speak with Ms. Desdemona Amendole, please?"

"Miss Desdemona is not at home."

"To whom am I speaking?"

"I'm the housekeeper, dearie."

"My name is Liss Ruskin. I'm the one taking care of Dandy and Dondi. I really need to get hold of Desdemona."

"Sorry, dearie. I've no idea where she is. She packed her bags and left right after her mother's funeral."

"Perhaps she's headed back to Maine to pick up the dogs?"

A snort of laughter greeted this suggestion. "Not likely! And if she does come for them, I'd think twice about letting her take them. She's madder than a wet hen about that provision in her mother's will."

"What provision?" Liss asked.

"Why, the one where Deidre Amendole specified that Dandy and Dondi are to live out the rest of their natural lives in the manner to which they are accustomed. Unless Miss Desdemona can find a loophole, or they're killed in a tragic accident, she's going be stuck taking care of them for years to come."

On that ominous note, the housekeeper broke the connection.

Liss set her phone aside, shaking her head in disbelief. As if Dandy knew Liss had been talking about her, the Scottie licked her hand. When the little dog rolled over onto her back, Liss tickled her tummy, provoking a rapturous wriggle.

"Don't worry. I'm not about to let anything happen to you or Dondi." She repeated what the housekeeper had told her for Dan and Sherri's benefit.

"What a wretched woman!" Sherri exclaimed.

"Is there some legal way to prevent her from taking the dogs?" Liss asked.

"Probably not. You have no hard evidence that she means them harm. And you don't know exactly what that will says. Maybe there's something in it to discourage Desdemona from trying anything underhanded. You know—any suspicion of foul play and the entire estate goes to the home for unwed cats."

"I just wish I knew where Desdemona is right now." Liss felt as if the Scotties were facing threats from all sides and only hoped her protection would be enough to keep them safe.

Dan offered Sherri a hand to haul her up off the sofa. "We've got to hit the road. I don't want to keep Margaret waiting."

"You look like you're about to pop." Liss regarded her friend's enormous baby bump with wary eyes.

"Not yet." Sherri grinned. "Trust me. I've done this before."

Liss saw them on their way, a little surprised that Dan wasn't trying to convince her to go with them. It was reassuring that he trusted her to handle herself, even though she could tell that he was worried about her. She'd feel the same if their situations were reversed.

The word *trust* had come up a lot lately, Liss mused. Who did she trust at Five Mountains? That was a darned good question.

She was looking for her list of suspects when her glance fell on a small patch of white all but hidden between the desk and the wall. Curious, she caught hold of the visible corner and tugged, revealing a piece of 8½ x 11 copy paper folded in thirds.

"Well, what do we have here?" Liss asked Dondi, who seemed to think she'd retrieved the page for his entertainment. It certainly wasn't her suspect list.

Unfolded, the paper revealed itself to be a printout of a travel itinerary. The name of the passenger was Desdemona R. Amendole.

"Speak of the devil," Liss murmured.

She thought back and recalled papers spilling out of Desdemona's purse the day she left for Ohio. This had probably been one of them, overlooked when she scooped up the others. Liss was about to toss it into the wastepaper basket when a date caught her eye.

Desdemona had said she flew to Maine after Dandy disappeared. That would have been late on Monday or very early the following Tuesday. But the itinerary told a different story. Desdemona Amendole had arrived in Portland on Sunday, the day before the dognapping.

She'd lied, but why? And what had she been doing during an extra twenty-four hours in Maine?

Two strikes, Liss thought. Two lies, the one

about an honorarium being the first. She remembered how twitchy Desdemona had been that day at the condo. Then again, she'd been fidgeting when she visited Liss at Moosetookalook Scottish Emporium, too. A nervous disposition didn't mean she was guilty of anything.

She looked at the itinerary again, just to make sure she wasn't mistaken. She wasn't. And this time, she noticed something else. Desdemona had booked a round trip. She'd planned all along to leave when she did. Taking her mother's body home for burial had not been the reason she'd chosen that day to fly back to Ohio.

Three strikes?

Liss heard the shouting as she passed Willetta's room on her way to record the results show. The singer sounded hoarse, but she definitely had her voice back.

"I know you did it!" Willetta screeched.

"I did not!" Iris shouted back. "You've got no reason to pick on me." She let out a loud shriek, as if Willetta might be about to do her bodily harm.

Liss pounded on the door. "Willetta! Let me in! It's Liss Ruskin!"

It was Iris who jerked it open, a terrified look on her face. "I never did anything to anybody!"

"Liar!" Willetta shouted. "Bitch!"

Something flew across the room and crashed into a wall. Both Liss and Iris ducked, even though the object came nowhere near hitting either one of them.

With a wail, Iris pushed past Liss and fled to the safety of her own room. Liss drew in a deep, steadying breath and stepped into Willetta's suite, pulling the two dog carriers after her.

"Hold your fire. I'm on your side."

Arm raised, hand gripping a hairbrush, Willetta glared at her. Slowly, she lowered her weapon.

"Are you okay?" Liss asked.

"I'm pissed off." Willetta's voice lowered to a hoarse whisper.

"You should rest your voice."

"Why? Nobody's going to hear me sing now, are they?"

Liss didn't argue with her. Instead, she asked another question. "Why do you think Iris is the one who doctored your cough drop?"

"I found one of her earrings."

"In here?"

Willetta nodded.

"It could have been planted." She held up a hand to stop Willetta's automatic protest. "Whoever vandalized Mo's props left behind a dog harness to make it look as if Mo was the one who took Dandy."

Willetta put down the hairbrush. "You think Iris was framed?"

It pained Liss to listen to her speak. "Did you ask her where she last saw that particular earring?

She must have dozens of pairs, and she's not the neatest person in the world."

"I didn't give her a chance to say much of anything," Willetta admitted. "I accused her. She burst into tears. I told her to cut it out, and the shouting match escalated from there."

"I'm not ruling Iris out," Liss said. "Neither Hal Quarles nor Oscar Yates has been the victim of any dirty tricks. Of course, a stand-up comic doesn't have any props to damage and there are two people guarding the magician's tricks, so maybe that explains it."

"Lucky them." Willetta went to stand in front of the mirror, checking the line of her gown and patting a strand of hair back into place. "I may as well get this over with. I think I can guess who's going home after this week's results show."

They went down to the ballroom together.

If Roy Eastmont had planned on eliminating someone other than Willetta, he didn't let on. Instead, he reminded everyone that the "shock" of having one of the leaders voted off would be excellent for ratings.

When the expected result was announced, Willetta bore up like the professional she was, smiling through her tears as she said good-bye to those still in the competition and allowing herself to be photographed packing her bags. Mo, Liss, and the two dogs were instructed to drop by her suite to show what good friends they all were.

Liss stopped off in her own room long enough to leave the carriers and attach leashes to collars. Mo left as soon as the dogs arrived, eyes streaming from her allergy rather than her sorrow over Willetta's departure. Liss lingered after the camera crew had gone, watching Valentine Veilleux snap a few more stills.

"Thanks, Willetta," the photographer said, slipping the lens cap back into place on her camera. "You need any help *un*packing?"

Willetta dumped the contents of her suitcase onto the bed. "Done."

Dandy trotted over to investigate and was gently shooed away.

It took Liss a minute to catch on to the fact that no one who was eliminated could leave. They had to be on hand until Friday, when the final results show would include one last performance by each of them. "Do the others come here, too? The acts that were eliminated before the show changed venues?"

"Of course." Willetta finished cramming underwear back into a drawer and began to hang up the blouses she'd folded so neatly when she'd packed for the cameras. "They'll start trickling in tomorrow."

Oh, great, Liss thought. *More suspects.* Who knew where they'd all been in the interim. Maybe revenge, not greed, had been the motive behind all the malicious mischief. She checked her rampaging imagination, reminding herself that there was a simple way to find out who'd had the opportunity to doctor Willetta's cough drops.

"Who had the opportunity to doctor your cough drops?" she asked.

Willetta closed the closet door. "I've been thinking about that. It could have been Iris. I'm not letting her off the hook just yet. And I did find one of her earrings in here. But how could she know which cough drop I'd pull out of the package?"

"Maybe you should toss the rest," Valentine suggested. "Just to be on the safe side."

"Already done. Right down the toilet."

Curling her legs under her as she settled into the chair beside the bed, Liss bit back the suggestion she'd been about to make. It was no longer possible to have the remaining lozenges tested for contaminants. Instead, she asked a question: "Has Iris ever been in your suite? Other than earlier today, I mean."

"Sure. Once or twice. So were Mo and Elise. But not here in the bedroom, which is where I found the earring."

"Still, she could have lost it a while ago. Maybe housekeeping found it on the floor in the front room and put it on your dresser, or wherever it was that you had the bag of cough drops."

"More likely it was planted," Valentine said from her perch on the windowsill. The setting sun behind her made her strawberry-blond hair into a golden nimbus.

Still intent on restoring her possessions to drawers and dresser top, Willetta shrugged. "Like I said, I've been thinking. I can't remember when it was I last saw her wearing that pair—the ones that look like little anchors. Maybe it doesn't matter, not if only a single cough drop was tampered with. I just took the one with me to the ballroom."

"That's right," Liss said. "You were holding it in your hand in the elevator. Did you hang on to it the whole time?"

"That's the thing." She straightened, hands on hips, shaking her head at her own carelessness. "Hal Quarles asked me to give him a hand. The back of his jacket was bunched up. Turned out one of his suspenders was twisted. I put the cough drop down on the prop table so I could straighten it out for him. Turned my back on it. If someone was waiting for their chance, there was time enough to pick it up, unwrap it, doctor it, and wrap it again."

"Whoever it was would have had to be quick." Valentine sounded doubtful.

"Whoever is doing these things is good at seizing an opportunity." Liss ticked them off on her fingers. "Taking Dandy. Damaging Mo's props. Phoning in a phony complaint against Eudora. And now, tampering with your cough drop."

"You missed one," Valentine said. "The Great Umberto's magic cabinet is missing." Her lips quirked. "You know—the one Iris steps into to do her disappearing act. It just . . . disappeared."

Liss frowned. "They already used that trick. Stealing the cabinet won't set them back in the least."

"Most of the dirty tricks didn't work," Valentine pointed out. "That is, they didn't cause anyone to drop out or be eliminated."

"Except me." Willetta opened the bottom drawer of the dresser and pulled out a bottle she had not bothered to retrieve and tuck into her suitcase when she'd been pretending to pack.

Liss had never heard of Old Overholt, but she accepted an inch of the rye whiskey in one of the suite's water tumblers when Willetta handed it to her and was pleasantly surprised by the taste.

Valentine proposed the toast: "Here's to finding out who dunnit."

"And squashing that sucker flat," Willetta added.

The three of them clinked glasses and drank to it.

The party broke up a short time later when Dandy and Dondi showed signs of needing to go out. Valentine left with Liss and the Scotties.

"Park or pee pads?" she asked.

Liss was already heading for the elevator. "The pee pads are handy, I admit, but housekeeping hasn't been taking the used ones away with the other trash."

Valentine smothered a laugh. "Can you blame them? Ick."

"But what am I supposed to do with them?" Liss's answering grin was rueful. "I guess I can take them home with me and dispose of them at the Moosetookalook town dump."

"I've got a better idea," Valentine said as they exited the hotel and walked toward the statue of the skier. "Give me a lift there and I'll arrange for you to dispose of them at the dump here in Orlin. I'm supposed to show up there tomorrow morning at eight."

Orlin was the town in which Five Mountains Ski Resort was located, although few visitors from away, like Valentine, ever knew that. "What on earth for?"

The "park" was less inviting than it had been. The sunny day had left it awash in mud and slush. The pee pads were looking better and better as Dandy and Dondi plunged right into the muck. They were going to need baths when they got back to their suite, and so was she if they decided to shake themselves in her vicinity. Liss took a prudent step back.

"I've taken on a small extra job," Valentine explained as they watched the two Scotties frolic. "The town of Orlin hired me to shoot photos for a civic calendar. Town office. Fire house.

Historical society museum. Dump. I can get to the other places on my bike, but the transfer station is a ways out of town. Going by car would make the trip much easier."

"It must be inconvenient not having a car."

Valentine shrugged. "Most of the time I visit locations in the RV. For short trips, the bike is adequate."

"Except when it rains."

"There is that."

Their conversation reminded Liss of something Margaret had said, and she ventured another question. "Can I interest you in a photo shoot at a local historic hotel before you move on?"

"I'm always open to new opportunities. Where is it?"

"Moosetookalook. Just down the road a piece." She chuckled. "I can also take you to *our* transfer station, if you want to make comparisons. My husband and I load all our trash and recyclables into the truck and visit there every other weekend."

"Then you *have* to agree to drive me tomorrow," Valentine insisted with a straight face. "I obviously need a technical adviser. What do you say? Are you in?"

Liss laughed. "Why not? I could use a dose of reality that doesn't have the word *television* after it."

Chapter Ten

As Liss had secretly hoped, Dan returned that evening to stay the night. Although this was the first time he'd met either of the Scotties, they both took to him at once. It didn't hurt that he'd brought dog treats.

"How's Margaret?" Liss asked when he'd divested himself of his coat and lavished sufficient affection on Dandy and Dondi to hold them for a while.

"She's fine. She sends her love. And she asked me to remind you that she's looking forward to watching the show when it airs and to seeing you win."

"If she only knew!"

"More trouble?"

Liss filled him in on the missing cabinet, Willetta's suspicions about Iris, and Desdemona's itinerary. Once again, to his credit, he did not lobby her to quit *Variety Live* and come home. She almost wished he would. Aside from her concern about the safety of two little dogs, she still felt guilty for abandoning her aunt.

"Who's staying with Margaret?" she asked.

"She has a lot of friends, Liss. They rallied as soon as the Moosetookalook grapevine got the word out. Maud has moved into the spare room for the next day or two. And Audrey Greenwood has promised to spend time with her tomorrow."

Maud was Maud Dennison, the retired schoolteacher who ran Dan's co-op, Carrabassett County Wood Crafts, in the building next door to Moosetookalook Scottish Emporium and Margaret's upstairs apartment. Audrey the vet, Liss's cochair for the March Madness Mud-Season Sale, was reliable, too. Liss couldn't have asked for anyone better to look after her aunt, but she still felt like a bad niece. She'd seen the trouble Margaret was having that day in the shop. She couldn't help feeling she should have insisted, then and there, on knowing what was really wrong with her.

"What about when Maud and Audrey are at work?"

"Sherri will check in periodically and she's not the only one." Dan rattled off a half dozen names of friends who'd volunteered, including Sherri's father, Ernie Willett, who'd been Margaret's high-school sweetheart and still had a soft spot for her in an otherwise crusty and curmudgeonly nature. Dan's father, Joe Ruskin, who was Margaret's boss, was also on the list.

A knock at the door heralded the arrival of room service. Liss had ordered Dan's favorite foods in anticipation of his arrival. It crossed her mind, as they sat down at the suite's dining table, that someone could have tampered with their meal, but she pushed that unpalatable thought aside at once. There was a difference between being cautious and descending into paranoia!

They'd barely finished eating when her cell phone rang. "Sherri," she said as her friend's home number came up on the screen. She answered the call.

After the usual greetings and inquiries, Sherri got to the point. "Remember George Henderson?" she asked.

"Your pal, the medical examiner?" Liss activated the speaker-phone function so Dan could hear.

"*Retired* ME, but yeah. He stays in touch with his old buddies at the state crime lab, so I paid him a visit and in casual conversation—"

"Of course."

"—I posed a hypothetical question. Apparently the ME who did Deidre Amendole's autopsy spotted something that can't be accounted for by any of the pills they found in her condo. Another drug—a *different* drug—may have played a role in her death, but they won't know for sure until the toxicology comes back."

"Do they consider her death a homicide?"

"Not officially, but I think you should. And if it's tied to everything else that's been going on there, you need to be very careful who you trust." Unspoken was the warning that someone who'd killed once wouldn't hesitate to kill again, especially if he or she thought Liss was getting close to discovering the truth.

"Maybe Desdemona did Mommy in for the inheritance." Liss sounded flip but felt anything but.

And as much as she'd have liked to believe that Deidre's daughter was the villain, given the plans Desdemona apparently had for the two Scottish terriers, Liss was very much afraid Sherri was right. Everything that had happened at Five Mountains was connected. It was all too possible that the fear of being arrested for dognapping had led one of the other contestants to silence Deidre before she could make her accusation public.

After Liss hung up, she shared her troubled thoughts with Dan. "It seems so preposterous," she added. "Deidre might have had her suspicions, but how could she have come up with proof so quickly? She died less than twenty-four hours after I returned Dandy to her."

Dan had left the table for the sofa and now shifted to make room for her. Dandy and Dondi already had possession of the other end. "Say that Deidre found some compelling reason to believe she knew which of them took Dandy. I might not watch *Variety Live*, but I'd have to be living in a bubble not to know that reality shows, especially those that involve competitions, thrive on feuds."

"Feuds and romances," Liss agreed. "More than one hot affair has developed during a competition like this one."

Dan's eyebrows lifted. "The Great Umberto?"

"He certainly wasn't carrying on with Deidre. She was old enough to be his mother. Besides, as far as I can tell, he's all talk and no action, nothing more than a congenital flirt."

"So we're back to feud." He slung an arm around Liss's shoulders, and she felt some of the tension drain out of her. "From what you've told me, Roy Eastmont wouldn't be above egging on rivals."

"He sees conflict as a surefire way to attract viewers."

"These days, a celebrity would have to go a long way to cause a public outcry."

"Any publicity is good publicity? Maybe, but I'm pretty sure murder steps over the line." She shuddered. "At least, I hope it does."

Dan held her closer, nestled against him from head to toe. "Deidre must have known how Eastmont operates. Wouldn't she share any evidence she had with him? And if she had anything to back up her claim, wouldn't she have gone to the police?"

"She only reported that Dandy had been stolen to hotel security and they, apparently, didn't take it very seriously."

"They must have done something or Sherri

wouldn't have been able to put you in touch with Deidre so quickly."

"That's true. Still, Deidre would have hesitated to approach them again. It's also possible she was still in the dark as to the villain's identity. But if the dognapper was convinced that she'd figure it out eventually, why not make a preemptive strike?"

"It had to be someone who knew she habitually took a lot of pills."

"Everyone seems to have known that."

With lazy motions, Dan stroked her arm, soothing her even though his words had the opposite effect. "Maybe Deidre did know who was guilty, but she didn't have any proof that would hold up in a court of law. If she was trying to get it, that could have tipped off the guilty party."

"We can speculate all we want, but it doesn't bring us any closer to figuring out who dunnit." Liss sighed and snuggled closer to Dan's reassuring warmth.

On the other side, she felt one of the dogs shift closer and reached out her hand. A warm, wet tongue licked her fingers. Tears sprang into her eyes, and her chest tightened as she thought of Deidre and how much she'd loved these little dogs. Murder was always horrible, but this one, over something so petty, had a heartlessness about it that was truly appalling.

The injustice of it ate at Liss. She knew it was not her responsibility to find Deidre's killer, but if she wanted closure for herself, she felt she had to do all she could to help the police figure out what had happened.

Focus on the intellectual puzzle, she ordered herself. That was the only way she knew to keep her emotions at bay. Emotions clouded judgment and led to making stupid mistakes.

"Is dognapping a felony, or just a misdemeanor?"

"No idea." Dan considered for a moment. "I suppose how serious a crime it is depends on the value of the stolen animal. Run off with a mutt and you might only get a slap on the wrist. Take a dog insured for a million bucks and you'd probably be arrested, brought to trial, and sentenced to time in jail."

"So maybe, just maybe, Deidre's suspicions posed a tangible threat to someone. Not just public humiliation, but a prison sentence. Do you suppose Deidre was foolish enough to let on that she thought she knew who took Dandy?" Liss turned her head to look at the little dog. Dandy had fallen asleep, trusting Liss to look after her.

"There's no point in trying to guess," Dan said. "Besides, it's still possible that the toxicology report will come back saying Deidre died of some easily explicable cause. It could happen," he protested when Liss twisted her head around to give him a skeptical look.

"Someone *did* take Dandy."

"That was a dirty trick," Dan agreed, "but the Scottie wasn't harmed. After Deidre dropped out of the show, her dog would probably have been returned to her."

"Would she?"

"Sure. Otherwise, why keep Dandy alive in the first place? If Dandy or Dondi was supposed to die, a fatal accident would have been easy enough to arrange. You said so yourself. That's why you've been keeping such a close eye on them."

Liss's thoughts returned to that night on the icy road. Dandy had been running loose. No collar. No one around.

Or had there been someone? She remembered the cracking sound she'd heard. A branch breaking under the weight of the freezing rain? Or, as she'd first thought, someone stepping on a twig.

Had Dandy escaped? Had the dognapper been trying to get her back? Or had the Scottie been driven out into the middle of nowhere and abandoned? The little dog could easily have died out there with no one the wiser.

Liss wanted to believe Dan's interpretation of events, but hiding the Scottie and returning for her later just didn't add up. Neither did someone chasing the little dog through the storm. The weather hadn't been bad in the afternoon, when Dandy had been taken from Deidre's condo, but it had been terrible by the time Liss almost hit her.

The dognapper was probably long gone by then.

"There was no place around there that could have been used as a prison for Dandy," she said aloud. "She wasn't supposed to be found. She wasn't supposed to survive."

Her arms wrapped around both dogs and Dan's arms holding her, Liss faced the reality of her situation head-on. If Deidre *had* been murdered, the most logical reason for the crime was to keep her quiet. That meant the killer was also the dognapper, which left the original motive for the crime unchanged—eliminate the competition. The way Liss saw it, she was in danger, but she also had one big advantage that Deidre had lacked.

Forewarned, as the old saying went, is forearmed.

Dan left for Moosetookalook early the next morning, too early to be introduced to Valentine Veilleux.

"Are you sure you can trust her?" he asked.

Reaching up to smooth away the frown lines in his forehead and, Liss hoped, the worry along with them, she attempted to reassure him. "Pretty sure. She has no reason to hurt anyone, and no motive to sabotage any of the acts. She's not a competitor."

"No motive that you know of." He hesitated before opening the door to the hallway. "It just strikes me as peculiar that she'd ask you along on a visit to the town dump, of all places."

"That jaunt will probably be the bright spot of my day." She kissed his cheek and then stepped back to make little shooing motions. "Go on. Hit the road. You've got orders to fill."

"Oh, it's you lecturing me on responsibilities now, is it?" Grinning, he swept her into his arms for a long, leisurely kiss.

After he'd gone, she stayed where she was, staring at the plain wooden door and the requisite hotel map and safety instructions. Slowly, the floorplan came into focus. A big *X* marked the suite she occupied. Bold letters spelled out *EXIT* next to the series of lines that indicated stairs.

Liss frowned. She knew where they came out. She hadn't considered it before, but on the afternoon Dandy had been taken, someone must have left the hotel, probably from this floor, and driven to the nearby condominiums in broad daylight. Had someone witnessed that departure? Had that same someone given Deidre a name? Liss posed those questions to Valentine a short time later.

"No idea," the photographer said.

Liss couldn't see her face. Valentine's head and shoulders had disappeared into the backseat of Liss's car so that she could stow her camera equipment next to the two carriers containing Dandy and Dondi and the plastic garbage bag containing the used pee pads. Satisfied that everything was secure, she slid into the passenger seat for the trip to the town landfill.

"You'll have to give me directions." Liss glanced her way, then looked again. Valentine's complexion was naturally pale, but this morning, in the bright sunlight, it looked ashen. "Are you okay?"

"Why wouldn't I be?"

"Whoa! Don't go all defensive on me."

"Sorry. Take a left out of the parking lot." She rattled off the rest of the instructions in a subdued voice.

Liss had no difficulty following them and before long came to a sign reading ORLIN TRANSFER STATION. She turned onto a narrow, uphill road sparsely flanked by single-family homes. After a quarter of a mile, a second sign directed her to hang a right and begin an even steeper climb. At the top of the rise were several large buildings and more signs. The road branched, becoming a one-way, one-lane drive that circled back on itself.

At her side, Liss heard Valentine breathe a sigh of relief.

Curious, she thought.

She applied the brakes and lowered her window when a man approached, signaling for them to stop. He wore the outdoor uniform common among Mainers from late fall until the temperature hit fifty or above in the spring—a quilt-lined coverall made of cotton duck with a corduroy collar and lots of zippers.

"We're not open until nine on Wednesday." He peered at the windshield. "And I don't see a permit. You can't recycle here unless you live in Orlin."

Valentine leaned across the seat far enough to pass a piece of paper to him. "I'm here to take pictures, although I'd count it a huge favor if you'd also let my friend leave off a small amount of trash."

The dump keeper studied the page so intently that Liss wondered just how well he could read. The suspicion on his jowly face was undiminished when he handed it back to Valentine. "What kind of trash?"

"Uh, they're called pee pads." Liss felt heat creep into her face. "Uh, sort of like big diapers?"

He didn't look happy, but apparently Valentine's paperwork was in order. He indicated the bin where she could discard her garbage and then stomped back inside the largest of the buildings.

"Now what?" Liss asked when her distasteful task had been accomplished.

"Now I take pictures." Valentine sounded more cheerful than she had on the drive from the hotel, but the way her gaze darted from side to side as she strode forward struck Liss as odd. For a professional photographer used to searching in strange places for interesting subject matter, she seemed extraordinarily jumpy.

A bulldozer and a beat-up old truck that obviously belonged to the dump keeper were the only other vehicles in sight. The only person was the town employee who'd checked Valentine's credentials. She felt comfortable leaving the dogs in the backseat of her car, the windows cracked open for air, while she trailed after Valentine. This transfer station—the old term *dump* was no longer politically correct, although people continued to use it—was similar to the one in Moosetookalook. Recycling was accomplished by the use of a single bin, no sorting required. A large sign attached to the building listed those materials that were accepted and those that were not. The rejects, together with bags of unrecyclable trash—clear plastic trash bags only!—eventually went into a landfill.

"It wasn't that long ago that recycling meant separating everything into piles and going from giant dumpster to giant dumpster to deposit newspapers and magazines in one, mixed paper in another, corrugated boxes in a third. There must have been a dozen different categories. If I remember right, there were separate bins for milk jugs, for detergent jugs, for aluminum cans, for metal cans—they had a magnet mounted nearby if you weren't sure which were which—and for brown paper bags. Or maybe those went in with corrugated boxes." Liss chuckled. "There was a big sign over that bin, warning you not to throw in any pizza boxes."

"Why not?"

"They might have food stuck to them. Clean cardboard only, if you please. And you'd better believe the dump keeper yelled at you if you put something in the wrong place."

"And before there were regulations—what were town dumps like then?"

"When I was a little kid, the dump was just a landfill. Everything went into it." She frowned, trying to remember. "There were always seagulls circling around, even though we're nowhere near the ocean. Scavengers."

"How . . . picturesque."

Liss was struck by Valentine's sarcastic tone of voice. "It's a lot less photogenic these days."

"Thank God." She kept taking pictures.

"Meaning?"

They'd come to the edge of the paved area, where their view encompassed the section where trash was buried. Some of it was biodegradable and would eventually become part of the ecosystem. Other items would be around forever. Liss felt a twinge of guilt about those pee pads, until she reminded herself that she hadn't been the one who'd bought them.

She glanced over her shoulder at her hatchback. It was still the only car parked at the transfer station. The dogs were safe. They wouldn't even be cold waiting in there, not the way the sun was beating down. If she and Valentine stayed much longer, she'd have to go open that window a little wider to keep them from getting too hot.

Valentine stopped taking pictures, but she made no move to leave. She continued to stare at the landfill, as if she saw something that wasn't there.

Her demeanor puzzled Liss. What was there about the town dump to make the other woman look so worried? She tried to see her surroundings through Valentine's photographer's eye. Once there would have been veritable mountains of trash where now only little molehills cropped up. She added gulls to her mental picture. White ones. There should be rats, too, she supposed. It had been quite the sport in the old days, going to the dump to take potshots at the rats.

And then it hit her. She knew what was bothering Valentine. Suppressing a laugh, she touched the other woman's arm, unsurprised when she jumped a foot and let out a little squeak of alarm.

"Let me guess—you read *Salem's Lot* at an impressionable age." That would certainly explain why she hadn't wanted to visit the dump alone.

Valentine's smile was rueful. "A little imagination is a dangerous thing. I don't suppose that old guy in the coveralls is really a vampire, but he gives me the creeps."

"It's broad daylight," Liss reminded her, pointing up toward the sun.

They had their backs to the barnlike building that housed the office and the recycling center. It took a surprising amount of willpower not to look over her shoulder, especially when Liss heard the sound of a car engine. Stephen King's powerful writing had stuck with her all these years, just as it had for Valentine.

"If I remember right, the dump keeper was the monster's first slurp."

"The vampire got lucky at the dump." Valentine shuddered. "I had nightmares for weeks after I read that book. I never felt the same again about rats, either."

"I'm pretty sure all the rats are long gone."

Valentine turned with a smile that looked forced. It faded when her gaze shifted past Liss's shoulder. Her eyes narrowed. "Not all of them."

Liss turned to look. The vehicle she'd heard had stopped at the area reserved for discarding lumber. A glance at her watch told Liss the transfer station still wasn't open for business, but the driver was already out of his car and working fast to unload what looked like a pile of broken boards from his trunk.

"Hey! You there!" yelled the dump keeper. "You got a permit?"

Without pausing to reply, the man slammed his now-empty trunk closed, jumped back into his car, and took off. He didn't notice Liss and Valentine, but Liss had a clear view of his face as he sped away. It was Hal Quarles.

Liss and Valentine exchanged a look and headed for the area Quarles had just left. It did not take long to inspect the wood he'd left behind. Liss took a piece of it away with her. It was obvious even to her untrained eyes that the wreckage had once been an item of furniture, and a very specific type of furniture at that.

She drove Valentine back to the hotel in thoughtful silence. They hadn't encountered one of Stephen King's vampires at the dump, but they might just have crossed paths with a murderer. What else could explain why Hal Quarles had been getting rid of the remains of the Great Umberto's magic cabinet?

By the time Liss and Valentine returned to the hotel, Hal Quarles had long since scurried inside. Liss was just as happy not to run into him in the parking lot. Confronting him about what they had seen was tempting, but probably not a smart thing to do.

"I'm going to give Dandy and Dondi a run before I go inside." Liss said, indicating the little parklike area with the statue of the skier. "It should be less messy than the last time we were there. It's still mud season, but there's nothing like a few hours of bright sunshine to start drying things out."

Valentine didn't answer her. She was staring at something in the opposite direction. "Isn't that the television reporter who was here the other day? Ballantyne? Berryman?"

"Barrigan. Troy Barrigan." All Liss saw was a back view of a man in rapid retreat. "That could have been him, but I didn't get a good enough look to be certain."

"If he's snooping around, it won't be good for the show."

"If he was worth his salt as an investigative reporter he wouldn't have filed that fluff piece after his last visit. He'd already guessed there was something fishy about Eastmont's claim that the show is recorded live."

"I think I'll see if I can catch him. I'd like to have a little chat with him." Valentine set off at a trot.

With a shrug, Liss hauled the two dog carriers to the edge of the parking lot and opened the doors to set the Scotties free. She didn't have their leashes with her, but Dandy and Dondi were well trained. She wasn't worried about either of them running away, and they'd come when she called.

A few minutes later, Iris Jansen came out of the back entrance to the hotel and crossed the parking lot in the direction of the magician's van. Spotting Liss and the Scotties, she changed course and joined them. "Hi," she said with her usual friendly smile. "You're up and at 'em early this morning."

"You don't know the half of it." Liss fingered the piece of wood she'd picked up at the transfer station and tucked into her coat pocket. Pulling it out, she showed it to Iris. "Does this look familiar?"

Iris's eyes widened. "It almost . . . but it couldn't be!"

"I'm afraid it could. Valentine and I just came from the town dump. She was taking pictures. While we were there, Hal Quarles drove in and unloaded a whole pile of broken bits just like this one."

"Hal Quarles? Why, that awful old man! This cabinet isn't going to be cheap to replace. We'll sue his socks off if he doesn't pay for it." Indignant, she started toward the hotel.

Liss caught her arm. "Don't be hasty, and don't confront him on your own."

"I was going to tell Oscar." Her eyes opened wider. "Do you think he's the one behind everything that's happened?"

"I don't know, but if he is, he could be dangerous."

Worry lines creasing her forehead, Iris hugged herself. She wore only a red knit sweater, but Liss didn't think it was the cold that was making her shiver. The day continued to warm up rapidly, springlike even though there was still snow on the ground.

"Is that where Valentine went?" Iris asked. "Did

she follow him? If it isn't safe for me, she's very brave to face him down on her own."

Liss supposed Iris had crossed paths with Valentine inside the hotel, although it had been the driveway along the side of the hotel that the photographer had followed in pursuit of Troy Barrigan. Who knew where the reporter had led her?

"She'd didn't go after Quarles," Liss said. "It was that TV reporter she wanted to catch up with. She thinks he's snooping around, trying to get the inside scoop on *Variety Live.*"

"Oh." Iris thought that over. "She's probably right."

Seeing Dandy approach, the magician's assistant abruptly crouched down and thrust both arms out toward the Scottie. "Come here, you sweet thing! Give Iris a hug!"

Startled, Dandy jumped backward into the parking lot. She squeezed between two cars and kept going when Iris gave a little squeal of distress.

"I'm so sorry, sweetie. Did I frighten you?" Iris went after her.

"Come here, Dandy," Liss called.

The little dog ignored Liss, much as she'd ignored Iris that first day in Deidre Amendole's condominium. Instead of returning to the safety of the wooded area, Dandy broke cover and took off in the direction of Valentine's RV. At the same time, Liss heard the unmistakable sound of an approaching car.

A station wagon, skis lashed to the top, came around the end of a row of parked cars. The teenaged boy behind the wheel was driving just a little too fast. For one horrible moment, Liss was certain Dandy would be hit.

Then, somehow, Iris was between the vehicle and the dog, waving her arms and shouting. An inch short of striking her, the station wagon screeched to a stop.

Dandy changed course and charged back toward Liss. She seemed to think they were playing a new game. Liss scooped the Scottie up and stuffed her inside her carrier in one movement. Her hands trembled as she fastened the latch. Dondi, oblivious to all the excitement, trotted up to his carrier and went inside on his own.

The teenager drove on, slowly, careful to select a slot on the far side of the parking lot. Iris, looking shaken, walked up to the bronze statue and leaned against it for support.

"That was one of the bravest, *stupidest* things I've ever seen," Liss said. "You could have been killed."

"It would have been my fault if Dandy was run over," Iris said. "How could I live with myself if that happened?"

Liss went up to her and hugged her. "Thank you."

Red-faced, Iris squirmed free. She gave a shaky laugh. "Honestly, I wasn't in any real danger. I've been trained as an escape artist. I can pick locks almost as well as Oscar can and I can even get out of the water tank on my own. Why, I'm practically indestructible."

Liss backed off, reluctant to embarrass Iris further, but she didn't buy the young woman's grandiose claims for a second. That had to be the adrenaline talking.

"We should probably go in now," Iris said. "It's almost time for dress rehearsal."

"I guess we'd better." Liss glanced at her watch. It was scheduled to start in less than an hour and she still had to pick up her costume. She also needed to find some way to show her gratitude for Iris's rescue of Dandy. At the very least, she'd send her a bouquet of flowers.

In the ballroom, areas had once again been taped off for practice. This time, Liss's outfit was a lovely ball gown in shades of rose and pale pink. They weren't colors she'd have chosen for herself, but the effect was pleasing.

"What, no neckline cut down to the belly button?" she'd asked Mel when she'd gotten her first good look at herself in the costume designer's full-length mirror.

"That's tomorrow," Mel had said with a straight face.

Liss wished she could be certain the other woman was joking.

There were taps on the shoes that went with the outfit. Tentatively, she tried out a few of the steps she'd been taught in a long-ago tap-dance class. The result didn't sound too awful. All things considered, Liss supposed she'd make a better showing today than she had as a kid. She had a photo somewhere, taken by her proud father, of a line of little girls in matching costumes—white satin, or more likely a fabric meant to look like satin, with high hats to match. She couldn't remember much about that recital beyond her opinion that the whole production was silly . . . unlike Scottish dancing, which had already become her passion.

Liss got a kick out of taking Dandy and Dondi through the next routine in Deidre's notebook. She was relieved when they caught on quickly. Her pleasure in their response was as much of a surprise to her as her newfound delight in wearing tap shoes. Was she really starting to feel as if she belonged in this competition?

Bemused, she tried to analyze her feelings. She would be disappointed if they didn't win. Not devastated, and not desperate enough to try to eliminate any of the other remaining contestants, but sad. Definitely sad.

"Huh," she said aloud, addressing the two dogs. "Go figure."

They cocked their heads, as if considering her comment.

"Okay, guys. One more time."

She was reaching for the PLAY button to start their music when a scream rent the air.

Liss froze. After a startled second of immobility, she raced toward the windows. The sound had come from outside.

A still, dark form lay half on the snow and half in the driveway below the windows.

Liss pointed to the production assistant. "Call 9-1-1." Then she was hoisting up her long skirt and running toward the nearest stairwell, the one that led straight down to the exit to the parking lot.

She was the first to arrive on the scene. Dropping to her knees, heedless of Mel's handiwork but careful not to jar the injured man, Liss leaned over his still form, reaching for the pulse point in his neck. Her fingers found bare skin and beneath it the faint flutter that told her he was still alive.

"Thank God," she whispered.

Only then did she take a closer look at his face. A gasp escaped her as she recognized him as Troy Barrigan, the television news reporter. His features were bruised and bloody but unmistakable.

When his lips moved. Liss bent closer, straining to hear. The whisper was so faint that she almost missed it. He said only one word.

"Pushed."

Chapter Eleven

"Oh my God," a woman shrieked. Judging by her maroon skirt and white blouse, she was one of the hotel employees. She stood less than a foot away, a cell phone pressed to her ear. "He must have fallen from a balcony."

Liss looked up. Her gaze stopped at the ballroom windows. Noses were all but pressed to the glass as the cast and crew of *Variety Live* watched a real-life drama play out before their eyes. Liss squinted, trying to make out their identities. Everyone seemed to be there. At least no one was conspicuously absent.

Other people had joined her at the side of the injured man. Liss recognized the security guard who had been involved in the incident with Eudora. He was checking Barrigan's vital signs and looked worried. Liss was pretty sure the reporter had lapsed into unconsciousness.

The wail of a siren reassured her. The EMTs were on the way. They'd need the police, too, but Liss hesitated to make that public just yet. It wasn't as if she knew *who* had pushed Troy Barrigan.

From a balcony? For the second time, she looked up at the building. On this side, the rooms on the fourth floor all had small balconies. One of them—her own—wrapped around the corner of the building. The other two were appended to the suites belonging to Oscar Yates and Roy Eastmont.

"Pushed," Barrigan had whispered.

From a balcony? Or from the roof? What was on the roof? How did someone get up there? More to the point, why would Barrigan have gone up there? And who could have followed him to push him off?

Valentine had been following him when Liss last saw him. Not Valentine, she told herself. Someone else. But who?

She had no answers, only questions. There was no one to ask, and when the paramedics arrived on the scene, they had their hands full with their patient. From their actions, Liss judged that Troy Barrigan was still breathing but in bad shape. She watched as they took precautions in case his neck or back was broken. When they'd done all they could to prevent further injury, they lifted him into the waiting ambulance to transport to the hospital in Fallstown, nearly an hour away by road.

"You're shivering, miss," the security guard said, touching her on the forearm. "You should go back inside."

His words brought her to her senses. She was doing no one any good standing out in the cold without a coat on. Worse, the longer she stayed here, the longer Dandy and Dondi were without her protection. Anything could have happened to them while she'd been distracted.

Common sense told her that a man had not been pushed from the fourth floor or the roof just to give someone an opportunity to harm the two Scotties, but she ran up the stairs as fast as she'd run down them. When the dogs were the first to greet her return to the ballroom, she was so relieved that she sank to the floor to gather Dandy and Dondi onto her lap.

Roy Eastmont, face pale and hands trembling, came up beside her. "Who was it?"

"That reporter. Troy Barrigan."

"Is he dead?"

Liss shook her head as she hugged Dandy. Dondi licked her cheek.

Turning away, Eastmont cleared his throat. "All right, everyone. Show's over. Back to work."

With varying degrees of reluctance, they returned to their designated rehearsal areas.

"Are you okay?" Mo Heedles knelt beside Liss, placing one cold hand on her forearm, bare below the three-quarter-length sleeves.

"Fine. I'll be fine."

"Is there anything I can do?"

Liss shook her head and buried her face in Dandy's neck.

She heard the rustle of fabric as Mo stood up and, in the background, the Great Umberto's low voice as he went into the patter that accompanied his magic act. A few minutes later, Mo's signature music started up.

Slowly, reluctantly, Liss got to her feet and returned to her own space, but she didn't turn on the upbeat tune for their number. It seemed disrespectful when a man was fighting for his life.

"That was the TV news guy?" Valentine joined Liss on the pretext of snapping more pictures of Dandy and Dondi.

Once again, Liss lowered herself to the floor, sitting cross-legged and gathering the Scotties to her. Belatedly, she saw that there were blood and mud stains on the long skirt of her rose-colored gown.

"Yes," she whispered.

She had to get hold of the police. She had to tell them what she knew. Unfortunately, she couldn't seem to summon up enough energy to stand, let alone to leave the ballroom in search of privacy to make a call.

After taking a photograph of the three of them from a few feet away, Valentine braced one knee on the floor and snapped a close-up. "Was everyone here when he . . . fell?"

"I don't know. I was busy rehearsing." She started to confirm Valentine's obvious assumption that he'd been pushed but stopped herself in time. Better to keep quiet until she'd talked to the police. She didn't know for certain where

Valentine had been when Barrigan took his nosedive.

"I'm not sure it matters." Valentine shoved her glasses up her nose, her brow creased in thought. "It wouldn't take long for someone to get from the roof to the ballroom. The emergency stairs go all the way up. It's waiting for this hotel's snail-paced elevators that makes people think everything is so far apart."

Liss read the look in Valentine's green eyes as easily as she saw the threads twine together in her own mind. What had happened to Barrigan had to be connected to the dirty tricks. Veteran television reporters were not pushed off buildings for no reason.

Abruptly, Valentine stood up. "Where's his cameraman?"

She didn't wait for an answer. Abandoning Liss, she headed for the exit.

Encumbered by her canine companions, Liss didn't try to go after her. She heaved herself slowly to her feet, hearing her bad knee pop as she did so. She'd kept up with her exercises, the ones she'd done daily ever since her surgery, but racing up and down stairs was not part of her regimen. She gave her leg a couple of experimental shakes before she put weight on it and was relieved to feel no pain. She coaxed the two dogs into their carriers and then followed Valentine's route toward the foyer.

"I'm done rehearsing," she told the production assistant standing just inside the exit.

"Please be back by one," the young woman said. "We're going to record the show and then the results show with only a fifteen-minute break in between."

Liss nodded in acknowledgment and took a few more steps before she stopped and turned. For the first time, she took a good look at Roy Eastmont's assistant. She was somewhere in her midtwenties, dark haired, with mild blue eyes, a pert nose, and a perpetually serious expression on her face.

"Do you have a name?" Liss asked.

The question surprised the PA into a laugh. "Of course I have a name, but nobody ever remembers what it is, not even Mr. Eastmont."

"Tell me. I'll remember."

"It's Jane. Jane Smith." When Liss's eyebrows shot up, Jane laughed again. "Really."

"Your parents must have had some sense of humor."

"You don't know the half of it. Still, it's better than Jane Doe, and I guarantee you that I absolutely never forget anyone else's name."

Intrigued, Liss took a step closer, her gaze settling on the clipboard Jane held. "And you keep track of who's where when, right?"

Jane nodded. "Sure. That's part of my job."

"Who was here . . . no, make that who *wasn't* in the ballroom when that man fell?"

Eyes widening as she took in the implications, Jane swallowed hard before letting her gaze drop to the top sheet on the clipboard. "The magic act hadn't set up yet. And Mr. Eastmont was running late. I think everyone else was here. Oh, no. Wait. The photographer hadn't come in yet, either."

"Valentine?" Liss's heart sank. So much for thinking Valentine Veilleux was the one person she could safely rely upon.

"I saw her exit the elevator just a second before I heard that horrifying scream," Jane added.

With heartfelt thanks, both to Jane and the powers that be, Liss left the ballroom with the dogs and returned to her suite. She was there when Valentine came looking for her a few minutes later.

"No camera crew," she reported. "Barrigan came back to the hotel alone."

"And nobody saw anything?"

"Not until he tried to fly."

"Did you catch up with him earlier?"

Valentine shook her head. "He'd done a better job of disappearing than our resident magician."

Liss reached for the phone.

"Who are you calling?" Valentine asked.

"An old friend."

She listened as the ringing stopped and voice mail picked up. Waiting for the beep, she took a deep breath, then plunged into her speech as soon as it sounded.

"Gordon, it's Liss," she said. "I'm not interfering, but I think you ought to know that Troy Barrigan, the TV news guy, is on his way to the hospital in Fallstown from Five Mountains. He was not injured by accident. I was the first one to get to him. He managed to gasp out one word—'pushed.'" She hesitated. "This may have something to do with Deidre Amendole's death."

She wondered briefly whether to say more. Perhaps she'd already said too much. She rattled off her cell-phone number, hung up, and turned to face Valentine.

The photographer was sitting on the floor, playing with the dogs. She glanced Liss's way with a questioning look.

"That message was for Gordon Tandy. He's a state police detective."

"I thought you said he was a friend."

"That, too."

"Handy," Valentine said, and went back to tossing a well-chewed tennis ball for Dandy to fetch.

Liss heard nothing from Gordon before it was time for the next episode of *Variety Live* to be recorded. Leaving Valentine to watch the Scotties, she paid a visit to Mel, the wardrobe mistress, who made emergency repairs to her gown by hacking off the damaged section. That left it short enough to show Liss's scar, but she was past caring about such trivial details. A pair of opaque panty hose covered up the worst of it.

After Valentine left, Liss ordered lunch from room service, fed the dogs, set out fresh pee pads, and tried to concentrate on the performance to come. It was a crucial one in the competition. It would determine which act would be the last to be eliminated before the finals. Tomorrow, Thursday, they'd record that show, in which the three remaining contestants would each have to perform twice. That meant two separate dances, and Liss had yet to go through Deidre's notes and learn the choreography.

The true finale, the final results show, was scheduled to be recorded on Friday.

Did Roy Eastmont already know who would win the champion of champions title? Liss felt certain that he *thought* he did, but until the last minute it was always possible that something would happen to change the results.

Much as she tried to concentrate on the show, Liss's mind kept circling back to Troy Barrigan. Was he fighting for his life in the hospital, or had he already lost that battle? Did anyone besides the person who had pushed him know why he'd been sneaking around the hotel? What had he suspected? *Who* had he suspected? What had led to such extreme measures to keep him from reporting what he'd discovered?

She had a splitting headache by the time she

returned to the ballroom to perform. No single suspect stood out in her mind. She was missing something, but what?

At the end of the second session of the day, the "live" results show, it was Hal Quarles who was eliminated. The three finalists were Deidre and her Dancing Doggies, the Great Umberto, and Mo Heedles.

While the requisite farewells and departure scenes were being shot, Liss tried to figure out how this lineup changed things. She watched Mo and Oscar Yates chat on the sidelines. As he seemed to in the presence of anyone, male or female, Yates laid on the charm. Some would call it flirting, Liss supposed. Whatever it was, Mo didn't seem to mind having his attention focused on her.

Liss looked around for Iris, expecting to find her glaring at Mo, eyes shooting daggers at the other woman, but Iris hadn't noticed the byplay between magician and juggler. She was commiserating with Hal Quarles for the benefit of the camera.

Hal was out. Mo was still in. Liss frowned, remembering that Valentine had said, early in their acquaintance, that Mo could be ruled out as a suspect because it was unlikely she would win even if Deidre did drop out of the competition. Yet here she was, in the finals.

She'd been a victim of the dirty trickster. The

destruction of her props had been particularly vicious. But was that really enough to exonerate her? She could have done all that damage herself. She would have known she could get replacements for her equipment.

Something else was nagging at the back of Liss's mind. It was only as she was putting Dandy and Dondi back into their carriers that she realized what it was. When Mo had come over to her, right after Liss had come back inside after trying to help Troy Barrigan, she'd stood right next to the Scotties for several minutes . . . and she hadn't sneezed once. Had the so-called allergy been a ploy? Had she pretended she had to keep her distance to convince Liss that she couldn't have been the one who'd stolen Dandy from Deidre's condo?

Deliberately, she dragged the carriers over to where Yates and Mo stood close together, big smiles on both their faces. A quick glance at Iris told Liss she was still blissfully unaware that she might have acquired a rival for the magician's affections.

"Hey, you two," Liss interrupted them, moving in close to Mo. "Congratulations on making the cut. May the best act win."

"Best? Or cutest?" Mo sent a pointed look at the carriers, now less than a foot away from her.

"Ladies, please. We all know the score. That's no reason not to be agreeable to one another. Ah!

Here's my lovely assistant. Ready to retire for the evening, my dear?"

Iris blossomed under his attentive gaze, becoming oblivious to the presence of anyone else. When they walked off together, arm in arm, Mo just shook her head.

"The blind leading the blind," she remarked. "Neither one of them can see what the other is really like."

"I'd say we're all putting up false fronts." She waited a beat. "Your allergy seems to have cleared up."

"I took an antihistamine. I got tired of sneezing every time I got within three feet of your furry little friends."

Her explanation made sense. It might even be the truth. Liss decided not to cross Mo off her list of suspects quite yet, but she had hopes of eliminating someone else from the running. When Quarles returned to his suite, she once again left Dandy and Dondi with Valentine and went to beard the lion in his den.

"What do you want?" Quarles demanded when he opened his door to her knock.

"Charming as always. May I come in?"

He stepped back to let her pass, but the disgruntled expression on his face didn't fade. "I'm not going to offer you refreshments. Say what you've got to say and go."

"Fine. I just have one question—what were you

doing at the dump with Oscar Yates's magic cabinet?"

His mouth dropped open. Then he swore with a creativity that had Liss blushing. Oddly, she did not sense anger in him, only chagrin and a certain amount of embarrassment. She waited until he ran out of words.

"Valentine and I were there at the transfer station this morning. We saw you unload the bits and pieces that were left and we looked at the remains of the cabinet after you had gone. There's no doubt about what it was. What I don't know is how you got hold of it."

His scowl deepened. For a moment, she didn't think he was going to answer her. Then all the hot air seemed to go out of him. He pulled out the desk chair and sat, gesturing for her to take the more comfortable well-padded armchair nearby.

"It was already in pieces when I found it."

"Where?"

"Here. Can you believe it? Someone got into my suite and hid what was left of it behind the sofa."

Liss glanced at that piece of furniture. "Not a very secure hiding place."

"Well, duh! I was supposed to find it. Or someone was. To make me look guilty of all the nasty little tricks that have been played on the others, I assume. 'It must have been Quarles all along,' they'd say. 'How else could he hope to win? And besides, those tactics fit right in with his nasty personality.' "

"You aren't exactly the friendliest one in the group."

"It's my *act!* I stay in character. Do you think I'm like that with my kids? My grandkids?"

"I didn't think you had any. I looked you up online."

"And I suppose you believe this show is aired live, too."

"Point taken. But you did try to get rid of the cabinet."

"Well, of course I did. Do you think I wanted to be accused of being behind everything that's happened, up to and including Deidre Amendole's death?"

"You've thought all along that she was murdered?" Surprised, Liss blurted out the question before she could think better of it.

He stared at his hands, curled into fists in his lap. "It seemed the only reasonable explanation. There's money to be made gambling on who wins, you know. Those who have bets down have a reason to make sure the act they're betting on wins." He glanced up. "You should see your face. Mouth hanging open. Eyes wide. You really are a little Pollyanna, aren't you?"

Aware that he was baiting her, falling back on the comfortable facade of an insult comic, Liss narrowed her eyes and closed her mouth with a snap, but still gave in to the urge to defend herself. "I'm not all that naive. You caught me off guard, that's all. Who is it that's betting?"

"Who isn't?"

"So the person behind all that's happened is someone who bet on him or herself? Or are you talking about some outside gambler?"

"I don't know and I don't want to know. Aside from trying to frame me, no one's done me any harm and I'd like to keep it that way. If you've got any sense, girlie, you'll stop asking questions. You might even consider dropping out of the competition, since it's been obvious since Dandy was stolen that your act can't be the one with the big money riding on it."

"What act is? The Great Umberto? Mo?"

A look of confusion crossed his weathered face. "Doesn't make much sense, does it? But I've told you all I know." He stood. "Time for you to leave. And do me a favor? Stay away from me. I don't want to be the innocent bystander who gets taken out when the shooting starts."

She left, her mind abuzz with new and frightening possibilities. If Quarles was right, then anyone, even the hotel security guard or the concierge or a member of the housekeeping staff, could be the one behind the dirty tricks. A real-life gangster seemed a long shot, the breed being pretty rare in rural Maine, but Hal Quarles's theory hadn't ruled out anything.

She looked over her shoulder more than once on her way to collect the Scotties from Valentine.

Back in her room a half hour later, Liss tried again to contact Desdemona. This time no one answered the phone. It was supposed to be Desdemona's cell, Liss remembered, but the last time she'd tried the number, the housekeeper had answered. Did that mean Desdemona had forgotten her phone when she left Ohio? Or had she mistakenly given Liss the number for Deidre's landline? Tossing her own phone onto the sofa, Liss wondered if it mattered. She couldn't trust anything anyone told her, anyway.

Her attempt to get hold of Gordon Tandy a short time later was also frustrating. He was either very busy or ignoring her calls. She had to be satisfied, once again, with leaving him a voice mail. She didn't try to explain why she'd called him again. She wasn't certain why she felt such a sense of urgency herself.

"This is Liss," she said after the beep. "Please call me. It's important." She rattled off her cell-phone number and added the one for her suite at the hotel before she hung up.

Her next phone call, to her aunt, went much better. Margaret sounded cheerful and impatient to get back to work at The Spruces.

"I hate being fussed over," she complained.

Liss sympathized and felt guilty all over again

for not being the one there in her aunt's apartment in Moosetookalook to do the fussing. It wasn't as if she had accomplished much by staying in the competition. She had no more idea who was behind the dirty tricks than she had at the beginning. Staying alert for danger every minute, fearful that she or the dogs would fall victim to some new attempt, was wearing her down.

"How are those adorable doggies?" Margaret asked.

"Sleeping. They sleep almost as much as cats do."

"I used to have a dog. Years ago. You probably don't remember."

"Not really." But Liss did remember that her aunt had not always lived in an apartment. At one time, when her husband and son were still living, she'd had a house with a yard—room for a dog. Did Margaret regret giving that up to live over the shop? Liss had never thought to ask.

They chatted a few minutes longer about inconsequential things. By the time she hung up, Liss was feeling restless. She'd expected Dan to turn up around suppertime to spend the night with her again. She'd been looking forward to being able to talk everything over with him. Valentine Veilleux made a good sounding board, and she'd often bounced ideas off Sherri in the past, but no one listened the way Dan did and no one understood her better. He was her closest friend as well as her husband. She took shameless advantage of his good nature.

Was that guilt she was feeling? Again?

"Just stop it," she said aloud.

Disgusted with herself, she picked up the room-service menu and amused herself picking out entrees Dan would enjoy. She was about to reach for the phone and order when someone rapped on the door.

For once, Liss didn't bother to look through the peephole first. She was certain she knew who stood on the other side. "It's about time you got here," she said, jerking open the door.

Only then did she remember that she'd given Dan his own key card. He'd have let himself in.

It was not her husband who stood in the doorway, glowering down at her. It was Gordon Tandy. And then, as if he'd realized that he was not the person she'd been expecting, his lips twitched with amusement. "May I come in?"

"Of course." Liss stepped back, thankful Gordon at least had the good manners not to laugh outright.

The dogs, awakened by the sound of voices, came to investigate the newcomer. They seemed to recognize him, especially after Gordon held out both hands for them to sniff. He was rewarded by permission to stroke.

When they were seated, Dandy and Dondi on the floor, Gordon on the sofa, and Liss in the chair facing him, the state police detective took out his notebook and a pen, a sure signal that he'd come on serious business. The stone face was back in place, too, although it cracked for just a moment to allow for the appearance of a look Liss could only describe as rueful.

"It seems I'm in the awkward position of needing to ask for your help," Gordon said. "I need an insider's view of what's been going on here."

"A few years ago, I'd have been thrilled to hear you admit that. Now, not so much. I'd truly rather not be caught in the middle."

"Why don't you tell me exactly what you're in the middle of, starting with how you came to witness an attempt on Troy Barrigan's life?"

"How is he?"

"Still alive, but in critical condition. He won't be answering any questions for a while, if ever."

Shaken, even though she'd been expecting to hear something of the sort, Liss could no longer sit still. She went to the kitchenette for a glass of ice water, carrying it back to her seat and taking the first sip before she began her story.

Gordon stopped her often, asking for clarification. Once she'd recounted what happened after Barrigan plunged past the ballroom windows, she went back to the beginning—finding Dandy—and brought Gordon up to the present and Hal Quarles's pet theory. By then,

Dandy was in her lap and Dondi had his head on Gordon's.

"Of course we don't know for certain that Deidre was murdered," she added, glancing at him for confirmation and meeting only the same stoic countenance he always wore during interviews.

The soft snick of the door opening was barely audible, but Liss heard it and saw that Gordon had, too. He glanced that way, gave the smallest of nods to acknowledge Dan's arrival, and returned his full attention to her, sending her a considering look. The silence stretched out long enough for Dan to come up behind her and place one hand on her shoulder. If she'd been a suspect in this case, Liss thought, she'd be squirming in her chair by now.

"There's nothing conclusive on the cause of Mrs. Amendole's death," Gordon said at last. "Not yet. As for Barrigan, unless he wakes up and can tell us who pushed him, we don't have much to go on."

"Did he fall from the roof?" Liss's hand went up to entwine with Dan's. He gave it a reassuring squeeze.

"Probably."

"Why would he go up there?"

"I'm hoping he'll be able to tell us that, but so far he's been unconscious or in surgery or heavily sedated."

"I assume you're talking about that TV newscaster who was injured here earlier today," Dan said. "I heard about it on the news on my way here. They said he was in a coma."

Liss snorted. It was a handy word for people to use but wasn't always accurate.

"He may be. Same result. No information from that source to help us discover what happened to him. He talked to Liss, right after it happened. He told her he was pushed." Gordon gently displaced Dondi and rose. "He was working on a story about *Variety Live*, and it wasn't a fluff piece. His cameraman says he was planning an exposé. Legally, it doesn't sound as if what this production is doing is fraud, but telling the public how they've been deceived wouldn't do much for the show's ratings."

"It was obvious to Barrigan that the show wasn't live." Liss remained where she was, with Dan beside her. "He could have exploded that bombshell in his first report."

"He was apparently holding off, gathering more information. The trouble is, he didn't share what he discovered." Shrugging into the jacket he'd taken off when he first arrived, Gordon clearly intended to leave matters there, explaining no more than he already had.

"Did someone check the balconies overlooking the driveway?"

Gordon didn't answer. She couldn't tell if that meant they had or they hadn't. She didn't suppose there would have been much to find. To judge by her own balcony, the housekeeping staff swept them clear of snow and tidied them up on a regular basis. It would have been possible to push Barrigan over the low railing without leaving a trace.

"Oscar Yates has one of the rooms opening out onto a balcony on that side from this floor. Roy Eastmont has the other. Both were late getting to the ballroom and missed seeing Barrigan fall."

Gordon didn't look surprised by this information and didn't bother taking his notebook back out to write it down. "Anything else you want to share?"

"I found Desdemona's itinerary. She arrived in Maine a day earlier than she said she did."

He didn't write that down, either, or ask to see the paper she'd discovered behind the desk.

"Did you ever get hold of her?"

Silence.

Liss sighed. "When do you think you'll know more about Deidre's death?"

"No idea." Gordon leveled his sternest gaze on each of them in turn. "I hope I don't need to remind you two that everything I've told you must stay confidential?"

"No, you don't." Dan spoke before Liss could, and threw in a scowl for good measure. Dandy licked their joined hands, her big eyes worried as she sensed the tension in the air.

"And you didn't tell us a heck of a lot. Was anything I told you helpful?" Even now that Liss had reviewed all the dirty tricks for Gordon's benefit, she was no closer to figuring out who was behind them.

His reply was frustratingly enigmatic. "You never know."

When Gordon had gone, Dan took the place he'd vacated on the sofa, absently stroking Dondi as he settled in. "You think all this ties together?"

"I do, and I think Gordon does, too, although it's hard to tell with him." She brought Dan up to speed on everything that had happened since he'd left that morning.

"So Hal Quarles thinks there's big money being wagered on the outcome? That sounds crazy to me."

"Crazy, but possible."

Dan was still shaking his head. "These dirty tricks have to be an inside job. Only one of the people connected to the show would have access to the others. Who else would know precisely what kind of damage to inflict to take an act out of the competition?"

"Maybe we need to combine motives. What if someone associated with the show is either betting on the outcome or being paid by an outsider who stands to win big?"

"Or lose big." Dan didn't look convinced. "There's another possibility, too. Barrigan's target was the show, Eastmont's baby. That gives Eastmont the motive to stop him."

"You think there are two separate individuals connected to this show who are capable of murder? I don't even want to think about that possibility!"

Liss reached for the room-service menu she'd abandoned when Gordon showed up and insisted that they drop the subject for the rest of the evening. The trouble was, she couldn't stop thinking about it.

There were only three acts left in the running. Since she knew she wasn't guilty, that ought to narrow down her list of suspects to the remaining competitors—Mo Heedles, Oscar Yates, and his assistant, Iris. She disregarded the fact that dirty tricks had been played on both those acts. A clever villain would make sure to be included among the victims.

Dirty tricks she could see. But murder? She knew that, in theory, anyone could kill, but she had trouble imagining Mo, Iris, or Oscar going to that extreme. And Iris had saved Dandy's life at the risk of her own. That wasn't the act of a person bent on eliminating the competition.

Liss looked up from her hamburger to see the worry in Dan's eyes. Even after what had happened to Troy Barrigan, he wouldn't ask her to drop out of the competition, but he wasn't happy that she was staying in it. She wasn't thrilled to be there herself, although she had no intention of quitting.

She reached across the table to take his hand. “Have I told you lately how much I love you?” she asked. “And how glad I am that you’re planning to stay the night?”

Chapter Twelve

The next morning, the state police were out in force. Once cast and crew were gathered in the ballroom for rehearsal, they were informed that they would be questioned individually about Troy Barrigan's fall. No one was to leave the ballroom without telling one of the troopers until everyone associated with *Variety Live* had accounted for their whereabouts the previous day.

"They don't think it was an accident, do they?" Valentine whispered to Liss.

"Neither did you."

The photographer looked troubled. "I had my suspicions, but it's a big jump—you should pardon the word choice—from a few dirty tricks to murder."

"Maybe this wasn't the first."

"The overdose that killed Deidre could have been an accident."

"Because she took too many pills by mistake?"

"Or because whoever slipped her those extra pills might not have realized how deadly they would be in combination with what she already had in her system. This attempt on Barrigan's life, though—if he was pushed, there's no way that could be unintentional. Even someone acting on impulse would have to realize the probable outcome of shoving someone from that height would be death. That the reporter is still alive is nothing short of a miracle."

Liss wasn't sure whether it was encouraging or scary that Valentine's thoughts so closely paralleled her own. "Who?" she asked. "And who has no alibi for all the other times?"

"No one's been keeping tabs on us," Valentine said. "Not even Jane."

As members of the cast and crew were called out one by one, those remaining in the ballroom were permitted to continue rehearsing. It was dress rehearsal for Liss, the Great Umberto, and Mo. In the afternoon, they'd record what was called the finale but was in fact the next to last show, in which they'd each perform twice. That meant two costumes. Liss was wearing the first, a tuxedo-style pants suit that clung tighter than that Catwoman outfit.

The final program of the season would be the last results show. It would feature a brief recap of performances by each of the twelve acts who'd started the season. The six who'd been eliminated before Liss came on board had arrived at Five Mountains Ski Resort the previous day, but not until after Barrigan was injured. This morning they were nowhere in sight. Liss supposed Gordon had informed them that they would not be allowed into the ballroom to rehearse until he and his men were done with those who had survived the first half of the season.

The state police appropriated several small rooms near the ballroom for their interviews. Liss was one of the first to be called out. She took the dogs with her.

"Anything new?" Gordon asked when he'd closed the door to give them privacy.

"No. Thank goodness. Is Barrigan still hanging on?"

"So far, so good. But he hasn't been able to tell us anything useful." He braced one hip on the conference table that took up most of the space in the small room. "I don't have any questions for you, Liss. I just didn't want to create suspicion by skipping you. As far as the others know, this is the first time you've talked to me and we don't know each other."

"Got it. Only Valentine Veilleux already knows you're an old friend."

A peculiar expression came over his face. "I'll keep that in mind."

Liss knew better than to try to question him. He'd just clam up. "Shall we talk about the weather or do you prefer sports?"

He cracked a smile. "Ah, chitchat—never my strong suit."

Her own smile was halfhearted. "And I'm not really up on my sports chatter. There's still basketball and hockey going on, right, but it's too late for football and too early for baseball—"

"It's never too early for baseball. Hasn't Dan been watching spring training?"

"He probably has." Liss felt her expression sour. "I haven't been home enough to notice." It wasn't that she disliked the Red Sox. Their games just seemed to take up an inordinate amount of time from March through the play-offs. And every single one of them was televised.

Gordon glanced at his watch, then looked around for the dogs. They were investigating a far corner of the small room, probably a spot where someone had once dropped food. "I think I've interrogated you long enough." He hesitated. "Good luck with the competition."

"I'll tell you a little secret," Liss said as she collected Dandy and Dondi. "Luck has nothing to do with it. Roy Eastmont already knows who the winner is going to be. It's always been Deidre and her Dancing Doggies."

"In that case, congratulations." His lips quirked. "Do you get a trophy?"

"Apparently. And then, if Desdemona shows up to reclaim the dogs, I inherit a whole new set of problems. She hates Dandy and Dondi. I have to figure out a way to keep them safe after the competition is over."

"You've heard from her?" His sudden alertness triggered an answering wariness in her.

"No. I told you. I tried calling a couple of times

with no luck, but I did find out that her intention was to euthanize Dandy and Dondi. There's a clause in her mother's will that may prevent that, but frankly I don't trust her to abide by it."

The contents of the will didn't seem to be news to Gordon. "I'd think," he said slowly, "that the point will be moot if you win the competition. Don't you have to follow up on your win?" At Liss's puzzled expression, he explained. "I just assumed that the winners of these televised competitions have to go on to make a series of promotional appearances."

"I don't think so," Liss said, but she had not previously considered the possibility.

Lost in contemplation, she returned to the ballroom. Was she obligated to do more than she'd bargained for? The disturbing image of herself, rapidly signing documents she'd scarcely had time to read, preyed on her mind and made it difficult to get back into the rhythm of rehearsing.

You have bigger concerns at the moment, she reminded herself.

Pushing worries about the future aside, she shifted her focus to the people around her. As the morning wore on, members of the cast and crew were shuffled in and out of the ballroom. Most looked relieved when they returned. Roy Eastmont was a glaring exception.

Sweating, his face pale, his hands unsteady as he gesticulated while giving Jane instructions, he gave every indication of having been overset by his encounter with the law. Liss wondered why. Did he have something more to hide than the bogus claims made by *Variety Live*? As far as she knew, deceiving the public wasn't a crime. "Live" was a lie. So was the fiction that votes from viewers affected the contestants' scores. But did anyone who watched television truly believe everything they saw in entertainment programming was real?

Liss hated feeling so jaded. She wanted to be able to trust the people around her, but she didn't dare take the risk. As she ran through her routine with Dandy and Dondi, she remained vigilant. Since Mo, Yates, and Iris were still in the competition, it followed that the three of them were the most likely suspects, but she kept Roy Eastmont on her watch list as well.

When she changed into her second costume—a multicolored, multilayered gauzy creation that only lacked a supply of pixie dust to turn her into one of Tinker Bell's BFFs—she ran through the other routine she'd be performing until she was sick of it. After rewarding Dandy and Dondi with dog treats and a cuddle, she coaxed them back into their carriers. That done, she sat on the floor beside them, unwrapped an energy bar to give her an excuse to stay put, and took stock of which members of the cast and crew were still in the ballroom.

The state police had been swift and efficient. They'd worked their way through almost everyone. Mel was still waiting her turn. So was Jane Smith. Roy Eastmont had left. So had Mo. Valentine was missing, too. Oscar and Iris continued to rehearse, and to judge by the ripe language that erupted from that direction, things were not going well.

"Concentrate!" The Great Umberto bellowed, both charm and charisma conspicuous by their absence.

Once the energy bar was history, Liss couldn't think of any more reasons to hang around. Lunch awaited, and then they'd all be back, once again recording "live" performances.

There was hardly anyone left in the foyer, but as she waited for the elevator, the door to the room Gordon was using for interviews swung open and Valentine came out. Liss was about to hail her when Gordon called her back. The two of them stood in the doorway, locked in an exchange of words so intense that it set Liss's antennae quivering. Although she strained to hear what they were saying, she was too far away to catch a single word.

The elevator dinged and the doors opened. She stepped inside, dragging the carriers behind her. By the time she turned around to punch the button for the fourth floor, the door to the interrogation room had closed. Unless they'd vanished into thin air, both Gordon and Valentine had gone back inside.

"Well, damn," Liss whispered as the elevator began to rise. "Does this mean I can't trust anybody?"

That evening, Dan showed up early. They had time for a leisurely supper, during which Liss gave him a brief account of her day. She skimmed over the parts she didn't want to dwell on—her concern about the papers she'd signed, her newborn suspicion of Valentine Veilleux, and her growing conviction that she was never going to figure out who was behind the dirty tricks. She'd meant to check alibis, but that wasn't easy to bring up in casual conversation. Casual conversation was darn near impossible in any case. Everyone was too fixated on their own next performance.

"So, the finale is in the bag and just the last results show is left?" Dan shoveled the last of his mashed potatoes into his mouth and reached for the beer he'd ordered to go with their meal.

"Right. Each of the twelve acts that started the season gives one reprise performance and then the winner is announced, supposedly based on call-in votes by viewers as well as the judges' scores." Surreptitiously, Liss fed the last small bites of her steak to Dandy and Dondi. Ever hopeful, they had been sitting beneath the table throughout the meal.

Dan leaned back in his chair and sent her a skeptical look.

"Yes, well, at least it will all be over once the champion of champions is crowned." She hoped. "Unfortunately, I have one more chore to do this evening. Everyone else will be wearing the same costume they wore for the first show but Deidre's outfit won't fit me. Mel, the wardrobe mistress, had to make something new." Liss glanced at her watch. "I have a fitting in about fifteen minutes."

"Where?" He started to replace their cutlery and dishes on the room-service tray, preparatory to leaving it in the hall to be picked up.

"Her suite." She gave him the number. "It doubles as the costume shop and wardrobe storage. I shouldn't be long. Maybe an hour?"

After putting the tray outside the door, Dan rescued his half-finished beer from the table and carried it with him to the sofa. "I knew there was a reason you were being so nice to me," he teased her. "You need a dog sitter."

Dandy and Dondi followed him to hop up and perch, one on his left and one on his right, looking for all the world as if they were waiting for him to turn on the TV.

"Yes, it was all an evil plot. Feed you. Get you drunk. Force you to do my bidding." Liss came up behind him to plant a kiss on the top of his head.

"Is that the best you can do?" He turned just enough to reach up, catch hold of her upper arms, and tumble her over the back of the sofa and into his lap. Liss shrieked. The dogs scattered. Then a little silence ensued, broken only by the faint sound of lips moving on lips.

"Mmm," Liss murmured when he let her up for air. "Maybe I could postpone the fitting."

He sat her up, a wicked grin on his face. "The sooner you go, the sooner you'll be back."

"Good point. Thanks for taking care of the Scotties. I will definitely find a way to repay you later." She fluttered her eyelashes at him as she got to her feet.

"No problem." Laughter lit his eyes as the two dogs returned in a rush, nearly tripping Liss up in the process.

She sent them a rueful look. "They're sweet little guys, but they do tend to get underfoot, especially when I'm getting dressed or undressed, and Valentine—"

When she broke off in midsentence, Dan's gaze sharpened. "Valentine . . . ?"

Liss shook her head. "Probably nothing. It's just that she looked so peculiar today when she was talking to Gordon Tandy. As if she had something to hide." She described what little she'd seen of their exchange.

"She's the photographer, right? That probably means she's pretty observant. Maybe she was just trying to decide if something she saw was important enough to share with the cops." He chuckled. "Either that, or she's been working undercover for them all along."

"Or maybe she's got a guilty secret." Liss sighed as she headed for the bathroom. "It's so hard to know who to trust. If I didn't have you to rely on, I don't know what I'd do."

She thought about that on her way to Mel's suite. She did rely on Dan, and he on her. Which was what made it so ridiculous that she hadn't yet told him about the papers she'd signed. The minute she returned, she promised herself, she'd explain the situation, and together, they'd decide what to do about it. Way too late, she'd realized that she should have been given copies of everything.

Mel had outdone herself. She'd produced a creation that was glittery and gaudy without being tasteless. The gown was royal blue in color, floor length but with slits in the sides of the skirt to give Liss room to execute the few simple dance steps Deidre's routine required. Best of all, it fit like a dream. Liss stared at herself in the full-length mirror.

"Wow. I look like Hollywood royalty."

"Nothing but the best for the woman at the top of the leaderboard."

Liss winced.

"What? You don't want to win?" After a curious glance from Liss's expression in the mirror to the one on her face, Mel busied herself with the few minor adjustments needed to make the costume perfect.

"Not so much." Liss hesitated. "Mel? What do you know about what comes next? I mean, does the champion of champions have an obligation to make appearances, do publicity, that sort of thing?"

"Didn't Mr. Eastmont talk to you about that?"

"No, he didn't. I, uh, signed some papers. I don't remember one that addressed events after the end of the season."

"How about 'standard postproduction publicity'? Did you agree to that?"

"Maybe. I'm not sure." The phrase had an ominously familiar ring.

"Deidre's contract would have covered it. Did you sign something that promised to honor her contractual obligations?"

"I don't think so, but I can't be certain. It was all done in such a rush. I thought I was being careful, but Eastmont was looming over me. I skimmed when I should have taken the time to analyze every word. If I'd really been smart about it, I'd have had a lawyer look over the papers before I signed anything."

"You'd be well paid, you know." Finished sticking pins in the hem, Mel stood.

"That would be a change. How much?"

"Don't hold me to this, but from what I've heard, it's a hundred thousand."

The sum had Liss's eyes widening. "If the show has that kind of money, they ought to be spending more on the contestants *during* the competition."

"Amen to that." Mel helped her out of the costume, transferring it to a padded hanger. "Healthier staff salaries would be good, too."

Liss bent over to unbuckle the shoes that went with the dress. How Mel managed to keep finding them in her size, let alone with taps on them, she had no idea, but that was not the question she asked once she'd kicked them off. "Did everyone but me know there would be a nice payday for the winner?"

Mel carried the gown into the connecting bedroom and placed it on the bed, where she'd already assembled the needle and thread she'd need to hem the skirt. "Sure. They all won their own seasons, didn't they? Of course, the appearance fees for those wins was only half what it'll be for the champion of champions."

Was the "reward" for winning sufficient temptation to explain everything that had happened? Liss pondered that question as she got dressed in the comfortable jeans and warm sweater she'd put on as soon as she returned to her suite after recording the finale. To someone living in small, rural Moosetookalook, Maine, it was a small fortune. To someone from away? Not so much.

"You know you're a shoo-in, right?"

"So I've been led to believe. And a hundred thousand dollars would be nice. We could pay off our mortgage. But I have other obligations and a life of my own apart from the dogs." Liss slid her feet, already encased in woolly socks, into the warmly lined moccasins that had served as both shoes and slippers during her stay at Five Mountains. "And what about Dandy and Dondi? They don't belong to me. Desdemona will probably demand two-thirds of the appearance fee if we have to fulfill that part of her mother's contract."

"Bummer," Mel said.

Liss gave a short laugh. "I thought about trying to throw the competition. I'm beginning to wish I *had* tried to turn in a poor performance."

"You think it would have made a difference?" Mel sounded skeptical.

"I don't know." Liss sighed. "It's too late now, anyway. The last performance has been recorded, along with the judges' scores." She'd been awarded all tens for her showing on the finale. The Great Umberto had also earned a perfect score. Mo's juggling act had received two tens and a nine.

"Hey, look on the bright side," Mel said with a grin.

"What bright side?"

"Maybe the viewer votes will make a difference."

"Yeah. Right." Waving farewell, Liss let herself out of the costume suite.

She stopped with her fingers still touching the door handle. Maybe Mel was on to something. Since the show was rigged, that explanation *would* account for someone else being named champion of champions. All she had to do was convince Roy Eastmont that an upset victory would boost ratings.

The *Variety Live* MC was not in his suite, but there weren't that many places he could have gone after dark on a cold night in mid-March. She checked the hotel dining room first. Her second stop was the hotel's sports bar. Eastmont had holed up alone in a corner booth to drown his sorrows.

He was not receptive to Liss's idea.

"The fans will love it," she insisted. "They'll think they really did make a difference."

"The fans want the doggies to win." He drained his glass and signaled the waitress for a refill.

"At least consider it. There are problems if I win. The dogs aren't mine."

"Deidre's doggies," he mumbled.

She waited while the empty glass was taken away and a full one placed in front of him. "Get you anything, honey?" the middle-aged waitress asked.

"I'm good."

Eastmont stared at her, bleary-eyed. "You *are* good, Deidre. You're the best. The champion of champions." He lifted his glass in a toast, slopping some of the liquid onto his hand before he took a long swallow.

"Oh, good grief!" She put a hand on his arm to stop him from lifting the glass a second time. "Listen to me. I'm not Deidre. And I don't own those two Scottish terriers. Desdemona does. And assuming Desdemona ever decides to surface again, she'll have a say in what they do after the last show airs. What if she doesn't *want* them doing PR work for the show?"

"Got to." Eastmont's words grew more slurred every time he spoke. "Got a contract."

"Deidre had a contract, and no matter what I signed when I came in as her substitute, it's not binding on Desdemona."

She watched him try and fail to process that thought. Forehead wrinkled, lips working, he stared at her as if he'd never seen her before. After a bit more cogitation, he asked, "What act are you?"

Liss sighed. "Deidre and her Dancing Doggies, but—"

"That's right!" He took another swig of his drink and slammed the glass down on the table with a resounding thump. "And it's all set. You listen up, Deidre. You signed a contract. I'll sue you if you don't fulfill your obligations."

Liss gave up. Since he kept calling her "Deidre," she couldn't be sure how much credit she should give to any statement he made. She'd have to tackle him again in the morning, when he'd be hung over instead of falling-down drunk. Oh, there was something to look forward to!

As she made her way back to the lobby, she was dimly aware of the presence of other members of the cast and crew. Preoccupied, she acknowledged greetings and waves but paid little attention to who was in the bar and who wasn't.

She needed to get back to her suite. She needed to talk things through with Dan.

Out of the blue, another thought momentarily stopped her in her tracks. Margaret! With so much else going on, she'd forgotten all about her ailing aunt. She hadn't even asked Dan for an update on her condition.

Guilt swamped her. Was it too late now to call? A glance at her watch told her it was already nine. She'd been gone longer than she intended. Dan would be wondering where she was.

She jabbed at the elevator button and waited. Nothing happened. The display above the doors told her that all the cars were on the second floor. Some kind of function must be taking place in the ballroom. Too impatient to wait any longer, Liss headed for the stairs.

Passing the back exit leading to the parking

lot, Liss started to climb. She felt a cold draft as someone used that door to enter the hotel. Intent on getting back to Dan, she didn't bother to look over her shoulder to see who it was.

When rapid footsteps pounded up the stairs behind her, Liss edged over to her right to give the other person room to get by. She was prepared for a tight squeeze, since the stairwell was narrow, but what happened next caught her completely off guard. Without warning, someone threw a blanket over her head, then seized her in a bear hug from behind and lifted her off her feet.

Liss tried to scream, but the heavy wool muffled her voice. With her arms immobilized and her legs next to useless, she was half carried, half dragged back down the stairs and out into the cold. An engine was running—a vehicle ready and waiting to take her away.

Struggling, Liss managed to kick the person holding her, but then there were more hands grabbing at her, pushing her in the direction they wanted her to go. Fighting at least two people, she gained her footing for an instant, but the surface of the parking lot was slick. She couldn't get traction. Blinded by the blanket over her head and upper body, she couldn't even figure out which way to run.

She was already panting when one of the people attempting to subdue her got the bright idea to smother her. A large hard hand clamped down over her nose and mouth, pressing the thick wool tight to her face and cutting off what little air she'd had. In the darkness beneath the wool, Liss's world faded to black.

Chapter Thirteen

Liss had no idea how long she was unconscious, but when she came to she was still wrapped tight from head to knees in the heavy blanket. Oxygen remained in short supply.

She fought down a flare of panic and tried to order her rattled thoughts. A cocoon of wool held her prisoner but she *could* breathe.

When she'd calmed sufficiently, she took stock. She was not in any pain, so she hadn't been damaged physically. She wasn't even tied up, although the blanket did a good job of holding her motionless. She was inside a vehicle. She could hear the engine and the sound the tires made on the road. Every time it hit a pothole or a frost heave, she felt it right down to her bones.

She had been kidnapped.

That staggering realization triggered a burst of anger, one that cleared the rest of the confusion out of her muddled brain. She'd been on her way back to the suite when someone had tossed this blanket over her head and made off with her.

Dan! He'd have missed her by now. He'd search. Sound the alarm. But he'd have no idea where to look for her. No one would.

Intent upon escape, she tried to sit up, only to discover that she had no leverage and no room to maneuver. Until she was pulled free of the cramped space where she was lying, she wasn't going anywhere.

The realization made her heartbeat accelerate. She tried to gulp in more air, but none was available. Afraid she would black out again, she willed herself to take small, even breaths. *Don't panic! Think!*

She was not tied up, she reminded herself. Put that in the plus column. She supposed her captors hadn't thought it necessary, since her hands were already immobilized by the folds of the blanket and the size of the area into which she'd been wedged.

And they'd made the mistake of leaving her feet free. It cheered her considerably to contemplate how much damage she could do with a few well-placed kicks. All she needed was an opportunity to deliver them.

Liss strained to hear, listening for voices, but no one spoke. The steady swish of tires over pavement told her they were on a paved road, but she supposed it was too much to hope for that a passing motorist would be able to see in to where she was stashed and notice an oddly shaped bundle. Even if one did, what were the odds he'd report it to the police?

She was not lying on the floor in the back of a

car, she decided. Her prison had to be a station wagon or a van . . . or an RV.

For an endless span, nothing changed. Then Liss felt the vehicle slow and wondered if they had reached their destination. Instead of stopping, the driver made a left turn onto a road in worse shape than the previous one. More potholes! Liss felt sure she'd have a splendid assortment of bruises by the time they stopped.

That was when it occurred to her that she might not have to worry about bruising.

Her kidnappers could be taking her somewhere far away from witnesses so they could *kill* her. Were they planning to bury her in the woods? It was not at all reassuring to feel the vehicle make yet another turn, this time onto what felt like a dirt road, rutted and uneven.

Liss tried to tell herself that if they'd meant to kill her, they'd have done it back at the hotel. Transporting a body had to be easier than dealing with a captive.

She wished she knew for certain who "they" were. There had been two people in the parking lot. Okay, yes, that and the van—she was sure it was a van now—suggested Oscar and Iris, working as a team. But she'd begun to think of Iris as a friend, and Iris had saved Dandy from being run over, at the risk of her own life.

Who else? Who would team up with the Great Umberto to take Liss out of the competition? Mo?

Had Iris been right to be jealous of the juggler?

Then again, maybe she was on the wrong track. Someone could have stolen the magician's van, or maybe this wasn't Oscar's vehicle. Liss didn't know what vehicles any of the others connected with *Variety Live* drove, except for Valentine.

It didn't matter. She had to leave evidence that she'd been held prisoner in *this* van. For later, she told herself, after she was safe at home and needed proof of what had happened to her. Grimly determined, she wriggled until she felt something other than wool with the tip of one finger. A tool box? Part of the van? She couldn't tell, but all that counted was that the surface she was touching would take fingerprints, a signpost saying, "Liss MacCrimmon Ruskin was here!"

A particularly violent bounce slammed Liss's head against a hard surface. She saw stars, and pain shot through her entire body. It took her a moment to realize that the van had stopped.

She held her breath. The side door opened, and a blast of cold air eddied around her feet and legs. Then strong hands gripped her ankles and tugged, pulling her straight out of the vehicle.

For just a second, her feet touched solid ground, but before she could put up a fight, the edges of the blanket were pulled tight and she was lifted into a fireman's carry. She tried kicking, but it had little effect. The arm clamped across the back of her knees defeated her best efforts. Head down, still blinded by the thick wool, her upper body bounced against her captor's back.

She heard snow crunch as he strode farther and farther away from the sound of the engine. Very faintly, she heard the unmistakable metallic thump of a heavy vehicle door being closed. A van. No doubt about it.

They stopped moving after what seemed an endless interval. For a moment he did nothing, said nothing. Liss was gathering herself to try kicking again when he lifted her off his shoulder. A second later, she went flying.

Thrown with such force, still wrapped in the blanket, Liss was unable to control how she landed. It was pure dumb luck that she didn't slam into a tree and that her shoulder struck the ground first, padding the landing for her head. The wind knocked out of her, senses reeling, desperate to drag in air, she struggled with the folds of wool.

The blanket was twisted beneath her, frustrating her efforts. By the time she managed to fight her way free and stagger to her feet, her captor had vanished. Her thrashing had covered the sound of his retreat. She couldn't tell which way he'd gone.

She was alone . . . in the middle of the woods . . . in the middle of the night.

This is so *not good.*

Liss had no idea where she was. It was pitch-dark. It was mid-March. There was still snow on the ground. It was cold, and she didn't even have a coat.

Wrapping the blanket around her for warmth, she stared up at the sky. Where was the moon? The North Star would work, too. But she was in a pine forest. Even in winter the evergreen branches were too thick to see much of anything overhead.

"Okay," she said aloud to bolster her courage. "Think positive. You're still alive."

Obviously, her captors hadn't wanted her dead, just out of the way. She wasn't going to dwell on what made her different from Deidre Amendole and Troy Barrigan. *Don't look a gift horse in the mouth. Or whatever.*

They'd driven most of the way here. That meant there was a road . . . somewhere. A dirt road, but there might be houses along it. And even though, at the time, it had seemed as if she'd been carried for miles, that road was probably not too far away.

Liss had been standing in one place for too long. Her feet, although they were encased in woolly socks and fur-lined moccasins, were already cold, and she didn't have a lot of confidence that the leather would keep out the wet.

"My kingdom for a pair of boots and a warm coat," she muttered. "And gloves. And a woolly hat."

She'd have to move soon, before she turned into an ice sculpture.

Liss blinked, realizing that her eyes had begun

to adjust to the darkness. She could see enough of her surroundings to make her think that, if she walked with care, she could probably avoid running head-on into a tree.

She put a hand out in front of her for extra protection and took a cautious step forward. In that moment, her sense of humor surfaced. She wasn't blind. She wasn't even nearsighted.

It was no wonder so few of the detectives in the mysteries she read wore glasses. Take the sleuth's spectacles away, and the poor, nearsighted boob would barely be able to function. She tried to picture Margery Allingham's Albert Campion in a situation like this one. He'd be hard-pressed to find his way out of the woods. So would Dorothy L. Sayers's Lord Peter, or even Ellery Queen.

Get a grip, Liss.

She took another tentative step and broke through the surface of the snow with a resounding crunch. She pulled her foot free, wishing she'd had the good sense to trade her moccasins for something sturdier. Even walking shoes that laced up would be an improvement. What if she lost one of the moccasins? Her foot would get wet. Wet and cold were a sure recipe for frostbite, and frostbite led to amputated toes.

Maybe she *should* stay put. Wasn't that what the guidebooks advised for lost hikers? Liss didn't want to end up walking in circles for hours on nd. She'd heard of skiers who'd gone off the marked trails and stayed warm overnight in snow caves. Somehow, she didn't think that would work. For one thing, what was on the ground here wasn't the right kind of snow to burrow into. To make matters worse, there had already been a couple of thaws this month. Puddles of cold water or patches of cold mud weren't any healthier to step into than plain old snow.

Staying put was not a good idea. Not in this case. Liss was already shivering beneath the blanket. She would freeze to death if she didn't do something to keep herself warm. That said, she decided she might as well try to find her way out of the woods.

With fear of hypothermia as a powerful motivator, Liss took another step forward. Once again, she heard a distinctive crunching sound, the same one she'd heard when her captor had been carrying her. He'd broken through the crust of snow, just as she had. That meant he'd punched holes in it, holes that must still be around her somewhere, marking the path he'd taken from the road. If she could locate them, they'd lead her right back to it.

Hoping her hands weren't already too cold to feel the breaks in the surface, Liss clutched the blanket more tightly around her and bent double to begin her search. She found the first of the footprints a few minutes later. After that, she had only to place her feet where he'd walked.

It was a long trek and not easy going. Liss stepped out of the moccasins more than once and stumbled half a dozen times, once landing on her knees and another time on her backside. Only knowing that there was a road at the end of the tracks, a road that would eventually lead her back to civilization, kept her moving forward.

Liss had no idea how much time passed before she staggered out of the woods and into the middle of a narrow dirt road. The relief that washed over her was quickly followed by a terrible sense of uncertainty. Which way should she turn?

Her back to the woods, she stood still and closed her eyes, trying to call up the memory of her captor pulling her out of the van. The woods behind her must have been on the same side as the door because she'd been carried straight away from the vehicle, not around it. That meant the van had been facing to her right. To retrace its route, she had to turn left. Taking a deep breath and squaring her shoulders, Liss set off in that direction.

Her pace was brisk at first, but it wasn't long before slow, plodding steps were the best she could manage. The light was better on the road—a half-moon hung in the sky, along with a canopy of stars—but when she came to a signpost, she could not make out what it said.

Its presence suggested that she was on a camp

road. That cut down her chance of finding people nearby but increased the odds that there were buildings, maybe even one that boasted a fireplace, a supply of firewood, a cupboard full of canned goods, and a closet containing odds and ends of warm, dry clothing.

She swayed slightly as she considered what to do. Then she caught sight of what she thought might be the reflection of moonlight off a glass window. If the camp was that close . . .

The drive leading up to it had not been plowed, but it was short. The camp had been built overlooking a lake. That was what she'd seen—moonlight on ice. Unfortunately, the building itself was no use to her. Only the chimney still stood. The place looked as if it had burned down years ago.

Discouraged, Liss retraced her steps to the dirt road and kept going. She told herself survival stories to keep her spirits up. There had been that man who broke his leg in a nighttime snowmobile accident. He'd crawled a mile back to a friend's house to get help. It had taken him four hours, but he'd made it. Of course, he'd known where he was to start with and in which direction to go to find help.

Miles of walking might lie ahead of her. That thought was discouraging, but Liss's choices were limited. She could keep going until she found the paved road, where there would be passing cars and maybe even houses with people in them. Or she could try again to find a camp she could break into. Either way, she would survive. Anything else was unthinkable.

Liss felt as if she'd been trudging along the uneven dirt road for hours when she came to a second signpost. She couldn't read what it said either, but once again she turned off the dirt road, hoping to find shelter and warmth. Instead, the path led her out onto a scenic overlook. She came within two steps of falling off a cliff and landing in the lake below.

Back on the dirt road, faced with a third signpost, she wasn't as quick to take a detour. Even if the lane did lead to a camp, she might not be able to break in. She felt weaker by the minute and was having a hard time just putting one foot in front of the other. At this time of year, no one would be living at their camp. There wouldn't be a working phone. The owners might not have left even basic supplies behind, given that camps were prime targets for thieves during the off-season.

Liss stayed on the dirt road, hoping she hadn't just made a fatal error.

Cold and tired and discouraged, she began to lose touch with reality. Maybe this was all a nightmare, she thought. Maybe she could change what was happening to her simply by willing it.

A full moon instead of a half-moon would be nice. Bright sunlight would be even better.

"Make it so," she said aloud, giving her best imitation of Jean-Luc Picard at the helm of the *Enterprise*.

Nothing happened.

"These droids are not the ones you're looking for," she muttered.

A giggle escaped her. She had a feeling that hysteria wasn't far behind.

This road has to lead somewhere, she told herself, and kept going.

When it finally did, she could scarcely believe it. One minute she was walking on dirt. The next she had reached the paved surface of a cross-road. Liss resisted the temptation to sink down on her knees and kiss the Tarvia.

Like a schoolchild about to cross the street, she stopped and looked both ways. She saw not a single sign of life—no lights, no mailboxes, no road signs. If it hadn't been for that half-moon reflecting off the snow on the ground, it would have been even harder to make out anything in the dark, empty landscape.

Liss stood still, indecisive once more. Which direction had the van turned to get from this road onto the camp road? Left? Or had that been the first turn they'd made, off what was probably the main road leading away from Five Mountains Ski Resort?

Swaying with exhaustion, her feet as heavy as frozen blocks of ice, she was still trying to make up her mind when she heard a faint but familiar sound. Her brain was so foggy that it took her a moment to identify it as the barking of a dog.

It's "the curious incident of the dog in the nighttime" all over again, she thought, channeling Sherlock Holmes. A second near-hysterical giggle escaped.

Then she remembered. The point of Sir Arthur Conan Doyle's story was that the dog *didn't* bark. This one was going at it big-time.

Turning in the direction of the sound, Liss moved with renewed vigor. She had a tangible goal to reach. A dog meant an owner, and an owner meant a house, and a house meant shelter, warmth, and a phone. She'd call Dan first. Then Gordon.

She had not yet spotted any buildings when a human voice shouted, "Shut up, you stupid dog!"

The barking ceased, but Liss kept going. Civilization was close. It had to be. And then, across an expanse of open field and through a stand of trees, she saw the most beautiful sight she could imagine—a light in a window. More by instinct than sight, she found the driveway that led to the house. It seemed to take forever to reach the far end.

The dog started to bark again. This time it sounded frantic. Belatedly, it occurred to Liss that the animal might not be friendly. That other bit of trivia about dogs in the night came back to her, bringing with it a sudden sense of dread: Scottish tradition said a dog howling in the night was an omen of approaching death. It didn't say *whose* death.

Liss was panting by the time she reached the three steps that led to a porch. Nothing had leapt out at her. The barking was off to her left. The light from the window illuminated just enough of the yard to give her a reassuring glimpse of a chain-link fence.

At the sight, Liss blinked and stumbled. She knew where she was. The dog was a Doberman, a guard dog with big teeth, but he was also safely confined. She even remembered that the animal was called Cujo, although the name of his owner eluded her.

As she staggered up the steps and onto the porch, she hoped that memory lapse wouldn't matter. She raked an ice-cold, trembling hand through her hair. The other still clutched the blanket, now much bedraggled, around a sweater-and-jeans-clad body that was likewise shaking like a leaf. Even her teeth were chattering. The way she looked, there was a good chance that her appearance alone would be enough to frighten the homeowner into slamming the door in her face. Wouldn't that be a pretty sight in the morning—a woman frozen to death in the dooryard!

No. Not going to happen. If worse came to worst, the householder would call the police to come get the crazy woman on her lawn.

Sagging against the doorframe, Liss used her last reserves of energy to knock. She wasn't sure the faint sound could be heard over the racket Cujo was making. She supposed it didn't matter. Sooner or later, someone would come out just to see why the Doberman was going nuts.

She knew whoever lived in the house was still up. That light she'd used as a homing beacon came from a downstairs room. In between the dog's increasingly frantic barks, she could hear the faint sounds of a laugh track. The TV was tuned to a sitcom.

The porch light came on, nearly blinding her. She was shading her eyes with her free hand when the woman she remembered from the day she'd tried to find Dandy's owner opened the door. Mrs. Bentley, that was it!

Before Liss could stammer out her name, Mrs. Bentley's eyes widened. "It's you!" she exclaimed. "The one who was asking about the Scottish terrier. The one who was on television in that news story about the snake."

By the time Dan Ruskin arrived to collect his wife, Liss was nearly back to normal and feeling alternately relieved and chagrined by the realization that her condition had been nowhere near as desperate as she'd imagined.

"You're sure you're okay?" Dan asked as he helped her into the passenger seat of his truck. The heater was going full blast. "I can drive to the hospital as easily as I can take you back to the resort."

Luxuriating in the warmth of the cab and the comfort of the warm winter jacket, lined gloves, and knitted hat Dan had brought for her, Liss sent a reassuring smile his way. "I'm fine. Really."

He looked doubtful . . . and worried . . . but he closed the door and circled around to the driver's side. "Resort it is, then. Sherri's there. I called her when I realized you were missing."

"I wasn't gone that long!" Forty-eight hours was the rule, since she was well over the age of consent. She didn't qualify for an Amber Alert.

Dan backed slowly down the driveway, past the barking dog. "True, but she was about to issue a BOLO when you called."

"What are friends for?" Liss murmured.

Once they were back on the road, Dan reached for her hand and gave it a squeeze. "You're *sure* you're—"

"I'm sure. I admit that it felt wicked cold when I was wandering around in the great outdoors but, according to Mrs. Bentley, the air temperature never dropped below freezing. It was a balmy forty degrees for most of the time I spent trying to get back to civilization. Frostbite isn't in the cards. It doesn't look as if I even developed a case of chilblains."

Her casual tone didn't fool Dan for a minute. "You're lucky you found that farmhouse when you did, and that Mrs. Bentley was so quick to sit you down in front of the woodstove and let you warm up slowly. You were probably in the early stages of hypothermia."

"I didn't get wet! I was just cold. That's all. It felt wonderful to hold both hands out toward the heat. And then Mrs. Bentley made me a mug of hot chocolate and insisted I drink every drop before she'd let me use her phone to call you."

"You didn't even have a coat."

"I was dressed in layers. I had on a polypropylene camisole next to my skin, guaranteed to wick away sweat."

He didn't laugh when she quoted the manufacturer's advertising slogan. "What if there'd been a wind? Nothing is proof against a severe wind chill."

Just thinking about that possibility made Liss shiver. "Okay. If there had been a brisk wind, what I had on wouldn't have made much difference. The cold would have penetrated right through blanket and sweater and camisole. But there was no wind. I'm fine! I kept moving. I even flipped the end of the blanket over my head to keep the heat in. I was in good health to start with. I survived. Okay?"

Liss stared at her hands, flexing the fingers just because she could. She didn't want to think about how much worse off she would be right now if she'd been unconscious when her kidnapper walked away. Or if she'd turned the wrong way on the paved road. Or lost a moccasin. Or taken a header off that scenic overlook. What if she hadn't heard Cujo barking? She could still be out wandering around, looking for shelter, gradually losing body heat. Even at forty degrees, hypothermia would have gotten her in the end.

At the intersection where they had a choice of turning toward Moosetookalook in one direction or Orlin and the ski resort in the other, Dan braked at the stop sign. Engine idling, he put the truck in park. There wasn't another car in sight, and he seemed to need a moment just to turn his head and look at her, to reassure himself that she was there and whole and safe. His voice was low and clogged with emotion.

"You want to tell me how you ended up in the middle of nowhere?"

"Someone threw a blanket over my head and drove me there."

His hands tightened on the steering wheel. He swallowed before he spoke. "Who?"

"I don't know. You must have asked around

when you realized I was gone. Did anyone see anything?"

"Not that they'd admit to. The bartender said you were talking to Roy Eastmont, but Eastmont was completely out of it. I couldn't get a lick of sense out of him. I did find out one thing, though. There was a problem with the elevators. They were all stuck on the second floor for about an hour. Someone apparently tampered with them. Don't ask me how. That's not my area of expertise."

"So they *knew* I'd take the stairs." Liss sat up straighter, suddenly more alert.

"They?"

"There were two people. One grabbed me, probably a man, but another helped, and probably drove the van."

"A van? You're sure it was a van?"

"Pretty sure, from the sound the sliding door at the side made and from the area I was scrunched into. There was some kind of cargo, I think. That's what kept me from moving around. That and the blanket."

If she didn't know better, she'd swear Dan had just growled. His face in the dim lights from the dashboard was a mask of anger.

"Uh, Dan—do you know something I don't?"

"I know that when Sherri and I were in the parking lot of the hotel we ran into two people just getting out of a van. They *said* they'd gone out for pizza."

"Let me guess—the Great Umberto and his lovely assistant?"

"Yeah." He shifted into drive and continued on toward the resort. He had his temper back under control, but his grip on the steering wheel was so tight that his knuckles showed white. "They looked like they were arguing about something before they caught sight of us and put on the smiles."

Liss sighed. So much for hoping Iris wasn't involved.

Chapter Fourteen

Sherri was waiting for them in the Amendole suite with Dandy and Dondi.

Dan steered his wife inside and deposited her on the sofa. "Look after her for me, will you?" he asked Sherri. "I'll be back shortly."

When he started for the door, Liss sprang to her feet and all but tackled him to stop him from leaving. "Dan! Don't you dare! I absolutely forbid you to confront Oscar Yates!"

He tried to take a step and found himself dragging her with him. "I'm just going to talk to him."

"It won't do any good. He'll deny knowing anything and then you'll get mad and hit him and then you'll be the one in jail for assault. If you think I'll bail you out, you need to think again."

He stopped trying to reach the door, but the grimly determined look in his eyes hadn't faded. Liss was afraid that the moment she let go of him, he'd take off again.

"I know you're angry, but we have no proof of anything."

"That's exactly why I want to confront the guy."

Sherri circled them, blocking the way to the door, and cleared her throat. "Sit down. Both of you. Talk first. Action, if needed, later."

"Back off, Sherri. You're out of your jurisdiction!"

Liss smacked his arm. Hard. "Don't you mouth off at her. You're the one who called her in. More important, she's right." She didn't loosen the grip she had on him with her other hand. "I'll sit down if you will."

She could all but hear the wheels grinding inside his brain, but after a long, tense moment, he nodded. Slowly, she released him and stepped back. Obediently, he went to the sofa and sat. The Scotties, who had been watching the entire exchange with great interest, trotted after him.

He patted the cushion next to him. "Now you."

But Liss shook her head. "First I need a hot shower, but when I come out we'll talk, calmly and rationally, about what happened to me."

"Go," Sherri said. "I'll play jailer. I've had experience." She sent Dan a stern look that had him throwing his hands up in mock surrender.

Ten minutes later, hair freshly blown dry, body encased in a nightgown and wrapped in a warm, ankle-length bathrobe, and wearing a clean pair of thick woolly socks, Liss was about to return to the front room of the suite when she heard a loud thump on the other side of the bedroom door. She rushed out, skidding to a stop at the astonishing sight of her husband sprawled full length on the floor near the door to the hallway.

"What on earth—"

Sherri offered Dan a hand to help him up, her face split in a grin that went from ear to ear. "That'll teach you." Shifting her gaze to Liss, she added, "He tried to make a run for it and tripped over a dog."

A disgruntled-looking Dan limped back to the sofa. "Sorry," he mumbled. "I got impatient."

"I thought I could trust you," Liss whispered, and burst into tears.

As moments of catharsis went, it was amazingly effective. When she was cried out, Liss felt much better. Better yet, her breakdown had convinced Dan she needed him close at hand. They sat together on the sofa, his arm around her shoulders, her cheek pressed against his chest.

"While you were in the shower," Sherri said, "Dan told me you think you were transported in a van. Given everything that's happened, that does suggest a pretty obvious suspect."

"The Great Umberto." Liss sat up a little straighter. "He's one of the finalists, so he had motive. What happened to me earlier tonight is the latest in this whole series of dirty tricks. The dognapping. The phony complaint against Eudora. The destruction of Mo's props. Willetta's cough drop. Only this one could have had much more serious consequences."

Sherri and Dan exchanged a look. He gestured for her to take the lead.

"I don't disagree," Sherri said, "but you're missing a couple of incidents from your list. Have you decided the dirty tricks are separate from Deidre Amendole's overdose and what happened to Troy Barrigan?"

"I don't know, but I've begun to think it's possible. It came to me in the shower. Well, sort of. It was the curious incident of the dog in the nighttime, except that this dog, Cujo, barked."

They looked at her as if she'd lost her mind.

"I'm getting ahead of myself. Here's the thing. The dog I heard tonight, the one whose barking led me to Mrs. Bentley's house so I could call Dan, made me think of something that happened the night I found Dandy. I heard a twig snap. It was loud as a rifle shot and startled me. My first thought at the time was that there was someone there, watching me from the shelter of the trees, but I called out and no one answered me, so then I figured it was just a branch breaking under the weight of the ice and snow. You know what a loud cracking sound that can make."

"And now?" Dan prompted her.

"Now I think there *was* someone watching. The person who took Dandy out into what must have seemed like the middle of nowhere."

"To turn her loose?" Sherri sounded skeptical.

Liss reached out to stroke the Scottie's back.

"That's the thing. I don't know. If I hadn't come along, Dandy might have been recaptured."

"And killed." Sherri's blunt words made Liss wince.

"Maybe not. Maybe the intention was to keep her confined somewhere long enough for Deidre to have to bow out of the competition." She lowered her head to her hands. Was that what she really thought or just what she hoped was true? "The thing is, I was dumped in the same area where Dandy was running loose."

Step by step, Liss told them what she remembered of her abduction and the long, bumpy ride to the place where she'd been abandoned. Sherri interjected questions, but nothing new emerged about Liss's captors, not even the relative size of the person who'd thrown the blanket over her head.

"I couldn't tell how tall he was, or anything about his build except that he was strong. He wrapped his arms around me and then had me in a fireman's carry."

"You're no lightweight, but neither of those actions take brute strength," Sherri pointed out. "If I had to, I could haul you a short distance over my shoulder and I'm six or seven inches shorter than you are."

"Uh-huh." Liss cast a doubtful look at Sherri's baby bump.

"Well not *now,*" her friend said, laughing, "but I

hefted a guy bigger and heavier than you are when I was at the police academy."

"I don't see what the problem is," Dan interrupted. "We already have likely suspects. That magician and his assistant. They were lying about going out for pizza. No box."

"Maybe they didn't get takeout."

"In Orlin? That's the only choice they'd have."

"Well, there's one way to find out." Sherri commenced the rocking motion necessary to heave herself up off the sofa.

"Dan is *not* going to confront him."

"Nope. Neither am I. What we are going to do is check out that van. I want to look at the tires, see if there's any indication they were on a dirt road. We won't be able to get inside, but we can shine a flashlight around the interior, maybe figure out where you were wedged in."

Liss brightened. "I left fingerprints inside!" With everything else that had happened, she'd forgotten until that moment. "Maybe we should call Gordon first. I was planning to, after I phoned Dan, but Mrs. Bentley was making such a fuss over me that I thought I'd better wait. He's already investigating Deidre Amendole's death as suspicious, especially since Desdemona seems to have disappeared, and Troy Barrigan's fall wasn't an accident, it was attempted murder."

Sherri shook her head. "Not just attempted anymore. Troy Barrigan died earlier this evening."

• • •

With an effort, Sherri straightened and turned off her flashlight. "The magician's van has been driven over slushy roads, but there's no way for me to tell when or which ones. I'm sorry guys, but unless Liss is sure she was transported in this vehicle, there isn't enough evidence for me to ask for a search warrant."

"I couldn't see anything inside to confirm this is the right van." Liss had shone the light everywhere the beam would reach, but with the Great Umberto's props stored inside, it was difficult to tell where there might be spaces. He'd told her a few days earlier that he was no longer keeping his equipment in the van, but he might have had perfectly innocent reasons for changing his mind.

"She was kidnapped." Dan's voice was low and dangerous. "That's a serious crime. There must be some way to justify looking for the fingerprints she left inside the van. Find them, and there's your proof that this was how they got her out into the woods."

Liss placed one hand on her husband's arm. She could feel the tension in him even through the layers of fabric. Dan didn't often lose his temper, but he was on the verge of it now. "Let it go," she whispered. "We'll figure something out."

"Liss, face facts. The guy could have poisoned Deidre Amendole. It was probably his balcony

Barrigan took the header from. You're not safe as long as he's at large. It's time to call Gordon Tandy."

Both Liss and Sherri stared at him. Illuminated by the security lighting in the hotel parking lot, his face wore a stark, determined look.

"It's the middle of the night," Sherri protested, "and no matter what we suspect, this doesn't qualify as an emergency."

"The alternative is that I march up to the Great Umberto's suite and beat on him until he confesses." Dan already had his cell phone in his hand. "What's Tandy's number?"

"Okay. We'll call him," Liss said. "But let's do it inside, where it's warm." She found Dan's stricken expression heartwarming. "I'm fine. You're not putting me at risk. I just don't see any point in hanging around outside. Besides, the dogs are alone in the suite. After everything that's happened, I'm not comfortable leaving them there unprotected."

In the end, it was Sherri who made the call to Gordon. Liss listened to her explain the situation without much hope that the state police detective would be persuaded to do anything. She had seen nothing and heard less. Even though kidnapping was a much more serious crime than vandalism or theft, and might or might not be tied to one, or two, murders, they didn't have one iota of incriminating evidence against Oscar Yates and Iris Jansen.

Liss wasn't surprised when, after apologizing a second time to Gordon for waking him up, Sherri reported that he agreed with the conclusion they'd already reached.

"He said he'd be here first thing in the morning, but that unless the magician is willing to let the state police dust for fingerprints without a warrant, he doesn't have much chance of getting into that van." She directed her next words to Dan. "He suggested that we keep Liss's return quiet, for her own safety. Lots of people know she went missing because we were asking everybody we could think of if they'd seen her, but by now they've all gone to bed. It should be easy enough for her to keep out of sight."

"Better yet, she could leave," Dan said. "I don't see any reason for her to stay here longer. She'll be safe back home in Moosetookalook."

"She's right here," Liss reminded them.

"You can bring the dogs," Dan added. "Lumpkin and Glenora will just have to accept the situation."

All at once, Liss's long, traumatic day caught up with her. She slumped on the sofa she'd been sharing with Dandy and Dondi.

Troy Barrigan was dead. Murdered. If everything that had happened was connected, and she supposed it must be, then she *was* in mortal danger. If she gave in, gave up, went home, she'd be safe and so would the Scotties. That was the practical plan, the one based on common sense.

"I can't do it."

Neither Dan nor Sherri looked surprised.

"Well, it was worth a try," Dan said.

Closing her eyes, Liss had to will herself to think about the alternative. "Tomorrow we record the last results show," she said, talking it through. "All twelve acts that started the season are supposed to reprise their performances before Roy Eastmont narrows the field to two and then makes the big announcement—the act fans supposedly chose to be champion of champions. The three finalists perform last. That means I could wait until the very end to show up. Whoever thinks I'm still wandering around in the woods will be startled whenever I make my appearance, don't you think?"

"I think *startled* is a mild word for it," Sherri said. "The reaction could run the gamut from gobsmacked all the way to dangerous."

Liss paid her no mind. She liked this plan, and she was certain she'd be safe with so many people around. "Oscar Yates may be enough of a professional to hide his shock at seeing me," she mused aloud, "but Iris is an open book. She's sure to do or say something incriminating, and then you *will* have probable cause to search the van."

With a good night's sleep behind her, Liss was more certain than ever that the person who'd thrown the blanket over her head and half smothered her had been Oscar Yates. She still had plenty of unanswered questions. Why Iris had agreed to drive the van wasn't one of them. That poor girl was so infatuated with the Great Umberto that she'd do anything he asked of her.

Could he have switched Deidre's pills? And Willetta's cough drop? No trick at all for a magician who used sleight of hand on a daily basis. Ditto getting into a locked room to vandalize Mo's props. The phony phone call accusing Eudora of attacking a hotel guest must have been a piece of cake compared to the rest of what he'd done. Of course he'd had to sacrifice a valuable piece of equipment to make himself seem a victim rather than a suspect. That did puzzle Liss. Why hadn't he destroyed something less valuable than his vanishing cabinet? And, come to think of it, why had he planted Iris's earring in Willetta's suite?

Maybe he was being a little *too* clever, she decided. The fact remained that he'd had opportunity and means. As for motive, he had more than one. He wanted to win, or he wouldn't have agreed to participate in the champion of champions series. There was the money he'd get for appearances and the publicity those would generate for his act, as well as for *Variety Live*. Oh, yes. He had motive. Opportunity, means, and motive, the trifecta that pointed to guilt. All she . . . they . . . had to do now was find a way to prove the case against him.

She breezed out of the bedroom to find Dan and Sherri, who'd stayed the night, just finishing a hearty room-service breakfast. They stopped talking when they saw her.

"What?" Seeing a glance pass between them, Liss narrowed her eyes. They were going to try to talk her out of her plan. She held up one hand, palm out. "Never mind. Not a word until I've had some coffee. *Lots* of coffee."

Ten minutes later, she felt better equipped to face opposition. She turned to Dan and gestured for him to begin.

"It's dangerous. You don't know how Yates will react to seeing you."

"That's kind of the point."

But Dan was shaking his head. "I can make an educated guess. The guy has an ego as big as Chicago. He thinks he's manipulated everyone, that his illusions have succeeded in fooling us. He'll put on the charm, count on his charisma to give him the win over Mo Heedles once you're a no-show. But anyone who could do the things he's done has a darker side beneath all that charisma and charm. If you're right about him, he's killed twice. He'll have no compunction about killing again if he's threatened."

Liss put down the piece of toast in her hand, her appetite suddenly gone. "If he'd wanted me dead, he had plenty of opportunity to kill me last night. He didn't. I don't think he killed the reporter. Much as I hate the idea of a second villain, it makes much more sense for Roy Eastmont to have pushed Barrigan off a balcony. His suite is on that side of the hotel, too, and he had the most to lose if Barrigan exposed the truth about *Variety Live.*"

Liss laid out the details of her newest theory for Sherri and Dan. The final piece of logic was that the reason Eastmont had gotten stinking drunk was because he felt guilty about what he'd done.

"That doesn't mean you'll be safe if you suddenly reappear and cost the Great Umberto everything he's been working toward." Dan stabbed his fork into a sausage with unnecessary force.

The dogs beneath the table went on alert, certain that there were table scraps, intentional or otherwise, in the offing.

"So, *what* then?" Liss asked. "We just let him get away with everything he's done?"

"Of course not. Give Gordon Tandy a chance to accumulate more evidence, enough to get that warrant. Then the state police will find your fingerprints in the van and Yates will be arrested." Sherri's was the voice of reason, but Liss wasn't any more ready to listen to her than she was to hear what Dan had to say. Her mind was made up.

"He hasn't called back, has he? You said yourself that there isn't probable cause."

"Not yet."

"It won't do any good if Yates has time to clean the interior of the van."

"Why should he? He thinks your hands were covered by that blanket." Sherri's eyes widened. "The blanket! Do you still have it?"

"It's in the truck," Dan said. "Why?"

"If we're lucky, there will be something on it, a hair maybe, to prove it belonged to Oscar Yates. I'll make sure it gets to the state police lab."

"But you don't have anything to match that hair to," Liss objected, breaking a slice of bacon in half and giving the pieces to Dandy and Dondi. "Unless I pluck one from his beard. That would be fun."

"Are you out of your mind?" Dan's fists thumped down onto the table. "Even if he didn't push that reporter to his death, he deliberately poisoned Deidre Amendole. Okay, maybe he gave you a break, although I'm not so sure about that. You said he threw you down. He didn't care if you were injured."

Liss had been thinking about that. She suspected she owed her survival to Iris. It made sense that she'd had no knowledge of Yates's schemes until the very end, when he needed her help to get Liss away from the hotel. He wouldn't have wanted her to think him capable of murder. He'd have assured her that Liss was not dead, that she would make her way to safety, but not in time to appear in the final show of the season.

"No beard plucking," Liss promised. She'd only been half-serious anyhow.

"I'm sure Gordon can come up with some way to get a sample of his DNA," Sherri put in.

"I still think having you show up at the taping is a bad idea," Dan grumbled. "Yates is not going to take kindly to having you ruin everything for him."

"I'll be perfectly safe with so many people around," Liss insisted for what felt like the hundredth time. "You two will be there. I'll bet my next income-tax refund that Gordon will be, too. The place will probably be lousy with cops. Safe as houses."

Whatever Dan intended to say next, he was cut off by a knock at the door. Everyone froze.

"Probably one of the cast or crew stopping by to ask if you've been found," Sherri whispered.

"I don't want anyone knowing I'm back. They might let it slip to the wrong person."

"It could be Gordon," Dan said.

Liss pushed back her chair and hurried to the peephole. If not Gordon, then she expected to see Valentine on the other side, or perhaps Jane or Mel or Willetta.

For a moment she didn't recognize the person who stood there. Then her visitor turned slightly, bringing familiar features into view. With a gasp of surprise, and before she took the time to think about what she was doing, Liss opened the door to Desdemona Amendole.

Chapter Fifteen

Desdemona had brought luggage.

A lot of luggage.

And she looked as if she hadn't slept in days.

Liss was still trying to get a coherent story out of her when Gordon Tandy arrived on the scene to tell them he had not been able to get a search warrant for the van. The moment he caught sight of Desdemona, he politely but firmly asked Dan, Sherri, and Liss to either leave the suite or go wait in the bedroom with the door closed. He had an interrogation to conduct.

Ten minutes passed, then another ten. The coffee Liss had brought with her into the bedroom had gone cold. "What is taking him so long? And why can't we be out there?"

Looking up from the current edition of *Down East*, supplied by the hotel, Sherri sent her a pitying look. "What did you expect? You know how the state police operate."

"Yes, of course I do. But I don't think Desdemona was behind any of our troubles, and she certainly wasn't the one who carried me into the woods. She's not strong enough."

Dan spoke from the window, where he'd been

passing the time staring out at the ski slopes. "She was here when her mother died."

"Are we going to start this again? I thought we all agreed that Oscar Yates was the villain here, except for maybe Roy Eastmont being the one who pushed the reporter off the balcony."

"Yates had help. Maybe it was Desdemona driving the van, not Iris at all."

Mouth open, an objection on the tip of her tongue, Liss would have argued the point had Gordon not knocked on the bedroom door at that precise moment and asked them to rejoin him in the suite's front room. A disgruntled-looking Desdemona sat on the sofa, scowling fiercely at the dogs, who had not been banished during her interrogation. They were trying to comfort her, obviously the last thing she wanted. She shoved Dandy away and swatted at Dondi.

"You're not getting them back," Liss said.

For a moment, Desdemona looked confused. "Oh, you mean the dogs? They're all yours. Do whatever you want with them."

"What about the provision in your mother's will?"

The other woman's face twisted into a mask of hatred. "That old bitch can't make me do anything now, not after the way she cheated me out of my inheritance."

"The late Mrs. Amendole's . . . business ventures did not go as well as she'd hoped."

Gordon pulled one of the chairs away from the dining table, turned it around, and straddled it. His folded arms rested on the wooden back. "The money set aside for the care of her dogs is no longer available."

"*None* of the money is left. There was supposed to be enough to last me the rest of my life."

"Are you saying you intentionally gave your mother an overdose so you could inherit her money?" Liss looked from Desdemona to Gordon and back again. She didn't expect either one of them to answer her question, but she did notice that Desdemona wasn't in handcuffs. Did that mean she was off the hook for Deidre's death?

Desdemona heaved a great sigh. "I did not kill my mother. Her *accidental* overdose was just a lucky break for me, or so I thought. Turns out the only money left was her life insurance, just enough to pay for her funeral." Her hands were still, folded in her lap, but her foot jiggled in an erratic rhythm.

"Deidre Amendole had a gambling problem," Gordon said.

"She lost everything." Desdemona's voice rose in a self-pitying whine. "Even the title to our house!"

"That's unfortunate." Liss took the chair opposite Desdemona. Wary of being kicked, she pulled both feet up and curled them beneath her.

"You knew nothing about this?" Dan sounded skeptical.

"Oh, I had an inkling that something was wrong, but I had no idea just how bad things really were. I knew she'd bet a bundle—as it turned out, her last bundle—on herself to win the champion of champions title on *Variety Live.*"

Enlightenment dawned. "So that's why you wanted me to substitute for her in the act. Why you lied about the honorarium and your concern about being sued."

"I knew the fix was in. Eastmont had been paid to make sure Deidre and her Dancing Doggies won. But it turns out that the wager was for *Deidre* to take the prize. No Deidre, no jackpot."

"Good grief." Liss struggled to take in all the ramifications. Hal Quarles had been right about the gambling, but it didn't have anything to do with the dirty tricks or Troy Barrigan's death or her own abduction.

Dan leaned against the counter in the kitchenette, keeping his thoughts to himself, while Sherri busied herself with the coffeemaker. In the lull after this latest bombshell, she handed steaming cups to Liss, Gordon, and Desdemona.

"If the outcome of *Variety Live* no longer matters," Sherri asked, "why did you come back to Five Mountains?"

"Where else was I supposed to go?" Desdemona thrust the cup back at her. "I need something stronger than this. Call room service and order up a bottle of vodka."

"Excuse me? That isn't your call."

Drawing herself up, Desdemona glared at Liss. "The hell it isn't. This suite is in *my* name. *Variety Live*, or rather this hotel, is footing the bills through tomorrow, for the publicity when the show airs. Maybe I can stay even longer if the act wins."

"*That's* why you came here?" Liss knew she sounded incredulous, but she was having a hard time processing Desdemona's presence, let alone the surprises she kept springing on them.

"Why not? The debt collectors were starting to drive me nuts. I'd already gotten an eviction notice." She shrugged. "My plane ticket back to Portland was paid for. Why not use it? I figured this would be a quiet place where I could hole up and figure out what to do next." She directed a sour look at Gordon Tandy. "Obviously, I was mistaken."

"Don't you mean a quiet place to hide out?" Making a disapproving sound, Sherri lowered herself onto the arm of Liss's chair. Both of Desdemona's lower limbs were jittering when she shifted to glare at the two women. Sherri gave them a pointed look. "What's with the twitching?"

"If you must know, I suffer from restless leg syndrome."

So, not nerves, after all. Or guilt. Sipping the coffee Sherri had brought her, Liss studied

Desdemona's thin, wan face. She'd clearly had a rough week. Liss felt a little sorry for her . . . until Dondi sniffed the toe of her boot and Desdemona kicked him.

"You were in Maine a day earlier than you let on—before Dandy went missing. Are you sure you had nothing to do with the dognapping?"

"Of course I didn't. I wanted the win. I had . . . my own reasons to visit Portland."

Liss waited.

"A job prospect, if you must know. Modeling. Something Valentine Veilleux set up for me. It fell through. Story of my life!"

"I've already verified her alibi," Gordon said.

Liss shifted in her chair to see him better, lowering her feet to the floor. "Speaking of Valentine, why were you giving her such a hard time when you questioned her the other day?"

"I don't think—"

"Come on, Gordon. Give a little. I'd like to be able to trust *one* person connected with this show."

The frown on his face was not encouraging, but then he shrugged. "It's hardly confidential. You could have done an Internet search and found it for yourself, or even asked Ms. Veilleux."

She caught the flash of amusement in his expression and braced herself for what was coming.

"You and she have a lot in common. On an

earlier assignment, because she travels around the way she does, with no fixed address, the police took a hard look at her as a suspect in a murder case. She ended up proving her innocence and at the same time providing them with the crucial evidence they needed to solve the crime."

"What does Valentine have to do with anything?" Desdemona looked as sulky as a child denied a treat, now that no one was paying any attention to her.

"I take it you haven't kept up with what's been happening here. The dognapping was only the first of a series of . . . unfortunate events." Leaving out what had happened to Troy Barrigan, Liss gave her a brief recap of the dirty tricks. "I believe Oscar Yates was responsible for all of them," Liss added.

"Well, imagine that!" Desdemona leaned back against the sofa cushions, a sardonic smile on her thin lips. "Talk about pulling the wool over everyone's eyes!"

A sudden, suffocating memory of that blanket cutting off her supply of air had Liss going rigid. With exaggerated care, she set aside her now-empty coffee cup. "In case you missed the point, the obvious conclusion is that your mother may have been murdered by another of these attempts at sabotage that went horribly wrong."

"Maybe. Maybe not."

Gordon started to speak, and Liss interrupted:

"Yes, I know. Still waiting for the toxicology reports! But it's a good bet she was."

Liss derived a moment's satisfaction from seeing Desdemona's wince at the turn of phrase. She wasn't about to apologize for her choice of words. Desdemona's treatment of the two Scotties paled compared to her callous attitude toward human life. Maybe she hadn't gotten along with her mother. Maybe she did feel betrayed by Deidre. But the mere possibility that the woman who'd given birth to her had been murdered should have been enough to spark strong emotion—if not outrage or horror, then at least shock.

"I will be performing with the dogs this afternoon," Liss said. "In fact, I should go collect my costume from Mel."

"What happened to keeping out of sight?" Gordon asked.

"What happened to your search warrant?"

"Working on it. Let me handle this, Liss."

She shook her head. "I've already been through all the arguments with Dan and Sherri, Gordon. And, by the way, I don't think Oscar Yates pushed Troy Barrigan." She explained her rationale for suspecting Roy Eastmont and got the reaction she expected—an unrevealing expression set in stone.

Gordon looked at his watch. He was already familiar with the schedule for recording the final show of the *Variety Live* season. "I don't want you showing your face until the last possible minute. Is that understood?"

"My costume?"

"I'll get it, and convince the wardrobe mistress to keep her mouth shut about you being back."

The mental image of Gordon delivering her glamorous royal-blue gown—she pictured him in a bellhop's uniform—made Liss smile. "Deal."

"The wheels of justice grind exceedingly slow."

Liss knew she was misquoting, but she was pretty sure she had the gist of the sentiment. It was almost time to go down to the ballroom for the final "live" results show, and they hadn't heard a peep out of Gordon Tandy or anyone else in law enforcement since Gordon dropped off her costume. Sherri didn't count. She hadn't returned to Moosetookalook but was sticking by her friend's side, as was Dan.

"Some bodyguard," Liss teased her. "I'd like to see you chasing the bad guys with that, um, protuberance."

"What? Junior here?" She patted her baby bump. "He's going to grow up and follow in his mom and dad's footsteps. Just you wait and see."

"Local police chief like you or sheriff's deputy like Pete?"

"Who knows? Maybe he'll run for sheriff. Penny Lassiter will have retired by the time he's old enough."

“He might rebel—join the state police . . . or even the FBI.”

“Bite your tongue!”

“I’m glad you two are in such a good mood,” Dan said, interrupting their banter. “It’s final decision time. Go or stay put?”

“I haven’t changed my mind. I just have to slip into my costume and I’m good. Right guys?” Liss addressed the question to the two Scotties. Dandy gave a short, loud bark. Dondi wagged his tail.

Fifteen minutes later, pulling the dogs’ carriers behind her and flanked by Sherri and Dan, Liss reached the entrance to the ballroom. Desdemona had remained in the suite. As soon as Liss had dressed, she’d locked herself in the bedroom.

“Last chance to change your mind,” Dan said.

“No way. Go fade into the background, both of you.”

“I’ve got my cell phone on vibrate,” Sherri said. “If Gordon calls with news, you’ll see me slip out to the foyer to talk to him.”

“Got it. Now go.”

She gave them a few minutes to enter and get settled. Chairs had been set up behind the judges’ table for hotel employees to watch the show. Perhaps fifty people had gathered. All of them had to sign confidentiality agreements handed out by Jane Smith as they entered the ballroom.

“Ready or not, here we go.” She drew in a deep breath and stepped inside.

At first no one noticed her. Jane had turned her attention to lining up the contestants for the opening shot. The fact that Liss and the dogs hadn't appeared at the dress rehearsal that morning meant she'd had to cover up an empty space. Liss wondered what excuse Roy Eastmont had worked out to explain her absence. Then again, given the way this show was set up, maybe he was planning to fake it right up to the end. There was probably footage he could use for everything except awarding the trophy.

"Liss?" The incredulous voice at her elbow belonged to Valentine Veilleux.

Turning, Liss smiled and shrugged. "Long story."

"I'm so glad you're okay." Valentine took another step toward her, then stopped. "I'd give you a hug if I didn't have three cameras around my neck."

"That's okay." Her smile broadened into a grin as she remembered what Gordon had told her. Someday, when there was time, she'd have to ask Valentine about her previous brush with crime.

After a quick glance over her shoulder to assure that her friend's outcry hadn't attracted anyone else's attention, Liss stooped to open the carriers. Dandy and Dondi were used to the routine. They stuck close to her as she walked toward the stage.

"Showtime," she whispered.

Roy Eastmont's patented plastic smile stayed in

place, but his eyes widened ever so slightly when he caught sight of them. Jane was the next to notice. There was no doubt about her reaction—overwhelming relief.

"Right here," Jane called to her, taking hold of Willetta's arm with one hand and giving the ventriloquist a shove with the other. "This is where Deidre stood for the first show."

Liss was glad she didn't have to stand next to the Great Umberto. Oscar Yates was staring at her with a malevolence that sent chills down her spine, but that was nothing compared to the venomous look on Iris's face. Like a mother bear defending her cub, she took a step in front of the magician, almost as if he needed protection from Liss.

Liss had hoped for a more vocal reaction. A confession would have been nice, but she'd have settled for any kind of outburst. *"How did you get back here?"* or *"I thought you'd be dead by now!"*

No such luck. Liss took what consolation she could from the fact that her reappearance would keep the Great Umberto from winning by default.

No one else in the cast or crew appeared to be surprised or disturbed by the reappearance of "Deidre and her Dancing Doggies." Liss supposed they thought she'd been playing the prima donna by skipping rehearsal. Her act *was* supposed to be a shoo-in to win.

Just before the music came up and the lights narrowed to a series of spotlights, all trained on the master of ceremonies for his introductory patter, Liss cast her gaze toward the place where Dan and Sherri were supposed to be.

She had no trouble finding her husband and her best friend, but she did a double take when she realized they weren't the only familiar faces in the small audience. Sitting right next to them were Audrey Greenwood, the vet, and Margaret MacCrimmon Boyd. Liss's aunt sported a jaunty eye patch and a broad smile. Liss had no doubt she'd used her clout as events coordinator at The Spruces to talk the owners of Five Mountains into letting her in.

One by one, the acts reprised the performances they'd done on the season premiere. Liss was tenth on the program. She recreated Deidre's choreography without a hitch and was smiling as she returned to her place on the sidelines.

The Great Umberto didn't fare as well. Iris was clumsy, her attention divided between what she was supposed to be doing to sustain the illusion and keeping a watchful eye on Liss. What should have been a simple but clever routine spiraled rapidly into disaster. No one was surprised, when it came time to eliminate one of the three top-scoring acts, to hear Roy Eastmont announce that the magician had the lowest number of votes.

"No, he doesn't," Iris said in a carrying voice.

"It's all a sham. The viewer votes aren't even counted."

"Shut up, Iris," Yates hissed.

"But it's so unfair." The last word ended on a wail of despair that had Liss feeling sorry for her . . . until she added, "I did everything I could to help you win!"

Everything she could? On Yates's orders? Or did Iris mean—?

Before Liss had time to rearrange the possibilities, Roy Eastmont grabbed Liss's arm and hauled her up onto a small podium where Mo already stood. Dandy and Dondi trotted after them, lapping up the attention. Well, why not? They'd been here before. The last time, they'd won.

"Here it is," Eastmont intoned. "The moment we've all been waiting for. The viewer votes have been totaled alongside the scores given by our three judges. One act stands out above all the rest, the champion of champions on *Variety Live*. May I have the envelope, please?"

A young woman in a sexy, glittery costume appeared, bearing a large white envelope with a big golden seal affixed to the flap. She looked so confident in this role that it took Liss a moment to recognize her as the otherwise inconspicuous, although stupendously well-organized assistant to the producer, Jane Smith.

Eastmont took the envelope and held it up,

drawing out the moment. The wait was excruciating for Liss, not because she felt any sense of suspense, but because she was so annoyed by the MC's pretense. Although she had now begun to have the most dire suspicions about Iris Jansen, she was secretly glad that young woman had condemned the phoniness of the entire production.

The music designed to increase the crowd's anticipation ceased. In the hush that followed, Eastmont broke the seal and, with a flourish, removed a card from the envelope. He glanced at the name and did a double take so false Liss wondered that anyone could be deceived by it.

"Ladies and gentlemen," he announced, "the one, the only champion of champions of *Variety Live* is . . . Mo Heedles!"

To say the competitors, especially Mo, were stunned, was an understatement. For Liss, surprise was rapidly replaced by relief. She hugged the other woman, whispering heartfelt congratulations, and then stepped back to let Roy Eastmont present Mo with her trophy. It was as ugly a thing as Liss had ever seen, bulbous and twisted at the same time, all over gilt with tawdry-looking "jewels" embedded at random. She had no idea what it was supposed to represent.

It's over, she thought.

She was free. No promotional obligations to get out of. No envy from the other competitors to deal with. She even had legal possession of the Scotties. Desdemona had signed over their ownership during the long hours they'd had to wait for the recording session to begin.

"Come on, guys," Liss called. "Back into your carriers."

She'd just secured the latches when Gordon Tandy and a uniformed state police officer entered the ballroom. Liss glanced around, searching for two sets of people. Dan and Sherri stood by the bleachers talking with Audrey and Margaret. The Great Umberto and his assistant were over by the exit to the stairs. Liss watched as Gordon approached them. They were so wrapped up in a low-voiced argument—arms waving, bodies tense—that they didn't notice him until he was standing right next to them.

Judging it safe to leave the carriers where they were, Liss walked rapidly toward the scene of the action. She reached Oscar Yates in time to hear Gordon start to read the magician his rights.

Yates's naturally dark complexion went deathly pale. "No. No, you've got this all wrong."

Gordon finished the Miranda warning before he replied. "I don't think so, Mr. Yates. We've searched both your room and your van. Mr. Barrigan's prints were found in the former and Ms. Ruskin's in the latter."

"Barrigan?" The confusion on his face looked real. Then he shifted his gaze to Iris. "You stupid little girl! What did you do?"

Liss stared at the magician's assistant. *Iris? Iris* had done all this? The same Iris who'd risked her own life to keep Dandy from being run over in the parking lot?

Iris burst into tears. Always her fallback move, Liss thought, repositioning herself just as the uniformed officer who'd accompanied Gordon moved in on the young woman with his handcuffs at the ready. Seeing him coming, Iris bolted for the exit door, only to find Liss blocking her escape route.

"Give it up, Iris."

The hatred in the other woman's hazel eyes went a long way toward curing Liss of any inclination to believe in Iris Jansen's innocence. She no longer doubted that this rosy-cheeked, slightly baby-faced countenance belonged to a cold-blooded killer.

Iris flung herself at Liss, trying to shove her out of the way. Failing in that, Iris went at her with both fists. Liss got her arms up in time to fend off the blows, but one of Iris's dangly earrings caught her just below the left eye. That sharp little pain was the last straw.

Liss didn't like hurting people, but she liked being hurt herself even less. She hauled off and smacked Iris as hard as she could. Her open hand made contact with the side of her attacker's face, making her palm sting.

The other woman staggered backward, one hand

pressed to what would soon be a magnificent bruise on the jaw, and stepped straight into the long arms of the law. The snick of handcuffs locking into place assured Liss that she had been secured. That sound was immediately followed by a chandelier-rattling shriek of indignation.

A trifle breathless, dabbing at the blood on her cheek with the tissue Sherri handed her, Liss nodded her thanks to the trooper. Jane Smith, efficient as ever, had her cell phone out and was calling for hotel security to come and take over crowd control. Until then, Dan appeared to be the one she'd recruited to hold back the gawkers. He even shooed away Liss's Aunt Margaret.

"She's fine," Liss heard him say in a low, reassuring voice.

Gordon attempted to steer his two prisoners toward the stairs, but now it was the Great Umberto who made a bid for freedom. Using his skills as an escape artist, he'd picked the lock on the handcuffs.

Instead of making a run for it, he lunged at Iris, hands outstretched toward her throat. Gordon and the uniformed officer wrestled him away from her before he could close his fingers around her neck. Iris, frozen in the classic deer-in-the-headlights pose, just stared at them while Sherri took a firm grip on her arm. To make sure she didn't possess the same skills as her boss, Sherri took the precaution of double locking the handcuffs.

Oscar Yates continued to resist, making it next to impossible to maneuver him through the door to the stairwell. Although Liss had no idea why he thought *she* would be inclined to help him, he turned his pleading gaze toward her, his eyes deep pools filled with regret and despair, and cried out, "I had no idea she was involved in those dirty tricks until she stole my magic cabinet!"

"*That's* what tipped you off?" Liss knew she sounded incredulous, but why shouldn't she? She was still trying to adjust to the idea of Iris, of all people, as a criminal mastermind.

"Let's go, Yates," Gordon said.

Slippery as an eel, the prisoner nearly broke loose a second time. He'd have succeeded if the two men holding him hadn't been so much bigger and stronger than he was. After a brief, desperate struggle, he was once more held securely between them.

"I won't go quietly," he insisted. "Not until everyone understands that I didn't do anything wrong."

All around them, curious spectators pressed closer. The entire cast and crew had a vested interest in what was going on.

Liss suspected Gordon would just as soon drag Oscar Yates through the exit door and down the stairs, leaving Sherri to follow with Iris. The ballroom was hardly an approved venue for hearing a confession. On the other hand, no one wanted to be accused of police brutality, especially when several of those watching already had their cell phones out to record everything that happened.

"Back off," he shouted at the onlookers. "You are obstructing justice."

No one moved except Elise. With Eudora entwined around her body, the stripper slipped through the barrier Dan had been trying to establish and positioned herself directly in front of the stairwell door. "I want to hear what he has to say. I've got a right. So do the rest of us."

A murmur of agreement rose up from the crowd. Roy Eastmont pushed his way to the front to stand next to Jane Smith.

"Where's backup when you need it?" Gordon muttered under his breath.

The small tape recorder he extracted from his coat pocket with his free hand was a model that had been made nearly extinct by advances in technology, but it still worked. Any incriminating statement Yates insisted on making would be ruled admissible as evidence. To make certain of that, Gordon spoke first, identifying himself and the officer, the suspect, and the location, and repeating the Miranda warning for the benefit of the tape. He also named several of those who were close enough to overhear what the prisoner had to say: Liss, Sherri, Elise, Eastmont, Jane, and Dan.

"Okay, Yates," he said. "You have until reinforcements get here to say your piece."

"It was Iris. Iris was the only one who could have managed to get away with my equipment. When I confronted her, she admitted it, but then she talked me into believing that destroying the cabinet was necessary, all a part of Eastmont's plan to get publicity for the show."

"*My* plan?" Eastmont's squawk of outrage, together with the look of horror on his face, convinced Liss that he'd had no prior knowledge of Iris's activities.

Sweat beaded on the Great Umberto's forehead. All the charm, all the charisma leached away. "I didn't know she was capable of more than a bit of sabotage. I only agreed to help her abduct Liss Ruskin because she persuaded me that Liss had agreed to the plan. Iris said someone would rescue her shortly after we dropped her off."

"Then what was the point?" Liss asked.

"You were supposed to stay out of sight until after the results show. We were supposed to win."

"Convince me!" Suddenly furious, remembering all she'd been through, Liss got right in his face. "Explain away your hand over my mouth and nose, cutting off my air. Explain why you flung me away from you in the woods! I could have broken my neck if I'd landed wrong!"

"I-I got carried away," Yates stammered. "But there was snow. I knew you'd be okay."

"Snow is not always soft," Liss said through clenched teeth.

She didn't know whether to believe him or not. It would be just like a cowardly villain to try to put all the blame on a naive and infatuated young woman. On the other hand . . .

"Someone wanted to win, all right." Liss's mind whirled as she tried to work out what had really happened. "My absence when the final results show was recorded was supposed to mean that the Great Umberto would be named champion of champions. But I don't think Mr. Eastmont knew anything about it. I can guarantee you that no one was standing by to pick me up in the middle of nowhere. I had to walk out. If it had been any colder, or if I'd gotten wet, I'd be dead of exposure by now."

Yates opened his mouth, but no sound came out. The stricken look on his face almost made Liss feel sorry for him. Almost.

"Iris is the one who told me Liss was missing," Eastmont interjected. "First thing this morning. She woke me up to tell me."

The way the MC winced at the memory told Liss he'd still been recovering from his bender. She had a sneaking suspicion that Iris's thoughtlessness might have been what prompted Eastmont to declare Mo champion of champions rather than the Great Umberto.

Liss shifted her attention to Iris. She pouted, playing the little-girl card, but her act wasn't nearly as effective this time as it had been in the past.

Hotel security and Gordon's backup arrived at the same time. The innocent cast members were quickly dispersed, and Sherri was freed from her temporary duty as Iris's guard. Since Yates appeared to have said all he meant to and Iris maintained her silence, Gordon addressed Elise. She was still blocking the exit.

"If you wouldn't mind, Ms. Isley?"

But Elise did not step aside. Instead, she snarled at Iris. "Deidre trusted you. How could you *kill* her?"

Eudora, sensing her owner's agitation, lunged for the magician's assistant.

Iris shrank back against the state trooper who had hold of her arm. "It was an accident!" she shrieked.

"Deidre Amendole's death?" Liss asked before Gordon could intervene.

"Yes."

"And Troy Barrigan?"

Iris sent a venom-filled look her way, but this time she answered the question. "That was an accident, too. He followed me when I went to Oscar's suite to pick up a prop we'd forgotten. He forced his way in after me, asking questions about the show. I shoved him out onto the balcony and locked the door. I was going to go complain about him to the management, but he must have tried to climb onto one of the other balconies to get away. He fell."

With a little help from you, Liss thought. She could believe the reporter had caught up with Iris as she was entering Oscar Yates's suite and tried to talk to her, but the rest of her version of events just didn't ring true.

"I bet that reporter discovered the same thing I did." Elise stepped close to Iris once more, stroking Eudora with one hand to keep the big snake calm. "I've been asking questions. It wasn't all that hard to locate the waiter you paid to pretend to be a guest. He called in a complaint about my python. He thought it was all a big joke."

"Did Troy Barrigan talk to that waiter?" Liss asked. "Is that why he confronted you?" It made her stomach twist to think that such a little thing could have caused the reporter's death.

"We'll take it from here, Liss," Gordon interrupted in that firm cop voice that brooked no argument.

Without further ado, the Great Umberto and his assistant were led out. Excitement over, the crowd melted away, leaving only Sherri and Dan standing near the stairwell door with Liss.

"Iris," Sherri murmured, shaking her head. "Talk about your least likely suspect! Didn't you tell me she risked her own life to save Dandy's?"

Liss shuddered at the memory. "Apparently, she's good at creating illusions. I should have paid more attention to her the first time I met her. Dandy refused to go near her."

"Let me see if I've got this straight," Dan said. "Iris has been infatuated with Oscar Yates for a long time, even though he never showed the least romantic interest in her?"

"Right. He treated her like a younger sister. It looks to me as if she decided she'd do anything to help him win, but I suspect that she also wanted him to realize that the win was due to her efforts. I suppose she thought that if he was sufficiently grateful to her, in her debt, he'd look at her differently." He certainly had, Liss thought, but not the way she'd hoped.

"I can see the reason behind the dirty tricks. Sort of," Sherri said. "But why murder two people? Surely it wasn't necessary to go that far just to win this cockamamy competition."

"I don't imagine she meant to kill Deidre. It was probably an accident, just as she claimed. She wanted to make Deidre sick enough to drop out and overestimated the amount of whatever drug she gave her. With Deidre dead, though, Iris was at risk to lose everything if anyone suspected what she'd done."

"But Barrigan wasn't on to her about that, was he?" Dan asked.

"We'll never know. If he found out that she was behind one dirty trick, it's possible he had his suspicions about the rest." She turned to Sherri. "Do they have enough on her to make the charges stick?"

"You can trust Gordon for that," Sherri assured her. "He'll sort it out. And unless I miss my guess, Yates is going to spill his guts to prove he wasn't her willing accomplice."

"You think he was telling the truth?" Dan asked.

"He sounded pretty convincing to me," Liss said. "If he hadn't realized that Iris was the only one who could have stolen his disappearing cabinet, she probably wouldn't have involved him in her schemes at all."

The risk of taking credit for their win would have been too great once murder entered the picture. Liss shuddered at the realization that the outcome of her kidnapping could have been much different if Iris had still been acting on her own. Iris would never have left Liss alive in that lonely spot in the Maine woods.

She had probably intended for Dandy to die, too. When she'd set the Scottie free out in the middle of nowhere, she could never have imagined that the little dog would be found and returned to Deidre. Of course she hadn't stuck around to make sure. Not with the lousy weather that evening. Liss had been wrong about that. Iris would have hightailed it back to the hotel as quickly as she could so she could act the part of Deidre's sympathetic friend.

Reminded of her canine partners, Liss started back toward the spot where she'd parked Dandy and Dondi in their carriers. Margaret was there ahead of her, sitting on the floor beside the empty containers. Both dogs were in her lap.

They looked natural together, and blessedly ordinary. No one was trying to kill anyone else. Liss walked faster. Ordinary was good. Ordinary was *great!* She didn't need happily ever after, but a loving environment was nothing to sneeze at.

Margaret looked up with a sappy smile on her face when Liss came to an abrupt halt beside her. "Dan tells me these little darlings need a new home."

"You?"

"Why not?"

"Well, let me see. Number one, you live in an apartment. Number two, you work odd hours."

"True, but my niece just happens to run the shop that's right downstairs from where I live. Do you think she might be persuaded to let them outside from time to time? I was thinking that I could fence in that grassy area at the back of the building."

Margaret's enthusiasm was irresistible. Liss

grinned back at her. "Sounds like a plan. Well behaved as they are, I might even be willing to let Dandy and Dondi keep me company in the shop while I work."

"Watch out!" Margaret warned with mock sincerity. "Cute as they are, the next thing you know you'll be wanting to change the name of the place to Moosetookalook *Scotties* Emporium."

A Note from the Author

Some time ago, I received an e-mail from a reader who asked if I might one day use a Scottish terrier as a character in one of Liss MacCrimmon's adventures. I thought that sounded like a fine idea, and when the time came to write this novel, I asked that reader, Carolyn Grande, if she would serve as my Scottish terrier adviser, answering questions and telling me stories about her own Scotties. I am extremely grateful for her input. Any errors in portraying Dandy and Dondi are mine.

I'd also like to thank Mo Heedles, generous high bidder at the Malice Domestic charity auction in May 2014. She won the right to name a character in this novel, although I'm the one who decided which character she would be. In my book, Mo is definitely a winner!

Center Point Large Print
600 Brooks Road / PO Box 1
Thorndike, ME 04986-0001 USA

(207) 568-3717

US & Canada:
1 800 929-9108
www.centerpointlargeprint.com